The Last Martini

A NOVEL

JOHN CHIERICHELLA

Copyright © 2024 John Chierichella

Paperback: 979-8-9909647-9-2
Ebook: 979-8-9909647-8-5

All rights reserved. No part of this publication may be reproduced, distributed, or transmitted in any form or by any electronic or mechanical means, without the prior written permission of the publisher, except in the case of brief quotations embodied in critical reviews and certain other noncommercial uses permitted by copyright law.

Ordering Information:

Books to Life Marketing Ltd
128 City Road, London, EC1V 2NX, UK

Printed in the United States of America

Chapter 1

NICOLE WALKED BACK to the house from the mailbox that sat at the end of their driveway. She dumped the mail on the kitchen table and poured herself a cup of coffee before taking stock of what the Postal Service had delivered this morning. She found the usual bundle of catalogs and a number of offers for life insurance, extended automobile warranties, and solicitations of funds from the various schools that she and Jack had attended. Buried in that pile of irrelevance was a square envelope, addressed in elegant cursive to "Mr. and Mrs. John Beaumont." The return address embossed on the flap of the envelope told her it was from "The Millers," her neighbors on the adjoining five-acre plot.

"The Millers." Ted and Maryanne Miller were good friends. In fact, Maryanne was Nikki's best friend, one with whom she could share her feelings, including her frustrations and sorrows regarding her marriage to Jack. Maryanne was a good listener. She was non-judgmental and she refrained from offering advice unless and until asked. Nikki and Maryanne had spent many an hour sitting on the edge of each other's swimming pools with a glass of wine talking about life, love, hopes, and unrealized dreams. Most of those unrealized dreams belonged to Nikki. Not all, but most.

Nikki and Jack had socialized with the Millers frequently—movies, dinners, the theater, backyard barbecues, pool parties. They were easy to be with and, in Nikki's opinion, just about the best-looking couple she had ever met. Ted was a professional photographer and videographer. He was tall and blessed with the kind of craggy good looks that Nikki found to be very attractive. He had a thick mane of dark brown hair atop his head, but anyone who looked when he headed for the pool—and Nikki was one who always did—could see that his torso was relatively hairless. He had a well-toned physique. He obviously worked out regularly, but he did not overdo it. He was nicely muscled, without body builder bulk. He was also the life of any party, always up to date on current events, local community affairs, the latest movies and music, and a wonderful storyteller. He was on the A List for any party in Highland Estates. Nikki envied Maryanne Miller. She had chosen well from the pool of available suitors. Nikki often wondered what it would be like to be married to Ted and to share her body with him on a regular basis. She suspected that she was not the only woman in Highland Estates who harbored that fantasy.

Maryanne was every bit the "catch" that Ted was, even more. She was dark and beautiful. Her family roots were in Malta, and her olive-toned skin suggested that lineage. Her raven hair barely touched her shoulders, framing a face that could have appeared on the cover of Vogue. She was slender but nicely curved, with long legs that could draw and hold the attention of even the most critical leg man. Nikki often thought that Maryanne would make an inspired choice for Aphrodite if they were casting a movie about Greek mythology. Her intelligence matched her looks. She was a wizard with numbers and was a rising star at a large accounting firm.

She was well-spoken, witty, and gracious. And she could laugh like a sailor when a joke tickled her fancy. Everyone, including Nikki's husband Jack, thought that Maryanne was as close to perfect as a woman could be.

Jack did not seem to understand how his frequent comments about Maryanne hurt his wife. Yes, Maryanne was gorgeous, but Nikki was no slouch in the looks department. She, too, was slender and she worked hard to keep herself attractive for Jack. Although she had always maintained a flat stomach, her recent foray into martial arts classes had transformed her core. Aerobics kept her legs firm and nicely shaped. Work with light weights had given her arms and shoulders some nice definition. She wore her ash blonde hair in a shag, even though she knew it was out of style. She liked it. It was easy to maintain, and she liked the way it framed her face. It was a good face, not beautiful, not gorgeous, somewhat imperfect, and it betrayed the fact that Nikki had, at one time, suffered a broken nose. All in all, it was the nice face of the archetypal "girl next door," pretty enough to draw attention, with striking violet eyes.

Nikki knew she was no match for Maryanne Miller, but then again, who was? Nikki's self-appraisal, which was overly critical, was that, at the age of 34, she wasn't half bad. If Jack would take some time to get off the road and look at her, he might realize that she was a pretty good catch and that some of his comments about Maryanne could be applied equally to his own wife. Nicole would be a lot happier if Jack would comment on Nikki the way he commented on Maryanne and if he would look at Nikki the way he looked at his neighbor. But he didn't, and Nikki no longer thought he ever would.

Nikki slid a knife under the flap and opened the envelope. It was an invitation to a "Summer Kick-Off" party a week from Saturday. "Cocktails at 6, Dinner at 7, Pool and Poolside Festivities to Follow." Nikki wanted to go, but Jack would not return until the end of the week following the party, and she was not up for a party of married couples at which she might be the only single. As much as she liked Ted and Maryanne, and she truly adored them, she knew she would spend a fair portion of her evening explaining to their guests why Jack was not there, how important his job was, and how important this particular business trip was. It was not her idea of a fun evening.

She hit Maryanne's number on her cell phone to communicate her "regrets." But Maryanne would not take "No" for an answer.

"C'mon, Nikki. I'll see to it that you have fun. Emily Morton is handling the catering and she'll have Danny Dunphy tending bar. You've always liked his Greyhounds. I'll make sure we have plenty of Grey Goose and grapefruit juice."

"Maryanne, do you know what it is like always to be making excuses for your husband's absence? It becomes embarrassing."

"No. I don't have that problem. Ted's job doesn't involve a lot of travel. One of the things we talked about before we got married was making sure that work did not become more important than us."

"It's too late for that with Jack."

"Then he's an idiot. He's choosing a strange bed in a hotel room over a familiar bed with you by his side. Hell, Nikki, most men would choose you over work every time. I would."

"That's sweet, Maryanne, but it doesn't change the fact that he won't be here for the party."

"And his not being here doesn't change the fact that you're entitled to a social life. He can't expect you to sit at home and watch old movies when your best friends have invited you to a nice party right next door. Look, Nikki, pick out a cocktail dress that shows off those legs of yours.

I'll do the same and we can make the men leer at us while their wives look daggers at their husbands. And bring your bikini, the black one you wore last time we came over to your place for a swim. Show off that new body you've created at the dojo. There won't be a single man at the party who will be disappointed."

"I don't wear that suit in public, Maryanne."

"You should. You work hard to maintain your body. You should be proud of it."

"I am. But there's a difference between taking pride in yourself and showing off. Why would I do that?

"Because you can, Nikki. Because it would be fun. You won't be alone. I'll pick out a nice bikini of my own to keep you company."

"And to make me look like the door prize?"

"Why do you do that, Nikki? Why do you sell yourself short? You're very attractive. Take my word for it."

"Jack would never let me wear a bikini to the party if he were here."

"He's not going to be here, Nikki. If he's going to bury himself in his work all the time, you need to give yourself the freedom to have some fun."

"But what will Jack say when he finds out? You know someone is going to get catty about this."

"Well, I guess the first question is whether you really care what he thinks, Nikki."

Nikki pondered that question, which went to the core of her relationship with Jack. She had reached the point where she really didn't care if she made him angry by displaying her feminine assets at a pool party. If men ogled her, so what? It might make her feel good about herself. And if it made Jack jealous or angry, so what? At this point, it was fairly clear that he did not care about her, not the way a loving husband should care about his wife. And she really did not care about him anymore, not the way a loving wife should care about her husband. She often wondered what made her stay in the marriage other than her Roman Catholic upbringing.

"OK, Maryanne, I'm in."

"Great. See you Saturday at 6, Nikki. We'll have fun. I promise."

Chapter 2

JACK USUALLY CALLED every day when he was on the road. The calls came like clockwork, at 5 PM in whatever time zone he happened to occupy on that day. Nikki understood the timing. He was calling before cocktails and dinner, leaving him free to enjoy the company of his clients, colleagues, and whomever for the evening. Nikki had no evidence to suggest that Jack was spending any of those evenings with female company, but she did wonder. Were all of these trips really necessary? Did they need to be so long? Was it only the lure of profits that kept him on the road? Why couldn't he come home on weekends and spend time with her? And why did he never call later in the evening, if only to suggest to her that he was not out on the town with another woman.

She had asked him these questions, all but the ones about female company. She was afraid to ask those questions because she was afraid of the answers. After all, Jack was an attractive man with a nicely contoured body. She knew that he had squired his fair share of girlfriends around town before marrying Nikki. She had no reason to believe that he did not have the same physical needs and urges as other men. For her, weeks without sex increased her desires exponentially. But she was struck by Jack's relative lack of interest in sex, even after two or more weeks on the road. More often than not, he would rebuff her overtures on his first night back, claiming fatigue, when she would have expected him to respond eagerly, with a hunger born of abstinence. But she did not ask any questions, accepting the rejection in painful silence, convinced that he had not been abstinent and that he had satisfied his needs with other women while on the road. It hurt. It hurt very much. Often, after Jack had drifted off to sleep, she would pull up the covers on her side of the bed, slide under, and cry.

As for the other questions about his travel, Jack's answers were always the same, delivered calmly as if he were a professor and she a student who had not done her homework.

"Yes, dear, these trips are necessary. It is important to spend time with clients, to be there, working at their facilities. That's where the records are, that's where the people are, that's where I can do my job most efficiently."

"Interrupting the trip to come home on Friday night and return Sunday night isn't practical. First, the clients don't want to pay for the extra airfare. Second, that's pretty hard on me physically."

"The trips are as long as they need to be. You know that sometimes, if it's on the East Coast, it's just a day trip. That's because I can complete the job in a single day. I fly out early and I return late, but I do get home the same day. Other trips simply require more time, particularly when I'm working for clients on the West Coast. I'm sorry but look around. Look at our home, look at our pool, look at your BMW, look in your closet, look in your jewelry cases. It's my travel workload that pays for all of that. The trips solidify my relationships with the clients. That keeps them coming back and it keeps the money flowing to provide all this."

She knew the answers by rote. She was particularly annoyed by his frequent focus on what his earnings had provided for her. She had told him often that those things were not as important to her as he was, as their marriage was. He gave her response the proverbial back of his hand, asserting dismissively that she could never abandon their expensive lifestyle. He made it sound like she was a whore who had sold herself to him for all of those things and was experiencing g remorse over the price of the bargain.

It was 8 PM, 5 PM in Los Angeles, where Jack was working this week, as he did so often. The telephone rang, right on schedule.

"Hi, Nikki. How are you?"

"I'm fine, Jack." Doing her best to sound engaged, she added "Missing me?"

Jack responded in what had become, by now, a customary monotone. "Of course."

"When will you be home?"

"Two weeks from Friday."

"Jack, Ted and Maryanne are giving a "Summer Kick-Off" party next Saturday. Not this Saturday, but Saturday the 22nd. It sounds like fun. Maryanne told me that Emily Morton is providing the food. You know she always puts on a good spread. And you say that Danny Dunphy makes the best Old Fashioned you've ever had. Isn't there any way you can come home on Friday the 21st and go to the party with me on that Saturday? I would love it if you could. I miss you. Please, Jack."

The sigh at the other end of the phone seemed to ask "Do we have to go through this again?" Jack dutifully responded to her comments. "Emily Morton? You're right. She always does a great job. Danny Dunphy? Great bartender. Sorry I'll miss them." But after those perfunctory comments, he simply gave her the standard Jack Beaumont dismissal, "You know I can't do that, Nikki."

"You don't have to charge the client for the airfare. Consider it a present to me to start the Summer." In her most seductive voice, she added, "I'll make it worth your while after the party. Promise."

He didn't even pretend to be interested in her overture. "Nikki, that would be a 36-hour turnaround. C'mon, give me a break."

"You can do it. And you can ease the travel if you return to LA on Monday, on that early morning flight. That would give us two full days together."

"Enough, Nikki. It's too hard and the notice is too short."

"Jack, we . . ."

" Stop it, Nikki. The answer is 'No.' Do you understand?"

"Yes, Jack. I understand. But you can't blame me for trying. You should be happy that after 10 years, I want you here with me."

"Are you going to the party?"

"I think so."

"Alone?"

"Of course, alone." Displaying a bit of spine, she added "Do you have a date to suggest for me?"

"You've always told me you hate going to these soirees solo. Why are going to this one?"

"Maryanne was kind of insistent. I don't want to disappoint her. She's my best friend."

"Then go. But please don't complain about your absentee husband. Sooner or later, those complaints all work their way back to me and I don't appreciate it, Nikki."

"People ask me where you are and why you couldn't make it, Jack. I try to be as matter of fact as I can when I respond. I can't control how the message gets translated as it makes its rounds."

"Well, try to do a better job. Look, you know I would make it if I could. I always have a good time with Maryanne. I would love to see her. She's an absolute 10. It's been too long. You should set something up for us with Maryanne and Ted."

Nikki thought to herself, "There it is again. He regrets not seeing Maryanne, but not me. Hell, I offered him carte blanche in the bedroom and he turned me down."

"What do you have on tap for the weekend, Jack?"

"Same old, same old. Review documents, prepare some interim interview summaries, meet the client for dinner on Saturday evening."

She did not inquire about his plans for Sunday. "Well, have as good a time as you can. I hope you find something fun to fill your time."

"Got to run. Have a good evening."

Nikki put down her phone. It had been long time since Jack closed these calls with even a token "I love you." This had not been a call from an absent lover who longed for her touch. With each trip over the years, particularly the trips to the West Coast, he seemed to grow more and more distant, more and more disinterested in her. She sat down and began to cry. Her marriage was all but over. As she pondered that fact, Nikki became more determined than ever to go to the Millers' party and to have a good time.

Chapter 3

IT WAS SATURDAY afternoon. Nikki stood in front of the full-length mirror in their bedroom and began to get ready for the Millers' party. She pulled on the black bikini that Maryanne had suggested and subjected her reflected image to scrutiny. As Maryanne had said, Nikki was her own worst critic, but standing there, even she had to admit she looked pretty good. Jack might have lost interest in her, and he might well be spending tonight with someone he found more appealing, but Nikki was confident that at least some of the men at the party would enjoy the view she provided and go home fantasizing about her. Again, she wasn't Maryanne Miller, but Nicole Beaumont wouldn't be too shabby as a consolation prize in their fantasies, would she?

For her cocktail party attire, Nikki started with black satin bikini briefs that she had purchased at Victoria's Secret back when she hoped the sight of her in such attire could help to entice Jack into bed. They had not seen much use lately, but they fit perfectly, and they looked marvelous. She had no reason to think that anyone would see them, except perhaps another woman who might share a room to change into their swimsuits. Nonetheless, they made her feel risqué and that was a welcome feeling to have every now and then.

To cover her satin briefs, she then chose a frock that never had failed to garner approving glances from male onlookers. It was a black dress that was fitted at the waist and flared into an A Line skirt that ended 3 inches above her knees. The bodice was pulled up by two straps that tied behind her neck. It showed off her toned arms, shoulders, and back to great effect. The dress left no room for a bra, a fact that made Nikki feel a bit naughty. Black pumps with three-inch heels would showcase her legs. A string of pearls would encircle her neck, pearl earrings would dangle from her ears, and, along with the diamonds that glittered on her left ring finger, a pearl bracelet would complete the jewelry ensemble.

Nikki stepped back to admire herself. No one would ever confuse her with Maryanne Miller, but Nikki Beaumont was somewhat charming in her own right. When the time came, she would grab a small, black clutch bag, throw her keys in, and add a few sprays of Yves Saint Laurent Black Opium. She had come a long way from her initial inclination to decline the Millers' invitation.

Chapter 4

THE MILLERS HAD gone to great efforts to make this party a success. Chinese lanterns had been strung on the patio and on the deck surrounding the pool. They lent an immediate festive air to the gathering. Music streamed from the Millers' Sonos system, offering a continuous flow of soft ballads from Frank Sinatra, Dean Martin, Tony Bennet, and Al Martino, with occasional soft vocals from someone born after 1940.

The bar was set up on the patio, immediately beyond the French Doors, and it held all top shelf spirits. This was not a crowd that looked for wine during the cocktail hour, but for those who did, Ted and Maryanne had laid in an ample supply of Joseph Phelps Insignia and Louis Jadot Corton Charlemagne. She approached the bar. Unfortunately, Danny Dunphy appeared to be a no show behind the bar and Nikki could only hope that the new man's mixology skills were up to the well-known Dunphy standard. She asked for her usual, a Greyhound. The bartender smiled approvingly. Whether he was smiling at her drink selection or at her, Nikki did not know. In any event, he took a tall glass, dropped in a grapefruit section, added the ice, and reached for the Grey Goose. He poured a jigger into the glass, filled it with grapefruit juice, and handed Nikki her cocktail. She thanked him, took a sip, and concluded that the bartender knew his stuff. She began to relax.

She walked into the dining room and saw further proof that no expense had been spared. On the sideboard was an array of appetizers, the centerpiece of which was a veritable mountain of Osetra caviar, flanked by the customary accoutrements—blinis, toast points, crème fraiche, sour cream, chopped onions, chopped egg whites, and chopped yolks. Looking at the caviar, Nikki recalled an Esquire cover that she saw while looking over Jack's shoulder. It was a photo of an Italian actress, Monica Bellucci, naked except for the predictable parts of her body that were strategically obscured by caviar. Nikki had whimsically asked Jack if he would like to cover her like that with caviar and remove it without using his hands. There were plenty of possible answers to that question, but the one she received was incredibly deflating—"That would be ridiculously expensive, a waste of money." Nikki dismissed that disheartening memory, spread some caviar and crème fraiche on a blini, ate it in two bites, and silently thanked God for friends like the Millers. She looked at the accompanying assortment of cheeses, vegetables, and dips, and had one more caviar-laden blini and some Stilton on a cracker. Then she turned to look at the dinner buffet.

The buffet had something for everyone, except perhaps a Vegan. Main courses included Beef Wellington, poached salmon, and stuffed chicken breasts. Two different quiches were available. There were fingerling potatoes, grilled peppers, roasted carrots, and a green salad that included romaine, spinach, radicchio, and arugula, along with cherry tomatoes, cucumbers, olives, and radishes, with a raspberry vinaigrette on the side.

The dessert tray offered tiramisu, peach cobbler, Italian cheesecake, and homemade vanilla ice cream. No one would go hungry tonight.

"Hi, Nikki." Ted's voice arrived from behind her. She turned to greet him, and they exchanged light kisses on the cheek, as good friends are wont to do. He held a low-ball glass with ice, green olives, and a clear liquid.

"Silver bullet, Ted?"

"You know me too well, Nikki. Bombay Sapphire martini, very dry, on the rocks, olives. The Millers' libation of choice. It is the drink that strengthens our marital bonds."

"I'm sure. Hey, where is your beautiful wife?"

"Around. Probably flirting with the guests. I'm sure she'll wander over here when she sees you. You're hard to miss. Say, what do you think of our little get together?"

"It's magnificent, Ted. But my God. I can't imagine how much this is costing you."

"Well, when Maryanne told me you were definitely coming, I doubled the budget to impress you."

"It worked. I am quite impressed."

"Then it was money well spent. Hey, am I correct that Jack will be unable to join us, leaving his lovely wife subject to the predations of her handsome but lecherous neighbor?"

"And who would that be, Ted?"

He smiled. "That hurt, Nikki. Cut me to the quick. Couldn't you let me down a bit more gently?"

"No. My rule is very simple when a guy comes on to me, Ted. The better looking he is, the more quickly I need to cut it off, lest his looks get the better of my judgment. And you, Ted Miller, are one good looking man. There, did that ease your pain?"

Ted smiled and thanked her for the explanation. "So, if Jack's not coming, does that mean I have the gorgeous Nicole Beaumont all to myself tonight?"

Nikki laughed and said, "I guess so if you don't count Maryanne and the three dozen or so guests you have here."

Ted grinned and said, "I'll take those odds. By the way, Nikki, have you noticed all the eyes that keep sneaking a glance at you? I mean, you always look good, but you look especially good tonight. Did you send Jack a photo so he could see what he was missing?"

"Ted, stop flirting."

"Do I have to? It's fun to flirt with someone as pretty as you, Nikki."

"I appreciate the compliment Ted, but how does Maryanne feel about your flirting with her best friend?"

"Maryanne is fine with it, Nikki." It was Maryanne's voice. Nikki turned around and saw her friend, stunning as usual in a purple dress with spaghetti straps that teased onlookers with a not-so-slight peek at her cleavage. The dress made only a half-hearted attempt to cover her thighs. Like Ted, she carried a martini, but hers looked like she had not touched it. Maryanne turned to her husband.

"Ted, you've flirted enough with Nikki for now. You can resume later. For now, go be a good host and mingle."

As Ted dutifully wandered off to work the crowd, Nikki took a step back to get a better look at Maryanne.

"Wow, Maryanne. I guess all those eyes that Ted says were fixated on me have a new target. And who can blame them. What a vision!"

Maryanne leaned in to give Nicole a friendly peck on the cheek.

"Glad you like it. But don't sell yourself short, Nikki. A lot of those eyes are still on you and the ones that have left will be back. I can't wait to see their reactions when you pull on that bikini."

"You'll be wearing yours too, won't you?"

"I said I would, and I'm a woman of my word. It'll be fun. Now, we should follow Ted's lead and do some socializing."

Before heading off to mingle, Nikki asked Maryanne if she really was OK with Ted's flirting. Maryanne said that she was, and that she found it amusing, but if it bothered Nikki, she would tell Ted to lay off.

"No need for that. If you're OK, I'm OK. Frankly, it's sort of ego boosting when my husband can't find any time for me and the best-looking man I know flirts with me. But I don't want Ted hurting your feelings."

"Not an issue. I actually find it kind of titillating. Now go mingle."

As Nikki ventured off into the crowd, she saw Charlie and Vicki Waters, who lived several lots down the road from the Beaumont house. They were an affable couple, somewhat older. Charlie owned several fast-food franchises of a national chain. Vicki worked in the administrative office of a local, private elementary school. They were people who seemed to be comfortable in their own skins, who made no effort to impress others. Nicole wished more people could be like them.

"How are things at the hospital, Nicole? Have things slowed down any?"

Nikki was a Registered Nurse and she worked at St. Peter's Hospital, which was a short drive from home.

"It's better, Vicki. Not as frantic as it was for a couple of years. Thanks for asking."

Charlie chimed in, "With all due respect, I'm not so sure nursing is the right calling for you, Nicole."

Nikki half-frowned when she responded, "Why is that, Charlie?"

He smiled a good natured smile. "Because one look at you and the patients' blood pressure must soar by 20 or 30 points."

As Vicki punched him playfully on the arm, Nikki said, "I think that's a compliment, Charlie, so thank you." Smiling back, she added, "Just so you know, I haven't killed a patient . . . not yet."

She gave Charlie a peck on the cheek, excused herself, and returned to the bar. When she turned around, she was looking at Aaron Long and his wife Samantha. Samantha was young, cute, and perky, and quite a bit younger than Aaron. She worked as an aerobics instructor at a local health club, and she looked every bit the part. Aaron was a jeweler and the President of the Highland Estates Homeowners' Association. After exchanging hellos, Nikki and Samantha moved over to give other guests ready access to the bar. Ted was at the head of the drink line, asking for two more gin martinis. When Aaron's turn came around, he ordered a bourbon and water for himself and a Cosmopolitan for his wife.

Samantha was, as usual, enthusiastic and chatty.

"Isn't this something?"

"Did you see that pile of caviar?"

"Don't you just love those lanterns?"

"Is Jack here? He's a sweetheart."

"Did you bring your swimsuit?"

"Did you feel the water? It's heated. It's really inviting."

Neither Aaron nor Nikki could get a word in edgewise, but that hardly mattered to Nikki. It was nice to have someone else carry the conversation. Nikki always found the Longs to be an odd couple—he was tall, she was short; he was older, she was much younger; he was cold and aloof, she was warm and engaging; he was always looking for an opportunity to display his intelligence; she projected the image of a sweet, good-hearted scatterbrain. Nikki wondered how they made it work. Then again, who was she to question how other folks made a go of their marriages when hers had so clearly gone off the rails?

A server in a white waistcoat rang a small bell to signal the guests that it was time to visit the buffet table. Everything on the table screamed out "Try me!" Nikki nonetheless limited herself to a slice of the Beef Wellington, a slice of the stuffed chicken breast, and some salad. She chose a seat at an empty patio table and asked the server for a glass of the Corton Charlemagne. No wine connoisseur would have selected a white burgundy to accompany Beef Wellington, but Nikki knew what she liked, and she liked white burgundy. Besides, it was a good match for the chicken breast.

She was soon joined by Pete Carmelo and his wife, Antonia. They lived on the far side of Highland Estates, with their three children. Pete also worked at St. Peter's, as the Head Pharmacist. They were Italian through and through, a fact that Pete acknowledged with a fair degree of self-deprecation, often lapsing into a hilarious imitation of the gangster dialect heard in Grade B film noir. It never failed to get a laugh from Nikki, and tonight was no exception. A steady flow of "deez," "dem," and "dose" tripped off his lips. His monologue culminated in the classic Italian method of insulting someone, "I say this with all due respect, and I mean no offense," and then pausing for effect before adding, "but you have shit for brains . . . and your mother's a whore." Nikki liked Pete.

She liked Antonia even more. Pretty as any Italian actress, Antonia could have walked right off the set of a romantic comedy filmed in Rome. She had been born in Italy, in a little town called Sala Consilina, in the province of Salerno. She had come to America in her early teens and had never completely erased her Italian accent. Nikki found her accent to be charming and she wondered if Antonia took offense at Pete's gangster dialect. If she did, she never showed it. In fact, from time to time she would use the same faux dialect when dishing back at Pete. Jack and Nikki had dined at the Carmelo household on several occasions. They were warm and genial hosts who always made Nikki and Jack feel welcome. And Antonia could cook with the best of them.

Antonia asked Nikki what she was drinking. When Nikki described it, Antonia asked Pete if he would get one for her from the bar. As Pete rose, he asked if he could get something for Nikki. She declined politely. He told his wife he was going to try a martini, since the Millers seemed to be enjoying theirs so much. The look on Antonia's face suggested that Pete had tried this before and that the experiment had not gone well.

"Really, Pete? A martini?"

"Just one, sweetheart, I promise. Just one."

"You heard him, Nikki. Are you going to back me up if goes back on his word?"

"I'll try, Antonia. But don't count on me too much." She winked at the pretty little Italian. "After all, I have to work with him come Monday."

As Pete headed for the bar, Art and Penny Hamilton sat down at the table. Art was a professor of sociology at the local college. He taught a well-attended "Easy A" class on "Deviant Behaviors," to which his students happily referred as "Sluts and Nuts." When Art got rolling with a drink or three under his belt, he could be highly entertaining on that topic. Unless, of course, you were a nut or a slut.

Penny was an émigré from New York. If you looked closely, you could tell that, when she was younger, she could well have been the Queen of the Prom. Age had etched a few lines on her face, but she was still quite attractive. She was likely a little heavier than she had been in the halcyon days of yesteryear, but not by much. And she was still comely enough to draw interest from some of Art's students. Rumors persisted that she reciprocated their interest from time to time.

Rumors aside, Penny was fun at parties, regaling her dinner partners with stories of her upbringing in Brooklyn. The stories purported to be true and were populated with characters worthy of a Damon Runyon story, folks with names like "Louie the Burner," "Three Finger Brown," "Stiletto Sal," "Frankie Fists," and "Mikey the Moron." She always liked to suggest that she had never really left Brooklyn completely behind and that she "knew people" who could do a favor or eliminate a problem. No one ever saw any proof of her claim but, then again, who would want to challenge her and be proven wrong?

At that point, Ted dropped by, discharging his responsibility as host to make sure his guests were having a good time. And somewhere between the first and last sip from his martini glass, Ted reminded everyone that the county Zoning Board would be meeting on Monday to review the request for a variance to permit construction of a mega-mall on an undeveloped tract adjacent to the state highway. He hoped for their support in opposing the variance. Having reminded those at the table of the upcoming hearing, Ted dutifully moved on from table to table, where he no doubt made sure they were well lubricated and having a wonderful time, where he occasionally kissed one or more of his female guests on the cheek, and where his reminder regarding Monday's Zoning Board hearing would be repeated.

Ted had long been opposed to the construction of the mall. He thought it would ruin the semi-rural character of the county, increase traffic to a level that the state highway and connecting roads could not handle, pollute the air, and undermine local businesses that would find it hard to compete with challengers situated in a one-stop-shop mega-mall. He had formed the "Citizens' Alliance for Preservation" in order to consolidate the dissenting locals into a united opposition. Even his most ardent supporters thought that Ted was tilting at windmills, that the approval of the variance was all but assured. Nonetheless, Ted would appear on behalf of the Alliance and argue their case to the Zoning Board.

As Ted withdrew from her table, Gary Forsythe asked if the empty chair next to Nikki was free. Gary ran his own business as a cabinetmaker and his craftsmanship was highly regarded. He had been widowed last Spring when his wife Cecilia had lost her battle with cancer at the age of 33.

Nikki had visited Cecilia frequently during the terminal stages of her illness and she gained a fair degree of admiration for Gary during that difficult time. Knowing that their time together was limited, he added staff at his business to free up time to spend with his wife. He was gentle, loving, and upbeat. He was careful to shed his tears in private and to greet Cecilia always with a smile. Nikki often thought that while Cecilia's life was unfairly cut short, she at least had the right partner with whom to share the time she had been given.

Nikki thought this might mark Gary's first return to the Highland Estates social scene since his wife's passing.

"Hi, Gary. It's good to see you again. How are you?"

"I'm doing better, Nikki. Thanks. Better with each passing day. I've been thinking for some time that I need to get out of the house for something other than work, and the Millers' invitation arrived at just the right time for me. How have you been? Where is Jack?"

Nicole said that she was fine, that work at the hospital kept her plenty busy, and that Jack was on another extended road trip for his law practice.

"That's too bad, Nikki. But it gives me the chance to have dinner with one of my favorite people. I can't tell you how much I appreciated your visits with Cecilia while she was sick. I don't know how you managed it with your shifts at the hospital, but those visits really brightened her days. And your help with the reception following the funeral was a godsend."

"I was happy to help, Gary. Cecilia was a sweetheart. I miss her." Inwardly, Nikki wondered how long it would take for Gary to reenter the dating scene. He would be quite a catch for any woman intelligent enough to accept his memories of Cecilia while helping him to create new ones with her. It was a role she would have been happy to pursue had she not been married.

All in all, Nikki was happy with the table. The conversation was light, humorous, snappy, and calm. Apart from Ted's friendly reminders regarding Monday's Zoning Board hearing,

politics never reared its ugly head. Nikki's dinner went down easy, as did the homemade vanilla ice cream.

Chapter 5

AS THE GUESTS were finishing dessert, Ted clinked on a water glass with a knife to get everyone's attention. He had changed to a pair of baggy board shorts, the kind you see on surfers, a University of Tennessee T-shirt, and shower shoes. He announced that the pool was now open for anyone who wanted to swim or soak, that the pool was heated to 82 degrees and that the spa was heated to 101 degrees. The bar would remain open, and servers were available to take drink orders, which would be delivered poolside. He pointed to a tall pile of lush towels and only half-jokingly stated that swimsuits were recommended but not mandatory. He then directed folks to two bedrooms that would serve as changing rooms, each of which had a temporary gender insignia on the door. With that, he pulled off his T-shirt, kicked off the shower shoes, and dove into the pool.

Nikki felt a hand on her shoulder. It was Maryanne.

"Show time, Nikki. Let's go to my bedroom to change."

Nikki was hesitant. She did not want to be the first woman in the pool. She asked Maryanne for a few minutes to see if others succumbed to the lure of the water. They did not wait long. Samantha Long was the first, wearing a polka dot bikini that gave ample proof of the benefits of aerobics. Samantha drew admiring looks from a number of male guests as she made her way from the changing room to join Ted in the pool. It pleased Nikki that she and Maryanne would not be the only bikini-clad swimmers, and she was happy that Samantha filled out that suit so well. Samantha had served as a well-endowed trail blazer who would make Nikki's choice of swim wear less scandalous.

Samantha and Ted seemed to have a good deal of fun splashing each other, horsing around, and hugging each other until she elected to move to the spa. She asked Ted to join her, but he declined. As she settled in for her solo soak, her eyes closed and steam rose to envelope her head and shoulders. Bubbles from the jets surrounded her and inflated the bra of her bikini, which did not need any artificial enhancement.

Pete and Antonia Carmelo both spent a fair amount of time in the pool before joining Samantha in the spa and then heading back to the pool. Although Nikki was sure that Antonia would have looked positively captivating in a bikini, she wore a modest, maroon, one-piece suit. Back in the pool, Pete jocularly warned Samantha about the dangers of parboiling, and she moved from the spa back to the pool, where she gave Pete a close hug and a kiss on the cheek to thank him for his "medical" advice. Antonia did not seem pleased. Eventually, they were joined by Penny Hamilton.

Aaron Long and Art Hamilton sat at an open table, closer to the water, observing their wives, imbibing fresh cocktails, and having what appeared to be a genial conversation. Nikki wondered what they were talking about. Perhaps Art was complimenting Samantha's swimsuit, which was in fact worthy of compliments. Perhaps Aaron was noting how impervious to

Father Time Penny's legs appeared to be, and they in fact were quite attractive. Or, and Nikki smiled at this thought, perhaps they were exploring and bonding over the concept of "nuts and sluts" and hypothesizing which of the party attendees fit into either or both of those categories. If local rumors had any validity, there were plenty of candidates.

Satisfied that she would have plenty of female company in the pool, Nikki turned to Maryanne and said, "OK. Let's get changed."

The Millers' bedroom was quite large. The centerpiece was a king-sized bed with a brass headboard. On the wall facing the bed was a big screen TV. The room extended past the sleeping area, and Maryanne explained that the door on the right led to the bathroom and one on the left to a large walk-in closet. Past those two doors, the bedroom ended with another door. Nikki asked where that door led and Maryanne said it was a combination study/home office, with desks and computers for both her and Ted when they had to bring work home.

Maryanne told Nikki she could change right there in the bedroom with her or, if she preferred privacy, she could use the study or the bathroom. Nikki had no qualms about stripping in front of her friend, but she did want to see the bathroom. Maryanne led the way. She explained that she and Ted regarded the shower as a bit of a playpen. It was 10-feet square, with two normal "Rain Forest" shower heads, and two high pressure pulsating shower heads with hoses to help rinse off you or your partner or, she added, to provide some "added stimulation." The front wall was glass, and it incorporated the entry door. The other three walls were tiled, and a built-in, two-foot-wide bench spanned the rear wall. The back wall also featured several shelves, on which Nikki saw an array of body washes, shampoos, shaving paraphernalia for both sexes, bar soap, and a pair of rather large dildos.

With her eyes focused on the sex toys, Nikki said "I could spend an hour in here, Maryanne."

"I often do, Nikki."

They went back to the bedroom proper to doff their cocktail attire and don their bikinis. Nikki put on the black bikini that Maryanne had suggested, and Maryanne nodded approvingly. Nikki added a zippered coral-colored Roman beach dress to wear on her stroll between the bedroom to the pool. It was fetching, extending to mid-thigh, but Maryanne jokingly scolded her for her cowardice.

Maryanne chose an orange bikini. The color assured Maryanne that no one with a working pair of eyes would miss the show she was putting on.

"Are you wearing anything over your suit, Maryanne?"

"Why, Nikki? Once I hit the pool, I'd take it off anyway, so what's the point?"

"I could lie and tell you it has to do with modesty, but it doesn't. Tell me, Maryanne, when I am wearing this cover-up, what do you see?"

"Your legs, of course."

"And what do you think?"

"That they are pretty damned nice to look at. That's what I think, Nikki. Pretty damned easy on the eyes."

"I'm glad you think so. Look, I'm not above showing off and if I'm going to show off I might as well showcase my best asset and I think my legs are my best asset. The men can look all they want until I get poolside, take off this little robe, and display the rest of the Nikki Beaumont package until I drop into the water."

"Which you don't do right away?"

"That's right. I sit on the edge of the pool with my legs dangling and my body in full view."

"You have a bit of the whore in you Nikki. I find this side of you to be very becoming. So, which of my guests are you planning to seduce while Jack enjoys the California sun?"

"We'll see, Maryanne. Look, it's all in good fun. I think if I were to walk out there without the cover-up some men might gawk, and their wives would immediately scold them and describe me in unflattering terms, which is what some of them are probably doing right now about Samantha Long. But since I'm covered up, the wives can't really scold, and I won't be standing up and showing off in this skimpy suit for very long when I get to the pool."

"I never knew you were such a tease, Nikki. I've never heard you talk like this."

"Well, yes, I guess I am being a bit of a tease, but I am glad Samantha broke the ice with her bikini. We won't seem so scandalous. With my cover-up, I'll be modest by comparison, a bit of a mystery until the cover-up comes off. Anyway, blame yourself, Maryanne. You're the one who told me to show folks what Jack's been ignoring. I'm just trying to enhance the show, make the presentation a bit more enticing."

"Imitation is the sincerest form of flattery, Nikki." With that, Maryanne went to her closet, grabbed a yellow cover-up, and pulled it on over her suit. She walked up to Nikki, held Nikki's face in her hands, and pressed her lips against Nikki's, firmly, allowing them to linger long enough to mean something. Before Nikki could process that kiss, Maryanne said, "Let's go."

Chapter 6

 fair amount of time sitting on the edge of the pool, letting anyone who was interested get a good view of how the martial arts had enhanced her core. Once she felt that her male admirers had taken in their fill, she dropped into the water and swam a few laps to work off some of the ice cream. Then she moved to the spa to enjoy the warmth and allow the jets to massage her back. After a long soak in the spa, she got out and pulled on her cover-up. She sat for a while and chatted with Gary Forsythe and Art and Penny Hamilton, trading jokes and talking about their summer vacation plans. Eventually, Nikki signaled to the waiter and asked for another Greyhound. It was her third, but why count? She lived next door. If she couldn't drive, she could walk home. By the time she finished her drink, all of the other guests had departed. Ted and Maryanne came and joined her at her table.

"Bartender's getting set to depart, ladies. Time for refills."

He ambled to the bar and coaxed the bartender into a Greyhound for Nikki and two martinis. Handing the glass to Maryanne, he said, "Bombay Sapphire, my love, just as you like it."

He waved goodnight to the bartender and turned back to the women. "Cheers. Enjoy your drinks. The bartender is leaving but have no fear. Your host is a competent mixologist, and I can cater to your every remaining need. And I do mean every remaining need."

Maryanne chided him good naturedly, "I think you're a little tipsy, Ted. And I don't think you're talking about our need for drinks."

"I am a bit tipsy, Maryanne, but not with alcohol. I am besotted by the beautiful women who sit in front of me. To one I am wed. For the other, I lust and hope she reciprocates that feeling."

Maryanne did not seem all that offended by Ted's overt flirting with Nikki. She had long since grown accustomed to his frisky bent, "Get back in the spa, Ted. Maybe the jets will shake you from that rhapsody."

"I'm going, my love, but only if you and Nikki join me, lest I drown."

The women laughed at what they regarded as one of Ted's typical, slightly stewed performances. They brought their drinks, and his, to the edge of the spa and joined him. Maryanne brought her phone and placed it within arm's reach, but beyond any likely splash from the spa.

The air temperature was beginning to fall. The warm water felt really good. They sipped on their drinks and reviewed the evening's festivities. They all agreed it was a fabulous party, even if Samantha Long got a little too free with her hands in the pool with Ted and, later, with Pete Carmelo. Ted played the role of a good host, returning her hug and planting a meaningless kiss on her cheek. Antonia was less accepting of Samantha's free spirited pool antics with Pete. Antonia had nipped that in the bud, gently insinuating herself between Pete and Samantha without causing a scene. Ted said that Maryanne and Nikki had been dazzling, at cocktails and at poolside. They both thanked him for the compliment and Nikki blew him a kiss.

Maryanne said that she was upset that Jack did not make any effort to attend.

"Look, it was a great party. We're good friends. Hell, we are best friends. He couldn't bend his schedule to get here? "

Nicole looked disconsolate. Maryanne regretted her speech and apologized immediately.

"You don't need to apologize, Maryanne. I've been through this with Jack many times. I'm just not his top priority."

At that point, Ted piped in.

"Forget about Jack. He's irrelevant tonight. Let's get some snapshots and selfies of this night because the party was such a blast and because we can show them to Jack later to make him wish he had been here. Maryanne, you sit on Nikki's left, and I'll sit on her right. We'll put our arms out behind her and put on some big smiles and you take a few selfies. Nikki can show them to Jack when he gets home to encourage him to come to the next party."

Nikki enjoyed the pose. She enjoyed feeling Ted's and Maryanne's arms against her back and shoulders. And she enjoyed being with them, smiling with them, and laughing with them.

Maryanne clicked a few shots and then she and Ted resumed their positions on the spa benches across from each other, with Nikki on the bench between theirs.

Maryanne said that she thought it would be fun if she sat on Ted's lap and asked Nikki to take the photo. Maryanne sat, her arms around his torso, with her face turned toward the camera, both of them smiling brightly. Nikki snapped a few shots and she saw Maryanne turn and kiss Ted. The kiss lasted quite some time, but Nikki did not find it at all off putting. To the contrary, she found it to be rather exciting. She caught the moment with the camera and laughed, "You're busted."

"Well then, let me bust you, Nikki. Get over here and climb on Ted's lap, facing the camera and giving me your best smile."

Nikki did as she was asked, popping up out of the water and onto Ted's lap. It dawned on her that it had been ages since she had sat on a man's lap. As Jack grew increasingly distant, the very thought of such intimacy became farfetched. But she liked sitting here, with her arms around her handsome friend, the warm water washing over both of them. Her smile for the camera was genuine. She might be behaving somewhat scandalously, but she was happy. She thanked Ted and started to leave when Maryanne said, "Not so fast. I want a picture of you kissing him. It will make great evidence if I ever decide to divorce him. Or, you can use it to make Jack jealous." Nikki knew it was inappropriate, but she saw little harm in it. Jack wasn't there to kiss her and, frankly, she needed to be kissed. Moreover, she had often daydreamed about kissing Ted—and more—and now here she was, in his lap, with her best friend urging her to kiss a man to whom she would gladly submit completely were he not married to her best friend.

Maybe it was the Greyhounds; maybe it was Jack's disinterest and increasingly icy posture; maybe it was the warmth of the water, the lanterns, or the full moon bathed in clouds; maybe it was all of them, conspiring to convince Nikki that it was all in good fun. She turned to Ted, moistened her lips, and pressed them against his. He did the same. It was a nice kiss, almost chaste, like the kiss a young couple would share at the end of their first date. Neither one of them sought more, but they both knew that their kiss had meaning. She allowed her lips to linger on his until Maryanne interjected, "Hey, you two, break if off or get a room." Nikki thought momentarily about a room, about spending the night with Ted, but she doubted that Maryanne was interested in lending out her husband for anything beyond a harmless kiss.

As Nikki hopped off Ted's lap and returned to her spot on the bench, Ted said "Let's round out the photos. Let me take a shot of you two, smiling at the camera. Who's going to sit on whose lap for this one?"

Maryanne beckoned Nikki to join her. Nikki hopped up on Maryanne's lap, put one arm around Maryanne for stability, and turned to face the camera.

"Smile, ladies," said Ted as he snapped busily away. "This could be one of my favorite photos of all time. I've photographed quite a few fashion models, but you two in those swimsuits may be the nicest array of eye candy I've ever photographed."

Nikki looked, listened, recalled the many compliments that Ted had passed her way tonight, and thought, "I wish Jack could make me feel as good about myself as Ted does." She knew it was sexist, but she liked it that Ted thought of her as eye candy. She decided to return the compliment.

"Oh, those photos of you and Maryanne will be far more enchanting. You two are the best-looking couple I've ever known. Can you send me one of those photos?"

"I'll send them all, Nikki. Souvenirs of our Summer Kick-Off party. I'm glad Maryanne was able to talk you into coming. Have you had a good time?"

"I've had great time, Ted." Nikki was still on Maryanne's lap. She turned toward Maryanne and thanked her. "I'm so appreciative, Maryanne. Thanks so much for nagging me into coming."

Nikki started to hop off, but Maryanne closed her arm gently around Nikki's waist to delay her departure.

"One more photo, Nikki. You kissed the host. How about a kiss for the hostess?"

Nikki was reluctant. She remembered the kiss that Maryanne had given her earlier that evening when they had changed into their swimsuits. It was not a kiss from someone who wanted to stay in the Friend Zone. Her mind flashed as well to the day last summer when Jack and Ted were off playing golf and she and Maryanne sat on the edge of the Beaumonts' pool. Maryanne was looking wistful, and, for a change, it was Nikki's turn to ask what was wrong.

"I have a question that I'm afraid to ask you, Nikki."

"Don't be silly, Maryanne. We're best friends. You can ask me anything."

Maryanne shifted to face Nikki a bit more directly. "You find Ted to be very attractive, don't you?"

"What woman wouldn't find him to be attractive, Maryanne?"

"And sexy?"

Nikki wasn't sure where this conversation was going, but she answered honestly, "Yes, and sexy."

"I see the way you look at him sometimes, Nikki. Do you ever fantasize about making love with my husband?"

"Maryanne, I would never . . ."

"That wasn't my question. Do you fantasize about Ted?"

Nikki was embarrassed, but she had told her friend that she could ask Nikki any question, and she was disinclined to lie. "Yes, Maryanne, I've thought about what it might be like with Ted. I think it's only natural given how distant and cold Jack has been for some time now and how attractive Ted is. I envy you. I envy the affection you two share and the passion to which that most likely translates in the bedroom. Do I fantasize? Yes. I'd be lying if I said I didn't."

"I think Ted feels the same way about you, Nikki. I have no doubt you could entice him into your bed with very little effort. Sometimes, I visualize you and Ted together. And when I do, you seem to be so happy."

"I'd never hurt you like that, Maryanne."

"Well, I know what an iceberg Jack has been toward you these last few years, and I know how much that hurts you. It would hardly be surprising for you to look for someone to fill the void that Jack has left in your life. And Ted would be a perfect someone to fill that void for you, Nikki. I know that. And I think I could accept it if you and Ted were to succumb to temptation."

"Maryanne, he's your husband. He's off limits. Don't talk like that."

The next question caught Nikki by complete surprise.

"Do you ever fantasize about me, Nikki?"

Nikki stared at Maryanne, speechless. Maryanne continued, somewhat haltingly, but in a highly emotional manner.

"I think about you. A lot, Nikki. A lot. I think of kissing you, holding you close to me, caressing you. I think of you and me together. And I wonder if there is any possibility of that coming to pass. Because I really want that. Maybe I can fill the void that Jack has created in your life. I would love to do that for you."

Nikki had thought about Maryanne in that way on more than one occasion, and the more that Jack distanced himself from Nikki, the more enamored she became of that possibility. Yes, she fantasized about Ted, but even more than that, she fantasized about Maryanne. But she could not bring herself to respond to Maryanne's advances. Nikki had never been with another woman. She was not prepared to deal with the distinct possibility that she was bisexual, even if Maryanne was the other half of the equation.

As Nikki struggled with how to phrase her response, Maryanne had turned and pointed to the doors that led to the Beaumonts' bedroom.

"The guys won't be back for hours. Let's spend some time together, Nikki. Please. If you don't enjoy it, I'll never bother you again. Let me love you."

"I'm flattered, Maryanne. Truly. If I wanted to be with any woman, it would be you. It could only be you. Don't think I haven't thought of you that way. I have and I do. But there is a big gap between thinking and doing. Can't we keep our friendship the way it is?" She hesitated for a few seconds before inadvertently letting her innermost thought slip out, "For now."

Maryanne pounced of those two words. "For now?"

"For now, Maryanne."

"How will I know if you change your mind?"

"You'll know. Believe me. You'll know."

Now, as she sat on Maryanne's lap in the moonlight, with the warm water of the spa washing over her legs, Nikki looked into Maryanne's eyes. That look told Maryanne, as clearly as any words could, that Nikki had changed her mind. But Nikki decided to leave no doubt in Maryanne's mind. "I've thought about you ever since our talk by my pool last summer, Maryanne. And I've regretted how I responded."

She turned her head toward Maryanne and kissed her. It was not the chaste kiss she had shared with Ted. It was a hungry, open-mouth kiss that said there would be more to come before this night was through. She slid her hand under Maryanne's bra and softly fondled her breast, toying with her nipple, which became excitingly hard. Maryanne returned the favor, to Nikki's delight.

Ted snapped away, enjoying the scene that was unfolding before him. He and Maryanne were open and frank about the attractions they felt for other people, and about their extra-marital activities, but they had never disclosed to each other the unimaginable lust they each felt for Nicole Beaumont. It was a secret that Ted harbored to avoid any interference with Maryanne's friendship with Nikki. Maryanne held it close because, while she had now and then enjoyed the pleasures of other women, she did not love any of them. Nikki was different.

Maryanne and Nikki disengaged, smiling at each other like two children who had just opened their first Christmas presents and wanted to see what else Santa had brought. Nikki looked at Ted, and then at Maryanne, "I don't want to spend tonight alone."

Maryanne smiled at her friend. "We were hoping you felt that way. We'd like to think our night has just begun, Nikki."

"So, there's room for me at the inn?"

Ted laughed. "There's room. There's always been room for you Nikki. Right between Maryanne and me on our bed. Will that do?"

"Like a dream come true."

They exited the spa, dried off as best they could, and headed off to Wonderland.

Chapter 7

NIKKI WAS EXCITED as she entered the bedroom. She had never participated in a threesome, and she attempted to visualize how, in what order, and in what combination their lovemaking might proceed. Maryanne took her by the hand and led her to the shower. She turned on the water and the steam began to rise.

"I don't like the taste of chlorine, Nikki. Let's wash that off before we get to the main event."

Maryanne slowly removed Nikki's bikini, first fondling her breasts as she removed the bra and then sliding down on her knees to remove the bottom half of the suit. As she did so, her hands gently massaged the front and back of Nikki's legs and allowed herself the freedom to insert her fingers into Nikki, who was already quite wet. When Maryanne stood, Nikki eagerly removed Maryanne's bra and returned the favor. As she did so, Nikki asked herself how she possibly could have rebuffed Maryanne's previous overture and why she waited a year to act on her desire for her friend. She removed Maryanne's bikini bottom in the same manner that Maryanne had, using her hands and fingers to stroke Maryanne's legs and probe her genitals. She then stood up, facing her friend. Nikki stepped forward so that there was no space between their bodies, wrapped her arms around Maryanne, and resurrected the kiss they had shared in the spa. Maryanne then took her by the hand and led her into the shower. Ted followed.

The women stood under one of the shower heads, Ted under the other, letting the hot water flow over them. Maryanne reached for a bottle of bath gel, squeezed a generous portion across the top of Nikki's shoulders and began to work it into a rich lather with which Maryanne massaged every part of Nikki's body, running her fingers slowly but deeply between her cheeks, and then lingering at the crevice between her thighs, where she occasionally penetrated with one or two fingers.

Nikki turned to allow Maryanne to lather her back when she saw Ted. He was unlike anything Nikki had ever seen. "Large" did not do him justice. He was huge, and his length was magnified by his thickness. She was awe struck. She could not take her eyes off him. She didn't know if he was intending Maryanne to be his first partner of the evening, but she hoped that Ted had his eyes on her. Maryanne kissed Nicole on the shoulders and said in a soft voice, "I think my husband wants you, Nikki. I do too, but I'll wait my turn."

Nikki had always liked oral sex, and it was the one offer she could make to Jack that might occasionally induce him into their bed. As she looked at Ted, she realized that this was an opportunity she could not, would not, let pass. She slid down to her knees and took him as deeply into her mouth as she physically could. She moved her lips up and down along the length of his shaft while he began to thrust gently, back and forth in her mouth, as she hoped he would in another part of her anatomy later that night. When his thrusts beg to quicken, his moans did likewise, and

Nicole realized that he was about to ejaculate. When he was done, Nicole stood up. Ted wrapped his arms around her, pulling her close to him. As the hot water cascaded over them, they kissed, holding the kiss for what seemed like an eternity.

At that point, Nicole turned around and faced Maryanne. Maryanne handed the bath gel to Nikki and murmured softly as Nikki visited every pore of Maryanne's body with rich lather and probing fingers. Nikki moved behind her, pressing her body against Maryanne's back while her arms wrapped around Maryanne's waist and moved down, across her stomach and to the top of her thighs. Nikki moved her left hand upward, to fondle Maryanne's breast and, as she did so, Maryanne began to feel a pleasant thrusting motion inside her. Nikki had taken one of the toys from the shelf and was slowly sliding it back and forth, each movement probing more deeply into the woman whose advances she had once rejected. It continued for several minutes when Maryanne asked Nikki to stop.

"Am I hurting you?"

"No, Nikki. I like it. And I like the fact that you enjoyed doing that to me you. I need to spend time alone with you and some of our bedroom toys. But I have other thoughts about how I want you to finish with me just now, and they don't involve any toys. Why don't we all rinse, towel off, and hop on the bed?"

Maryanne was the first to the bed. She grabbed a pillow, placed it under her bottom, and spread her legs as an invitation to Nikki. Although this was new to her, Nikki did not hesitate. She had visualized this for quite some time. She positioned herself between Maryanne's legs, inching forward until there was nowhere else to go. She kissed and licked Maryanne's external genitals and then slid her tongue inside, probing and searching, then flicking it side-to-side and up-and-down. She did so slowly at first, then more quickly, then slowly again. Suddenly, Nikki worked her way to non-stop warp speed inside Maryanne. With each change of pace of Nicole's tongue, Maryanne would writhe with pleasure, pleading for more. Maryanne's orgasm had no effect on Nikki's lovemaking. She continued to have her way with Maryanne until Maryanne's entire body had shuddered with excitement a number of times. When Nikki had finished, there was no need to ask if her partner had enjoyed it. Maryanne wrapped her arms around Nikki and said, as she tried to catch her breath, "That was worth waiting for."

Maryanne looked across Nikki's body to the far side of the bed. "Feeling neglected, Ted?" It was obvious that Nikki's and Maryanne's lovemaking had restored his vitality.

Nikki was enthralled by the sight of his erection. She asked Maryanne, "You or me?"

"You, sweetheart. You want him and he most assuredly wants you. And you've never had him. He's quite a treat."

Nikki crawled up against Ted and they embraced. He kissed her hungrily, with far more passion than he had kissed her in the spa. He then began to move down her body slowly, fondling her breasts and lingering while he took them in his mouth, using his tongue to tease her nipples, moving his hands down to his ultimate goal, and slowly inserting one, two, and three fingers in a way that made her moan. When he positioned his head between her legs, she gasped, then laid back to enjoy the continuous movement of his tongue inside her. She had no idea how long he tarried there, but it was a hell of a lot longer than Jack had ever spent on the rare, long-ago occasions when he indulged her needs. And Ted was a lot more enthusiastic, a lot more. Ted clearly wanted her, and it thrilled her to be wanted by a man after the continual cold shoulder she experienced at Jack's hands. She, in turn, wanted Ted. She needed Ted, and she entreated him to love her, to love her and please her the way he made love to and pleased Maryanne. The fact that Maryanne was watching did nothing to inhibit the enthusiasm with which Nikki made love to Ted. To the contrary, fucking her best friend's husband while her best friend watched with feral excitement transported Nikki to heretofore unknown levels of ecstasy. The nuns at Saint Theresa's Elementary School would have been shocked and horrified at Nikki's wanton disregard for the Sixth Commandment, but she was having too much fun to care about that.

Ted rose to his knees and positioned himself between her legs. She looked at the enormity of the pleasurable fate about to befall her, begged him to enter, and moaned with delight as he slowly did so. They began a rhythmic thrust that she wished would never end. She ran her hands up and down his chest and then pulled him down, close enough to allow her to kiss him.

Suddenly, he withdrew, rolled onto his back, and asked her to climb on. She lowered herself onto him, and they resumed the thrusting. The orgasms came. She did not keep count, but—in terms of numbers and pleasure—it was unlike anything Jack had ever elicited from her. When she was done, she realized that Ted was not finished. He rolled her over onto her back and reentered. Thrusting quick and hard, he finished in a rush of pleasure.

"My, Ted, have you ever made love to me like that?" Maryanne's eyebrow was raised, but she quickly allowed a smile to light up her face.

"Often, my love. Often. And you know it. But I have to say the show you two put on was a human erector set. If I couldn't get it done after watching you two, you would have had to check me for a pulse." Then, having caught his breath, he added, "Does anyone want another drink?"

Nikki was ready for another Greyhound. She pulled on her cover-up and went out to the bar to prepare one. Ted wrapped himself in a robe and followed but he was not ready for another cocktail.

"Ted, I don't know what to say. Maryanne is so lucky."

"Well, I think I've been pretty lucky tonight. You know, if Jack had been here, our little threesome would never have come to be. So, I think I should thank Jack Beaumont for doing everything he could to allow us to enjoy each other."

She placed her palm against his cheek and stroked it gently. "Frankly, Ted, I don't really care about Jack anymore."

"I hope you care about us, Nikki, Maryanne and me. What we had tonight doesn't need to be a one-night stand. Do you think I'm going to be able to erase this from my memory bank? Do you think Maryanne will?"

"I hope not. I know I won't."

Nikki thought for moment, then started to speak, but hesitated.

"What, Nikki?"

"Ted, I'm not the first woman that you and Maryanne have shared like this, am I?"

"No, Nikki, you're not. There have been a few. Not many. But you're the only one for whom both Maryanne and I have strong feelings. Do you have any doubt about that?"

"I've known about Maryanne's feelings for me for over a year. She told me." Nikki felt that Ted was entitled to know what she meant, so she recounted Maryanne's prior poolside advances. Ted did not seem surprised.

"Maryanne and I have never talked about those feelings, Nikki, but I have long believed she loves you."

"Then why the other women, Ted?"

"I'm no shrink, Nikki. I don't know. What I do know is I never saw her as energized by sex with any woman as she was with you tonight. And her excitement for you aroused in me an incredible craving for you."

"Is this the first time you've felt like that about me, Ted?" Nikki smiled as demurely as one can in light of the circumstances.

"Hardly." Then it was Ted's turn to smile. He added, "And I think you already knew the answer to that question."

"You know, Ted, I've fantasized about you quite often, but the reality exceeds the fantasy." She turned to face him, wrapped her arms around him, pressed her body against his, and kissed him with the ardor reserved for lovers.

Nikki was disconcerted by the fact that Maryanne had shared her charms with other women but realized that she only had herself to blame. If she had acted on her feelings for Maryanne, if she had accepted the love that Maryanne offered that day by the pool, she felt sure that Maryanne would have stopped looking elsewhere. As for Ted, Nikki was not totally surprised. After all, he was the best-looking man around, he spent time photographing many women, and she was sure any number of them had let him know they would enjoy his company. That didn't make it right, but it provided context. Nikki nonetheless decided to push a little on the "why" of tonight's escapade.

"And you, Ted? Surely, you're not in love with me? You have Maryanne."

"No, Nikki. I'm not in love with you. I love Maryanne. But I do have a deep affection for you. Apart from Maryanne, you may be the nicest, sweetest woman I've ever known. And please don't be offended, but I meant it when I said I lusted for you. I have for a long time."

"Don't apologize, Ted. But why do you need other women? Mary-anne strikes me as everything a man could ask for and, based on what

I've seen tonight, you don't have my problem. Jack is distant, cold, and disinterested in sex, at least sex with me. Maryanne is the exact opposite. She is as enthusiastic in bed as I could ever imagine."

"It's complicated, Nikki. But I'd rather not discuss it tonight. Tonight, with Maryanne and you, is as good as it possibly can get. Let's savor it."

He kissed her lightly on the cheek and they walked back to the bedroom. Maryanne was sitting up against the headboard, her arms wrapped around her knees. She flashed Nikki one of the most bewitching smiles she had ever seen.

"It's ironic," said Nikki. "I wasn't going to come to this party. Instead, I ended up having the most passionate night of my life, ever. It was intoxicating . . . exhilarating."

"The night isn't over, Nikki. I think Ted might have one more tiger in his tank. Ted?"

"I'm up for it."

Nikki and Maryanne laughed at the double entendre. Nikki asked, "What more is there to do in one night?"

"My Ted has always had a fascination with the back door, Nikki. Tell us, Ted, do you see any that fascinate you tonight?"

"Two, but I fear I don't have two in me, my love."

"Well, if it is to be only one, what's your preference? Tried and true? Or fresh and new?"

"That was quite poetic, Maryanne. Why don't you roll your pretty little bottom my way?"

"Don't I get a say?" Nikki's question startled her bedmates. "I haven't come this far to stop now. What's the saying, 'In for a dime, in for a dollar'?"

"Well, in this case," said Maryanne, "it's in for at least ten inches."

The alcohol and the pleasures she had already experienced had stripped Nikki of all inhibition. She turned her back to him and said, in her best telephone-sex voice, "Do you want this, Ted?"

"Do you really need to ask?"

"You're a photographer, Ted. How good is it, Ted, in your professional opinion?"

He looked at his wife and smiled. "I've only seen one better."

"Would you like to sample it?"

"Who wouldn't?"

Maryanne interjected, "If this is going to be the final event of the evening, I'd like to be involved as more than an onlooker."

With that she moved to Ted's side, knelt next to him, and bent to take him in her mouth. Maryanne tarried only long enough to be sure that Ted was rigid enough for what was to follow. When she disengaged, she grinned and looked up at Nikki. "I think he's ready now."

Nikki knelt on the bed and slid invitingly forward to rest on her forearms. Ted positioned himself behind. Maryanne began to apply K-Y Jelly to Nikki's point of entry to ease the penetration and minimize her discomfort. Maryanne applied it generously, slowly working the lubricant into Nikki as far as her slender fingers would reach. Nikki enjoyed the feel of Maryanne's fingers, until Maryanne withdrew them and spread more of the lubricant on Ted's erection, using a light touch. She marveled, as she always did, at the sight of what Nikki would soon enjoy. Maryanne appeared to approach her job wistfully, as if she would gladly exchange places with Nikki, which in fact she would. Nikki felt Ted's hands on her hips and then felt him enter and penetrate, ever so gradually. She murmured until she had accepted him completely. She continued to murmur as he moved his hands to the top of her thighs and pulled her back toward him. As he began to thrust, her murmurs turned to moans. He began gently, allowing her to become accustomed to the magnitude of the task for which she had volunteered, thrusting slowly until she responded by adopting his rhythm. She began repeatedly to call his name, in a whisper at first and then graduating to a series of unrelenting demands for "More." As she did so, their pace quickened and he exploded inside her.

Nikki had asked Jack to indulge her curiosity regarding anal sex on more than one occasion, but he had always responded that he found the thought to be distasteful. She accepted his rejection of her overtures at face value, but she did wonder from time to time whether he found it to be equally distasteful with whatever woman, or women, occupied his nights in Los Angeles. Nonetheless, Nikki would occasionally daydream about it, hoping against hope that Jack would change his mind. Now, she no longer needed to daydream. Jack no longer mattered. Ted had given life to her daydream and Nikki liked it; she liked it a lot. She looked forward enthusiastically to the next time she would receive Ted Miller like this.

Nikki had lost all track of time, but she was thirsty. She offered to pour a fresh Bombay Sapphire martini for Ted and Maryanne while she fetched another Greyhound for herself. She asked Maryanne if she wanted to switch to a Greyhound to give her a boost of Vitamin C, but Maryanne said she would hold the Grapefruit juice for the morning and stick to the martini for now. Ted concurred. As she headed off to the bar, she heard Ted instructing her to "Just coat the ice with the vermouth and pour it off through the strainer, Nikki, if you please."

She arrived at the bar and was happy to see that there was still enough ice for the three drinks she was about to make. She made a tall Greyhound, light with very little Grey Goose and plenty of grapefruit juice. She found the dry vermouth, poured it over ice in a shaker and then drained it off. She poured the Bombay into the shaker, capped it and shook it vigorously. She filled Ted's and Maryanne's glasses with fresh ice and poured the elixir into the glasses. After how Ted and Maryanne had pleased her tonight, she wanted to make sure she mixed their drinks just how they liked them. As she added the olives, she allowed her mind to drift forward, to a future without Jack in which she would be happy to prepare post-coital martinis for Ted and Maryanne Miller. She even fantasized about moving in with the Millers and creating a "throuple" in which they might live happily ever after. She would raise that possibility with them tomorrow, prepared for rejection but excited by the possibility and curious to see their reaction. Or, she might just suggest that she stay with the Millers when Jack went on his never-ending California sojourns, so that she could finally enjoy on a regular basis the passion that her husband had denied her for the better part of their marriage. After all, she was fairly confident that Jack spent his California evenings with one or more objects of his desire. Why shouldn't she enjoy the same flexibility? Whether that would come to pass, time would tell. Maybe Nikki was being presumptuous. Maybe the Millers had no interest in any kind of permanent relationship with her. Whatever the future might hold, she thanked God for his gift to her of the Millers, if only for this night.

Nikki broke her reverie and returned to the bedroom. She asked if she could take a shower before retiring. Ted answered, "mi casa su casa." She kissed him goodnight and he watched as she completed the same ritual with a somewhat more prolonged kiss with Maryanne. Nikki handed them their drinks and raised hers.

"Maybe this is all a dream. Maybe I'll wake up in the morning, all alone in my bed and crying because I wanted it to be real and it wasn't. But

I hope not. I never knew it could be like this and I want it to be like this again and again, with you."

She took a swig of her drink to toast the night. Ted and Maryanne did the same, imbibing most of their martinis in a single gulp. No doubt to facilitate a good night's sleep.

Nikki headed off to the shower. She lingered for a while on the bench, indulging herself with one of Maryanne's toys while the warm water washed over her. The thought of Maryanne playing with her like this filled her mind. By the time she returned to the bedroom, Ted and Maryanne were both sound asleep. She crawled between them and summoned Morpheus, entertaining thoughts of some morning delight with one or both of her neighbors.

Chapter 8

THE EARLY MORNING sun filtered through the slats on the bedroom blinds. Nikki was the first to arise and she was looking forward to another taste of Maryanne. She rolled onto her side to face Maryanne's back and draped her arm over Maryanne's waist. She ran her hand down the front of Maryanne's thigh. Maryanne did not respond.

"Maryanne don't play hard to get with me. I need some Maryanne for breakfast. Or should I see what Ted has on the menu?"

No response. Nikki brushed away Maryanne's raven locks and kissed the nape of her neck. Nothing. Something was wrong. Nikki placed her trained nurse's fingers against Maryanne's jugular. No pulse. For an instant, Nikki froze in place, absorbing the horror of what lay before her. Maryanne was dead.

Nikki turned to deliver the news to Ted. He was in no condition to receive it. He, too, was dead.

Chapter 9

NIKKI BEGAN TO cry uncontrollably. She found it difficult to communicate with the 911 operator over her sobs, but she eventually regained her composure sufficiently to let the operator know that there were two dead persons at 2170 Highland Estates North; that the deceased were the owners of the property, Ted and Maryanne Miller; that her name was Nicole Beaumont; that so far as she knew she was the only person in the house; and that she would wait there until the police arrived.

Nikki realized that she could not greet the gendarmes in her birthday suit. She had two choices. The bikini and beach dress or her cocktail attire. Either one would speak volumes to the police about her activities of the preceding evening, particularly when they noticed the glassware for three on the nightstands. She opted for the cocktail dress. She thought about moving the Greyhound glasses to the patio to make the appearances of a threesome less obvious, but she quickly decided against moving anything. Jack had always snickered about supposedly intelligent people who lied to the police or disturbed evidence when they otherwise had nothing to hide. "It's the cover-up that always gets them," he would say. While she had decided last night that her future had no further room for Jack, he was a good lawyer and she heeded his longstanding counsel in this regard. She relocated to the foyer and waited for the authorities to arrive.

She did not wait long. Two detectives arrived first, followed in quick order by the medical examiner and a forensics team. Inspector James Milliken introduced himself to Nikki and then introduced his partner, Sergeant Joanne Tracey. He asked Nikki where the bodies were and, when she pointed the way, still crying, he asked her to wait in the living room with Sergeant Tracey while he organized his team. He asked the medical examiner for the usual preliminaries, the approximate time of death and the likely cause of death. He directed the forensics team to rope off the bedroom and treat it as a crime scene until they could determine otherwise. Sergeant Tracey did not speak to her. Nikki simply looked at the floor in front of her as tears continued to streak her face. Sergeant Tracey studied Nikki's face as they sat together and, as Nikki continued to cry, the sergeant handed Nikki a pocket package of Kleenex. Otherwise, the sergeant sat impassively waiting for direction from Milliken.

When he returned to the living room, he asked Nikki if she felt up to a few questions. Before answering him, she asked why they were treating the bedroom as a crime scene. He responded that when there were unexplained deaths it was their practice to treat the site as a crime scene so that evidence could be preserved until the cause of death could be determined.

"And you suspect foul play here, Inspector?"

"Well, Mrs. Beaumont, we have two relatively young and healthy people who died in the same bed on the same night. The likelihood that they both suffered fatal heart attacks at the same time strikes me as pretty darn remote."

"And how does that affect me, Inspector?"

"It depends, Mrs. Beaumont. Are you willing to answer a few questions?"

"We can try. No guarantees."

He furrowed his brow at her answer. She noticed the querulous look on his face and added, "My husband is a lawyer."

The Inspector quickly discarded any pretense of friendliness. "Look, Mrs. Beaumont, we're not here to do anything except gather some facts. So, let's take it one question at a time, OK?"

"Sure. I'm not trying to be difficult, Inspector. I'm happy to help, but you've characterized this as a crime scene and I know I have rights. Let's just see where this goes."

"From the look of the premises, there was a party here last night. Is that right?

Nikki considered for a moment congratulating the Inspector for his firm grasp of the obvious until her reason put a halt to any such sarcasm. Instead, she simply answered, "Yes."

"Was there a particular reason for the party?"

"Well, the invitation indicated it was a party to kick off the summer. Cocktails, a buffet dinner, and swimming."

"You attended?"

"Yes."

"I see you are wearing a wedding ring. Did your husband attend too?"

"No. He is in Los Angeles on business."

"You found the Millers this morning?"

"I discovered that they were dead this morning, yes."

"What time did you come to the Millers' house this morning?"

"I didn't."

"You didn't come here this morning?"

"No. I did not go home last night, Inspector."

"I guess that would explain the dress you are wearing, huh?"

"It would."

"Pardon my indelicacy, Mrs. Beaumont, but where did you spend the night?"

"In the bedroom."

"Alone?"

"No."

Nikki knew there was no way to avoid the events of last night. She had not done anything wrong, at least not criminally wrong. She supposed that a large number of folks would regard her love for Maryanne and her desire for Ted as immoral. She didn't, not given the state of her marriage. She also supposed that Jack might pounce on her infidelity as the basis for divorcing her and moving into the open with whatever woman he had been keeping on the side. Forensic evidence would place Nikki in the shower, in the bedroom, and on the bed. She was sure DNA would establish the nature of their bedroom festivities. She decided to cooperate with respect to the facts that would be easily corroborated by the forensics. If Milliken or Tracey went over that line, she would play it by ear.

"Look, Inspector. I spent the night with the Millers. Call it what you will, a threesome, a ménage a trois. When we had finished, I slept between them on the bed. When I woke up, they were dead, and I called 911."

"Was anyone else in the house while you three were in the bedroom?"

"I don't think so. It looked like the caterers had packed up and left. The bar was still set up, but the bartender was gone."

"Did the three of you turn in at the same time?"

"No. I took a shower and then joined them in bed."

"How long were you in the shower, Mrs. Beaumont?"

"I didn't time it, Inspector but it was long. The hot water felt good. Maybe 15 or 20 minutes."

"Was either of the Millers awake when you came back to bed?"

"No, they both appeared to me to be asleep."

"Was anything out of place when you came back?"

"Like what?"

"Glassware, clothing, anything?"

"Not that I noticed, but I wasn't looking for anything like that. I was tired and ready for sleep."

"Did you wake up at all during the night?"

"No."

"Do you know if either of them got out of bed during the night?"

"I wouldn't know. I was asleep."

"Did you hear anything out of place during the night?"

"Again, I was asleep. I didn't awaken until after dawn. The sunlight woke me up."

"Where do you live, Mrs. Beaumont?"

"Next door, on the next lot." She pointed to her house from the window. "2172 Highland Estates North."

"Alright, Mrs. Beaumont, that's it for now. You can leave. We'll be in touch when we've finished here and when we've done a post mortem on the corpses."

"Thank you."

"One more thing, Mrs. Beaumont. Please don't launder or discard any of the clothing you wore last evening."

"Huh?"

"They may be evidence."

"Of what, Inspector?"

"We don't know yet."

"So, that's the way it is?" She looked at Sergeant Tracey, hoping to find a friendly face. She was disappointed. Inspector Milliken responded in a matter-of-fact voice, "Yes, Mrs. Beaumont. That's the way it is."

"Am I a suspect?"

"We're not even sure that a crime has been committed. But if the post mortem suggests foul play, Mrs. Beaumont, you may well be the last person to have seen the Millers alive. That would make you a person of interest, if not more. We'll be in touch."

Chapter 10

MILLIKEN STOOD IN the bedroom, trying to visualize the crime. "What do you have for me, Hank?"

Henry McIntosh was a forensic pathologist with the coroner's office. Over the course of his 15 years with the coroner, he had examined dozens of bodies. He knew his stuff.

"The bodies are not that cold, Jim. I'd put the time of death between 3 and 4 AM. No signs of a struggle, no marks on the bodies. It looks like they just stopped breathing and died in their sleep. We'll need to analyze the blood samples, but my guess right now would be some kind of poison or a drug overdose."

Inspector Milliken turned to his partner. "Did Nicole Beaumont strike you as a murderer, Joanne? I mean, what kind of killer spends her night cavorting with her neighbors and then poisons them?"

"Assuming that Hank is right about the poison, Jim. I don't think she did it. You're right, people don't just make love and then kill their partners. If they do, it's usually because of some argument that escalates and leaves marks of a struggle. As Hank said, no evidence of that here. Maybe they took something to help them sleep and, in an inebriated state, they overdosed. What have we got? She admits she spent the night with them, that they engaged in three-way consensual sex, that she left them to take a shower, that she came back to bed and slept between them, and that they were dead when she awoke. I know that people can be good actors, but it was obvious to me that she was devastated by this, that she was probably crying most of the time between the 911 call and our arrival. We should listen to the 911 recording. Also, I kept sneaking a peek at her while you and Hank went into the bedroom and she was still tearing up. No, Jim, I don't think she did it."

"Is this a matter of gender solidarity for you, Joanne? Are you identifying with Mrs. Beaumont?"

"Hard to do since I don't have a husband to cheat on, Jim. But there's something else that suggests to me she's not the perp. Let's assume she did it—assume she knowingly handed them drinks that would kill them. Why does she stay? Why does she climb into bed with two corpses, or two people about to become corpses? That's pretty creepy. I know I couldn't do it. Why didn't she just wipe the glasses, pack up her things, go home, and let the evidence grow stale until someone else discovered the bodies? Isn't that what the killer would have done?

"Who else had the opportunity, Joanne?"

"There is the time that Mrs. Beaumont was in the shower, Jim. Someone could have entered the bedroom during those 15 or 20 minutes and administered the poison then."

"I don't buy that hypothesis, Joanne. Do you think that Mrs. Beaumont and the Millers would have played their threesome games if anyone else was still in the house after the party broke up?"

"Maybe they didn't realize they had company."

"Oh, and the killer walks in and calmly poisons them? They don't try to fend him off? There's no struggle?"

"Maybe they're asleep and he injects them with a quick acting poison or an injection of air into their blood streams. They are dead before they can wake up and engage him."

"And he does this while Mrs. Beaumont is in the shower and could emerge at any time and catch him, or her, in the act? Pretty risky murder plan if you ask me."

"Jim, are you sure you aren't fixating on Mrs. Beaumont because she was cheating on her husband the way Lori did? That wouldn't mark her as a criminal, Jim. Be objective."

Milliken bristled at her suggestion. "I am being objective, Joanne. She is the only person we know who had the opportunity to do this."

"And her motive, Jim? Her motive for killing the two people who shared their bodies with her last night?"

"I don't know, Joanne. Look, let's collect all the physical evidence and wait for the medical report. Then we can figure out for sure if we have a crime and investigate. You stay here while the forensics team does its thing. Let's make sure we cover every inch of the bedroom, including closets and the shower. Where does that door at the far end of the bedroom go, the one past the shower door?"

Joanne walked to door and, rubber gloves in place, opened it.

"Looks like a study or home office, Jim."

"Maybe that's where your imaginary intruder hid, Joanne. Make sure forensics gives it a good looksee. I'm going back to the station."

"Ok, Jim. I'll catch a ride back with the forensics guys. See you later."

As he left, Sergeant Tracey concluded that she might have a hard time with Jim on this case. She could already sense that, when he looked at Nicole Beaumont, Jim Milliken saw the face of his ex-wife, the love of his life turned slut who cuckolded him at every turn. He had discovered her infidelities and confronted her with them. She feigned remorse and they attended couples counseling, during which she repledged her love and devotion to him. It did not last. Lori resumed her roving ways and the marriage collapsed.

Joanne felt sorry for Jim. He loved Lori, he probably still did, in some curious mixture of love and hate. He had done his best, but it wasn't enough for Lori. It left deep scars and he developed an abiding antipathy for wives who cheated on their husbands. Joanne would do her best to help him separate his personal bias regarding such women from the objective analysis that their jobs required. But she could see that Nicole Beaumont had entered this investigation with one, if not two strikes against her in the eyes of Jim Milliken.

Chapter 11

NIKKI DROVE THE short distance from the Millers' to her home. She undressed and sorted for safekeeping her cocktail dress, her satin panties, her hose, shoes, bikini, beach dress, and clutch purse. She placed the pearl jewelry in the purse and added her engagement and wedding rings to that collection. She was sure she would have no further need of the latter two. She stepped into the shower, as much to wake up as to clean up.

For all the bravado she had exhibited in dealing with Inspector Milliken, Nikki was scared. The Millers were dead. They were more than friends to her, and Nikki would never again be able to reciprocate the love for Maryanne that she allowed herself to acknowledge for the first time last night. If they were murdered, why was she spared? How could the killer enter the bedroom and risk the possibility that Nikki saw him? Was she in physical danger now? And the Inspector thought she might be the killer! It was crazy. She felt nothing but love and affection for Maryanne and Ted. They had never argued. There was no reason for her bear a grudge against either of them. What motive could the Inspector possibly have concocted to connect her as the killer?

She knew she needed help, but she did not know where to turn. Once she advised Jack of what had happened, their marriage would be over, but that did not bother her. It had died before last night. Last night she merely acted on her conviction that the marriage had long been dead. She had resolved to end it and to plan a future without Jack that somehow included the Millers. That future would never come to be. She did not look forward to the call with Jack, but it had to be done.

It was Sunday and it was still morning in Los Angeles. She called the hotel, but he did not answer. She called his cell, and he seem bothered by her interruption of whatever had been occupying his time.

"What do you want, Nikki?"

"Good morning to you, too, Jack. Where are you? I tried the hotel, but you didn't answer."

"The cell is always best, Nikki. You know that. What do you want?"

"I want some advice, Jack. Where are you?"

"I'm getting set to tee off with Randy Carmichael if you don't mind. Can't the advice wait until later?"

Nikki quickly realized that this golf game was the reason Jack did not want to come back for the Millers' party. Randy Carmichael was Jack's biggest client, one of the few that Jack had ever invited to their home.

"No, Jack. It can't wait. Ted and Maryanne are dead."

"What! What happened?"

"No one knows for sure. The police think they were poisoned."

"You've been talking to the police?"

"Yes, Jack. I was the one who reported it to the police."

"Where did it happen?"

"At their home, sometime after the party ended."

"What party?"

"The one you and I discussed early last week. The one I asked you to come home for."

"Oh, yeah. How did you come report it?"

"I was with them when they died, Jack."

"What?"

"You're not going to like this, I know, but you're going to hear it sooner or later. I spent the night with them."

"Do you mean what I think you mean, Nikki?

"Yes, Jack."

Jack's anger flared. "You God damned slut! I couldn't make the party, so you punished me by cheating with the Millers? You're a fucking tramp, Nikki, that's what you are."

Nikki had expected this response. After all, what does a man say when his wife says she cheated on him? Serenity is not a customary hallmark of such conversations.

"Jack, I know we're through, but I think you'll admit we've been through for quite some time. You have no interest in me. I don't know what woman has been entertaining you so thoroughly on these long trips to LA, but we both know you're no saint. At least now your girlfriend can come out into the open and play the role of the caring friend who comforted you while you dealt with the psychic scars inflicted by the slut you married. Right, Jack?"

"I guess your extramarital escapades have sullied your imagination, Nikki. Just because you cheat doesn't mean I have a woman on the side out here."

"Look, we can deal with all this later. Right now, I need a recommendation for a good criminal defense lawyer."

Jack turned on his most sarcastic tone of voice, "Why? Did you kill them?"

"That's not funny, Jack. Can you give me a name or two?"

"Yes, Nikki. Consider it my parting gift to you. Keep an eye on your texts. And while you're at it, you better find yourself a divorce lawyer."

Chapter 12

 Joanne Tracey knocked on the door to Milliken's office.

"Anything interesting, Joanne?"

"Depends on what interests you, Jim. Did you know that Ted Miller was a videographer?"

"No. All I know about Ted Miller is that he lived at 2170 Highland Estates North, that he was married to Maryanne Miller, that they gave a party last night, that he and his wife had a swinging night with Nicole Beaumont, and that he and his wife are dead. You got something to add to that, Joanne?"

"Yes, Jim. He made a video of last night's bedroom festivities."

"Kinky. Did you watch it? Did it rev your motor?"

"I'll let that last question pass, Jim. There's no call for that kind of piggish behavior. I'm your partner. I treat you with respect. I deserve the same."

"I'm sorry, Joanne. You're right. I apologize."

"OK. As for your first question, yes, I watched it. Evidently, it's a multi-camera system. The video started when they came into the bedroom, bathing suits on, followed them to the shower, back to bed, and through their various physical gymnastics. All three are accounted for throughout that period, no exceptions, until Mrs. Beaumont leaves at one point with Mr. Miller and returns, drink in hand. Mr. Miller gets frisky with Mrs. Beaumont again while Mrs. Miller watches. Mrs. Beaumont asks if they would like a nightcap, they say "Yes," and Mr. Miller calls after her with instructions on how he likes his martinis. After about ten minutes, Mrs. Beaumont comes back with a tray that holds three glasses. Two of the drinks look like martinis, the other I didn't recognize. Mrs. Beaumont says something affectionate, kisses each of them goodnight, and hands them their drinks. They drink a short toast; Mrs. Beaumont heads off for a 17-minute shower. She returns, crawls into bed between them, and goes off to dreamland. The screen goes dark."

"What conclusions do you draw from all this, Joanne?"

"If Hank is right about poison or drugs, the poison was probably delivered in those martinis. If they died from the injection of air bubbles, the video is pretty much irrelevant."

"Wait a second, Joanne. From what you've said, it appears the recorder was motion activated. It started when they came into the bedroom and it ended shortly after Mrs. Beaumont climbed into bed, right?"

"Yeah, so?"

"Doesn't that rule out the unknown intruder, Joanne? Wouldn't the intruder have tripped the video to resume, just as it did when our three-some showed up in the bedroom?"

"I guess that's right, Jim. We can have forensics check out the recording system. If it was still motion activated when Mrs. Beaumont turned in, that pretty much kills the intruder theory."

Milliken brightened. "And Mrs. Beaumont mixed the drinks, delivered them, and watched as they drank them. Pretty damned clear to me!"

"Jim, when she hands them the drinks, Mrs. Beaumont tells them she adores them and is looking forward to getting together with them like this again. Does that sound like someone who knows she just handed them a lethal cocktail?"

"Maybe she was planting an alibi."

"That would assume Mrs. Beaumont knew they were videotaping the threesome. No one mentions it."

"Miller could have mentioned it on the way to the bedroom. Right?"

"I suppose so."

"That's something we can explore when we next question her."

"That still leaves a big fat question of motive, Jim. Where is her motive?"

"Joanne, we're only 15 hours into this case. We'll find her motive."

"Jim, assuming it was poison and that it was served up in their martinis, isn't it possible that someone else laced the gin with poison, left, and allowed Mrs. Beaumont to serve unwittingly as their Angel of Death?"

"Who? Mrs. Beaumont said they were alone in the house."

"No, Jim. She said she thought everyone else had left. The house was quiet, they had had several drinks, and they were getting ready to hop into bed. Do you think they searched the house? Don't be ridiculous."

"And can you suggest a motive for anyone else to want the Millers out of the way, Sergeant Tracey?"

"Yes, Inspector Milliken. That study off the bedroom? Ted Miller had a library of videos much like the one involving Mrs. Beaumont. There are about 30 of them. I took a quick look. There's one of the Millers with another woman; most involve Mr. Miller with other women; but some are of Mr. Miller with other men."

"One or more of them may have had a motive, Joanne. But where is their opportunity? Mrs. Beaumont is the only person with an opportunity."

"Before you ask the DA to charge Nicole Beaumont with murder, don't you think we owe it to her, and to ourselves, to check out these recordings and see what kinds of motives the Millers' other bedmates might have? What if they were at the party? Wouldn't that at least give them an outside opportunity at slipping something into the Millers' drinks? Don't we have a duty to check out all of that?"

"Yes, we do. You're right." He then raised his eyebrows and laughed, "Who knows? Maybe it was simultaneous double heart attacks or a drug overdose. Does the video show the Millers downing any pills before they turn in?"

"No, Jim. Nothing apparent to suggest a drug overdose."

"OK, Joanne. Let's hear from Hank in the morning and figure out if there was really a crime. In the meantime, these videos stay under lock and key. You and I are going to be the only ones to review them. I don't want stories about these DVDs or, God forbid, one of the actual DVDs to leak. The folks on those videos were probably not violating any laws. They have rights."

"Where are we going to watch them, Jim, without any onlookers?"

"How about your place, Joanne? Your mother can chaperone us."

"Sure, my home office will do. But I'll need to lay in an extra supply of Mom's heart medicine."

"OK. For tonight, grab the videos and let's lock them in my safe. We'll figure out tomorrow when we are going to look at them."

He paused and then looked intently at Sergeant Tracey. "Maybe we won't need to if we have enough physical evidence linking Mrs. Beaumont to the killings."

Chapter 13

HANK MCINTOSH SAUNTERED into Jim Milliken's office around 10 AM. He appeared to have been up all night, which in fact was the case.

"Well, Jim, if you had double heart attacks in the office pool, you lost. They were poisoned."

"With what, Hank?"

"Phenobarbital."

"Hold on a second, Hank."

Jim called Joanne and asked her to come to his office.

"Have a seat, Joanne. Hank says they were poisoned with phenobarbital. Hank, continue please."

"Phenobarbital is a barbiturate used by some pretty famous people to off themselves. Marilyn Monroe, for one, killed herself by overdosing on phenobarbital. Reports say that Abby Hoffman and Margaux Hemingway did as well. Its most common form is a tablet, but it comes in a liquid form as well. We didn't find any bottles or vials on the floor or in the trash cans."

"How does it work, Hank?"

"It generally kills the victim painlessly. It produces drowsiness. It depresses the bodily mechanisms that make you breathe, and respiration becomes shallow and less frequent. Combine it with alcohol and it reduces blood pressure and depresses the part of the brain that controls beathing. Enough phenobarbital and enough alcohol and your sleep becomes eternal."

Joanne asked, "No pain?"

"No pain. They go to sleep and never wake up."

Joanne continued, "Is there any telltale odor?"

"I think you're asking me if they would have been able to detect it. Not likely. It's clear and odorless. It can have a bitter taste, but it can be flavored to eliminate the bitterness. And if they ingested it in a martini, the taste of the juniper berries and vermouth could easily have masked it. And, Joanne, these folks had a lot of alcohol in their system. I doubt their tastebuds were on high alert."

"How quickly does it begin to work, Hank?"

"It varies, Jim. Depends on the amount of food in the stomach. As quickly as 10 minutes; as long as an hour."

"And their stomachs?"

"They had eaten not too long before they died. But not very much. The drug could have started to take effect somewhere in the middle of that range, maybe 25 minutes after ingestion."

"Did you examine the glassware on their nightstands?"

"Yep. The short, low-ball glasses had strong traces of phenobarbital. The high-ball glass was clean."

"So, if they drank from those low-ball glasses, what?"

"Two plus two is four, Jim. If they drank from those glasses, that's what killed them."

"Time of death, Hank?"

"4 AM, give or take a half-hour, Jim."

"Any prints on those low-ball glasses?"

"Yeah. One glass had clear set of the man's prints. The other, his wife's. There were other prints on each glass. Looks like the thumb and first two fingers of the hand. We don't know who."

"Thanks, Hank. Let me know if anything else pops up. And go get some sleep."

Jim Milliken turned to his partner. "This wasn't some double suicide, Joanne. We definitely have a murder case on our hands. Let's solve it."

Chapter 14

JACK HAD TEXTED two recommendations to Nikki. He sent her names, nothing more, leaving her to sort out for herself their strengths, weaknesses, and experience. He was irate and the terse nature of his text reflected his anger.

Nikki was not bothered by the relatively uninformative nature of his message. He recommended them and that was enough for starters. She spent a good part of Sunday evening on the internet, finding out what she could about Harold Moreland and Maria Romano. Their websites suggested that they were the Second Coming of Perry Mason. But those were their websites, created by the lawyers in conjunction with web site designers and marketing experts to attract clients. She went behind the web sites to stories about their cases, looking for clues that might help her select the person who would defend her against Inspector Milliken's as yet unspoken allegations.

From what she read, Jack had not done her wrong on these recommendations. They were both experienced and accomplished criminal trial lawyers. Either one would likely represent her well, but there was something about Ms. Romano's web site photograph that suggested to Nikki that the woman in that photograph was a tough cookie. Nikki wanted a tough cookie on her side. She would try to get a meeting with Ms. Romano and see if they were a match.

She called bright and early on Monday. She explained to the receptionist that she had been referred to Ms. Romano by Jack Beaumont and that she was afraid that the police believed she had murdered two people. The receptionist put her through to Ms. Romano's secretary, who took her name, listened to the same explanation for the call that Nikki had given to the receptionist, and asked Nikki to hold.

"This is Maria Romano, Mrs. Beaumont. Let me ask you a few questions."

Ms. Romano was all business—Who died? Where? When? Why do the police suspect you? Have you spoken to the police? What did you tell them? Were your answers all truthful? After getting a synopsis of the facts, Ms. Romano asked if Nikki could come to her office that morning. She wanted Nikki out of the house before the police arrived to continue questioning her. If the police got there before she could leave, she was not to answer any questions. She should tell them she was on her way to see her lawyer. Ms. Romano stressed that, no matter what the police said, Nikki was under no obligation to answer any questions. She issued that advice three times and had Nikki repeat it back to her.

Nikki dressed for the meeting, left the house, got into her car and drove off. When she had gotten sufficiently away from home to avoid running into the police, she pulled off onto a side street and punched the attorney's address into her car's GPS.

She arrived at Ms. Romano's office in about 25 minutes. She was ushered into a nicely appointed conference room and offered her choice of beverage. Coffee seemed like the appropriate option.

Maria Romano entered the conference room about 30 seconds after Nikki's coffee arrived. She was impressive, tall, and clad in a charcoal gray pinstripe pantsuit with a simple white blouse beneath the blazer. Her black hair was cut short and she wore horn-rimmed glasses that somewhat masked a nice face. After a few pleasantries, Nikki remarked that the law-yer's manner was softer in person than she had been on the phone. Ms. Romano explained that she wanted to impress upon Nicole the urgency of the situation and the importance of avoiding any further communications with the police until they could talk.

Ms. Romano asked Nikki to tell her story as thoroughly as she could, sparing no details. She should let her lawyer decide what might be relevant and what might be meaningless, and her lawyer couldn't do that if Nicole skipped over some details.

"Remember, Mrs. Beaumont, everything we say here is privileged. The police, the DA, they don't get access to my notes. So please be thorough."

Nikki started, beginning with the invitation from the Millers. Ms. Romano told her it would be simpler to refer to her as "Maria," and asked how she should refer to Nikki.

"My friends call me 'Nikki.' I would prefer that to Mrs. Beaumont. You'll know why as this story unravels."

"OK, Nikki. Go on."

Maria took copious notes as Nikki spoke for over an hour. When she was done, Maria asked her a few questions about Nikki and Jack, Nikki and Ted, and Nikki and Maryanne. She asked about arguments, jealousies, and prior infidelities. She asked Nikki to recount as closely as she could her conversation with Ted en route to the bar and her goodnight words to the Millers.

Maria put down her pen.

"Nikki, we don't know what the police are going to do, but we do know they are going to want to talk to you again. You don't have to talk to them. They will lean on you to talk and tell you that, if you have nothing to hide, you have nothing to fear in talking to them. Ignore that. It's pure BS. They say it to embarrass you into talking. You tell them you are represented by counsel and give them my card. Here, take as many as you want. Tell them to call me if they want to speak with you and we'll set up a time and place and get you prepared. And do not speak to anyone about this. I do mean anyone, including your soon-to-be-ex-husband. Until I say otherwise, Nikki, it's you and me against the world. Understood?"

"Yes, Maria."

"OK. We're done for now. If you remember anything you left out, call me. My cell phone number is on my card and on the web site if you lose the card."

Chapter 15

MILLIKEN OUTLINED HIS plan for the investigation.

He would talk with the District Attorney about obtaining a warrant for a search of the Beaumonts' home. He knew that the DA would ask him what he was looking for and that a judge was not likely to approve a warrant for a scavenger hunt with no identifiable targets. Milliken knew what he was looking for—phenobarbital or anything related to phenobarbital, materials regarding poisons or drugs that could prove fatal if combined with alcohol, or drugs or poisons that could produce a painless death without any immediate or obvious physical reactions. Information relating to Ted and Maryanne Miller. He would want to search the bathrooms, bedrooms, computers, and garbage. He thought that would pass legal muster. And he wanted Mrs. Beaumont's clothing from Saturday night.

McIntosh would continue to analyze the physical evidence, including anything obtained under the aegis of the search warrant, looking for any information that might bear on the identity of the killer or the presence of another person in the bedroom or the study. The team would look for information regarding who attended the party and who catered the affair. They would return to the crime scene if and as necessary, looking for invitation lists, RSVPs, and catering contracts. That would give Milliken and Tracey a long list of potential interviewees who might have seen or heard something worthy of follow up.

A technician with experience in video recordings would analyze the machine and its motion activation status when Mrs. Beaumont retired for the evening.

Sergeant Tracey would find out what she could about Mrs. Beaumont from her employment records at St. Peters. If possible, she would interview her supervisors and co-workers, check on whether the hospital maintained any stores of phenobarbital and whether Mrs. Beaumont had access to those stores.

Milliken and Tracey would review the DVDs, focusing first on the video of Mrs. Beaumont and the Millers to embed its every nuance in their memory banks. After that, they would move on to Ted Miller's library of videos of other guests who had attended the party. Milliken reluctantly agreed with Tracey that their presence in the Millers' home that night did give them some opportunity for foul play and that, if the videos afforded them a motive, they should be investigated. Given Mrs. Beaumont's delivery of the lethal cocktails, however, Milliken told his partner that he was dubious those investigations would lead anywhere. He was convinced, he told her, that Mrs. Beaumont was guilty.

He asked his team members to report when they had finished their tasks or as and when they had found something of particular interest.

Chapter 16

SERGEANT TRACEY KNOCKED on Milliken's door the next morning.

"I've finished up at St. Peters, Jim. I'll be writing it up, but would you like to hear what I found?"

"Aren't you the efficient one, Joanne. Sure. Tell me what you have."

"OK. Several things. The hospital fingerprints its employees as part of the hiring process. They will give us a copy of Mrs. Beaumont's prints. I doubt we need them since the video puts her in the bedroom and the tainted glasses in her hands, but that would nail down that fact. No one had anything but good things to say about Mrs. Beaumont. Experienced and skilled nurse, great bedside manner . . ."

Milliken interrupted with the most sarcastic tone he could muster, "Well, you already observed that much, Joanne."

"Please, Jim." She continued, "Great bedside manner. Model employee. Extremely punctual. Effective trainer for new nurses."

"So she wins the Miss Congeniality award, Joanne. Some very affable people have committed some pretty horrible crimes. What about the drug, the phenobarbital?"

"It isn't used as much as it was in the past, but doctors still prescribe it and hospitals do maintain a supply in their central pharmacies and in some medication cabinets. Strict records are kept."

"Do nurses have access to the drugs, Joanne?"

"They can obtain medications from the central pharmacy with a physician's order. It's not an open shelf operation. The nurse presents the doctor's order, the pharmacist retrieves the medication, and records it in the pharmacy log."

"Did Mrs. Beaumont obtain any phenobarbital from the pharmacy?"

"No, Jim. We went back through the computer logs for the last year. Nothing."

"Was any phenobarbital unaccounted for?"

"No, Jim. Not from the central pharmacy and not from the medication cabinets. If she's our perp, she obtained the phenobarbital somewhere else. The DEA classifies it as a Schedule IV controlled substance, so she either created an audit trail when she got it through proper channels somewhere other than St. Pete's, or she obtained it from some illegitimate source. She strikes me as pretty intelligent. I don't think she's stupid enough to leave a trail. And if she didn't, and she used the black market, then linking her to the drug is going to be awfully hard."

"I see your point, Joanne. Maybe we can't put the phenobarbital in her hands, but we can put the drinks laced with the phenobarbital in her hands."

"Jim, I know it's a bit of a Hail Mary, but I put out a notice to every Police Department within a 100-mile radius, telling them we have a suspected phenobarbital poisoning and asking them to let us know if there have been any thefts of the drug."

"You're right, Joanne. It is a Hail Mary. But it's good police work."

"Thanks, Jim. One other fact I came across at St. Peters. The head pharmacist there is named Peter Carmelo. One of the names on the log of Ted Miller's videos is Antonia Carmelo. It will be interesting to see if they are married and if they were at the party."

"In due course, Joanne. In due course."

As Milliken was finishing with Tracey, Hank McIntosh popped his head in the door of Milliken's office.

"We finished our analysis of the liquor on the bar, Jim. All the bottles are clean, no evidence they contain anything not printed on their labels. Except one."

"The Bombay Sapphire gin, right?"

"Yes, Jim. It was loaded with phenobarbital. A martini made with that stuff was a passport to the afterworld."

"And we know who issued those passports, Joanne. She made the drinks; she delivered the drinks. She even made sure they drank them by offering a loving toast before she went off to the shower, where she could wait until the drug put them to sleep."

"But, according to the video, Jim, she asks Maryanne Miller if she wants a Greyhound, which is made with vodka and is the drink that Mrs. Beaumont made for herself. Does that sound like someone who wants to kill Mrs. Miller with a lethal martini?"

"Maybe not, Joanne. Maybe she wanted to spare Maryanne Miller. Maybe the target of her plan was Ted Miller. But when Mrs. Miller asked for another martini, what was Mrs. Beaumont going to do? Maybe she did not plan on killing both of them, but circumstances forced her hand."

"That's a nice story, Jim. But who put the barbiturate in the gin bottle?"

"C'mon, Joanne, stop defending her. She mixes the phenobarbital in the gin bottle before she makes the martinis. By the way, Sergeant, if she wanted to spare Mrs. Miller, she would have mixed the barbiturate in the drink intended for Mr. Miller. She didn't. She laced the bottle, which ensured that any martinis made from that point forward would be the last martinis those persons ever drank."

Joanne turned to Hank.

"Hank, when you said that there was no bottle or vial, were you talking about the bedroom?"

"The bedroom, the bathroom, the bedroom closet, the study."

"What about the area around the bar? The garbage?"

"The team is combing all that as we speak, Joanne."

Milliken was perturbed. "What is that going to prove?"

"Jim, if we find the medicinal vial and it has Mrs. Beaumont's fingerprints on it, your theory of the case seems to be airtight. But what if someone else's fingerprints are on it, Jim. Doesn't that tend to exonerate Mrs. Beaumont and point us in another direction?"

"And if there are no fingerprints, Sergeant? What does that prove?"

"It proves that whoever laced the gin wore gloves or wiped the vial clean before tossing it."

"That doesn't rule out Mrs. Beaumont, Joanne, does it?"

"Not if it's been wiped clean, Jim. No."

"And if there is no empty bottle, Joanne?"

"Same answer, Jim."

Chapter 17

NIKKI WAS DRINKING her first cup of coffee when the doorbell rang. Inspector Milliken handed her a search warrant.

"We have a warrant to search the premises, Mrs. Beaumont. It's signed by a judge. We will make a list of everything we take so we both have a record."

"Wait, Inspector. I want to call my lawyer. Hold off for a minute."

"Feel free to call your lawyer, Mrs. Beaumont, but we don't need to wait."

He turned to the crew he had brought and ushered them past the door.

"You know what we're looking for. Confine your search to that. It's all specified in the warrant. Be careful. Try not to break anything. Let's not disrupt anything that's not listed on the warrant."

"Inspector . . ." Nikki tried to get a word in, to no avail.

"Excuse me, Mrs. Beaumont, I've got a job to do."

Nikki called Maria Romano. She was not yet at the office, but the switchboard patched Nikki through to Maria's cell phone. She was in her car, on her way to the office.

"Calm down, Nikki. This is part of their standard playbook. They want to scare you and traumatize you by invading your home and making you feel helpless."

"They're doing a damn good job of that, Maria."

"Look, don't fight with them. I'm on my way. Make sure you get a complete manifest of what they take. Once they leave, we'll take a look and see if anything is missing that doesn't show up on the manifest and we'll make sure it gets added."

Nikki watched as members of Milliken's crew walked past with plastic bags that were filled with who knows what. Milliken called Nikki to the study, where a computer stood atop each of the two desks with which the room was appointed.

"Your husband is a lawyer, right? Which of these computers is his?" When Nikki pointed to the one at the far end of the room, the search team disconnected Nikki's computer and walked it down the stairs and out the door.

He asked the same questions regarding the file cabinets in the room and Nikki watched as her files left the room on a hand truck.

At that point, Maria Romano walked in and asked for a copy of the search warrant. She looked at it quickly, looked around the premises, and asked Milliken if he was done.

"Almost. Where are the clothes you wore Saturday night, Mrs. Beaumont?"

Nikki led him to the closet and reached up on shelf to retrieve the bag in which she had stashed them. As Milliken grabbed for it, Nikki pulled it back.

"My jewelry is in the clutch bag, Inspector. I'd like to keep it if you don't mind."

"I do mind, Mrs. Beaumont. It may be evidence."

Maria interjected. "What jewelry are we talking about, Nikki."

"My engagement ring, my wedding ring, a string of pearls, a pearl bracelet, and matching earrings. They're pretty valuable and I can see them disappearing without a trace once they hit the so-called evidence room."

Milliken turned red. "Are you impugning the integrity of the Police Department, Mrs. Beaumont?"

Romano bit back, "Are you impugning hers, Inspector?"

"Look, counselor . . ."

"Maria Romano is the name, Inspector Milliken. I just looked at the warrant. It specifies clothing, not jewelry. If you want to make an issue of this, let's get before a judge so you can explain how the police cannot investigate a case without confiscating a woman's wedding ring. That'll look good in the morning editions."

Sergeant Tracey tugged lightly on Milliken's sleeve and leaned in to say something that neither Nikki nor Maria could hear. Whatever it was, it helped. Milliken told Nikki to remove the jewelry from the bag.

After the police had left, Maria sat down with Nikki to go over the warrant.

"Looking at this, it seems that the police think the Millers were killed with a lethal dose of phenobarbital. They were looking for any evidence that you had some phenobarbital somewhere in the house or that you had been studying it as a possible murder weapon. Either phenobarbital or some other colorless, painless poison or drug that could be used to kill the Millers silently while they slept. Any chance they'll find anything like that, Nikki? Journal articles, a Google search history?"

"I don't think so, Maria. I've never even seen a bottle that said it contained phenobarbital. I'm not sure that any other nurse on my floor at St. Pete's has either."

"I hope your memory proves out."

"Maria, why did they leave Jack's stuff alone?"

"My assumption is they know he's a lawyer, they know he wasn't at the party, so he is not involved. If they grabbed his records under those circumstances, he would have gone running into court claiming that the police had abused their authority and compromised his clients' attorney-client privilege. I'd do the same. Milliken probably saw little profit for him in that fight."

"What do we do now?"

"The police will probably complete their analysis of the physical evidence and then want to interview you again. Remember, you don't answer any questions without me by your side, no matter how they sweet talk you. They may try to get you to loosen up by using the good cop-bad cop routine. I suppose that Sergeant Tracey will play the role of the good cop. Don't believe it. It's a role, not reality. If I'm not there, you have lockjaw, Nikki."

Chapter 18

HANK ENTERED JIM'S office with the same countenance that always accompanied an unsuccessful search for clues. "No luck on the garbage from the party, Jim. The boys combed through all the detritus of the party and found nothing. Whoever laced the gin took the bottle or vial with him or her when they left the Miller place."

"Which means that if Mrs. Beaumont did it, then she took the empty bottle with her when she went home Sunday morning."

"Sounds about right, Jim. We'll look at the fruits of the search warrant, but it's a longshot. If she took the bottle with her, she would have ditched it at her first opportunity. It, or pieces of it, could be anywhere now."

"Did we collect her garbage when we served the warrant?"

"Yes, inside and out. We're not done screening it."

"OK. Keep at it. Look, when she left, Mrs. Beaumont was wearing a cocktail dress and carrying a small bag with her bathing suit and beach dress and a clutch purse. Hank, can you have your boys examine the clothing, the bag and the purse for traces of phenobarbital? If she stuffed the bottle in there in a hurry maybe there was some residual leakage."

"Will do. By the way, Jim. The video was motion activated. And the motion sensor was active when Mrs. Beaumont turned in."

"And no one activated it after that?"

"She did, Jim. When she woke up and found them dead. You can see the horror on her face and hear her sobbing."

"She could have been acting, Hank."

"Then you better get ready to hand over the Oscar, Jim. I don't see it."

"Did you see that part of the video, Joanne?"

"No, Jim. I looked at the video quickly that day, after you left the crime scene. I didn't study it. I turned it off after Mrs. Beaumont went to sleep. Sorry."

Hank added, "We also found a cell phone on the wife's nightstand, Jim. Lots of selfies of the three of them cavorting and kissing in the hot tub. It all looked quite friendly, sorta' like foreplay for the main event in the bedroom."

Sergeant Tracey looked at her partner with a raised eyebrow.

"Isn't it time we looked elsewhere, Jim. No jury is going to look at these photos and the video and convict Mrs. Beaumont. Then add in as potential suspects the other playmates the Millers chose to video. Do you think the DA would even indict her?"

"I told you we would look at those videos and follow up with the *dramatis personae*, Joanne. We'll do that. But as of today, Nicole Beaumont had the best opportunity to commit this crime and she's the Number One suspect in my book. The motive will come out. It usually does when you start squeezing folks."

"Jim, you need to let go. You and I both know what's obscuring your judgment."

"Leave it alone, Joanne. Leave it."

"No, Jim, I won't. Be a good cop. Be objective. If you're not, I'm going to continue to call you on it."

Chapter 19

NIKKI HAD ASKED Maria if she could refer Nikki to a good divorce lawyer. Jack was a man who usually made good on his threats and Nikki knew she would need to be prepared. She punched in the number Maria had given her and asked for Sharon Riley. Maria described Sharon as a tough, no-nonsense advocate who got good results for her clients. Nikki did not speak to Sharon, but her secretary set up an appointment for the next afternoon.

Sharon Riley had never had an intake interview start with the would-be divorce client stating that she was being investigated for a double murder. It was quite a hook. She asked Nikki to tell her story from the beginning, reviewing her marital woes in chronological fashion, and ending with the events that precipitated Jack Beaumont's threat of divorce.

"I have to say, Mrs. Beaumont, your husband has a pretty ironclad claim of adultery. I mean, you admitted it to the police, and you admitted it to him."

"I know. I really don't care about the divorce. I've had it with him. He doesn't love me, and I no longer love him."

"Your conduct pretty much screams that, Mrs. Beaumont." Sharon Riley was not one to sugar coat the issue. "But you should know that, in this state, adultery is not only a ground for divorce, but it can also affect your alimony. Are you prepared for that?"

"I don't know. I have my own salary. I'm a nurse at St. Peter's Hospital. But my income is nothing compared to Jack's. Without alimony, I will need to make some big adjustments."

"How confident are you that he's been playing around in LA?"

"I suspect he is, but I don't have any proof, Ms. Riley."

"Are you willing to let me find your proof?"

"How?"

"He's still in LA, right? He didn't come home to support you in this police investigation?"

"No."

"Do you have a current photograph of your husband?"

"I can get you one."

"His hotel?"

"The Century Plaza."

"What client is he out there visiting?"

"I don't know the company name. 'Transnational' something. His main contact out there is someone named Randy Carmichael. He spent the Memorial Day weekend at our home once, a few years ago. But that's all I know. He seemed like a decent enough guy."

"It's enough."

"For what?"

"To find out where your husband goes after 5 PM, and with whom and where he spends his time between 5 PM and his morning alarm."

"You can do that?"

"I have people who can do that. Let's see if we can cross file for divorce on the basis of his adultery."

"Please do. I would derive great pleasure from wiping that sarcastic tone from his voice and any self-righteous smirk from his face."

"I hope we can oblige you in that regard, Mrs. Beaumont."

Chapter 20

INSPECTOR MILLIKEN REASSEMBLED his team to review the status of the investigation.

"Hank, any luck on the Beaumont woman's clothes? Any traces of phenobarbital?"

"Negative, Jim. Clean."

Sergeant Tracey could see a slight grimace cross the Inspector's face as McIntosh delivered his answer. Plainly, Milliken was hoping for the physical evidence to link Nicole Beaumont directly to the lethal medication.

Milliken looked at Norman Brewer, who had led the search warrant team. That well, too, had proven to be dry. No bottles or vials of phenobarbital, nor hard copy or electronic articles about the drug, and no search history relating to phenobarbital or to colorless drugs or poisons that could be used to kill people while they slept. The Millers were in Mrs. Beaumont's computerized Contacts, but the email traffic between them was pretty nondescript. Tracey noticed Milliken's jaw clench as Brewer reported the results of his team's review.

"OK. Have we found a guest list for the party?"

Sergeant Tracey told him that a search of the Miller house had yielded a guest list, an RSVP list, and information relating to the caterer. Milliken released everyone, retreated to his office, and asked Sergeant Tracey to join him.

"Did you run the guest list acceptances against the names on the videos you found in Mr. Miller's study?"

"Yes, Jim. We have several matches. There is a video of Penny Hamilton with Mr. Miller. She's married to Art Hamilton, who teaches at Coleman Valley College."

"What does he teach?"

"A sociology course in Deviant Behavior."

"Deviant Behavior. How apt."

"You can't make this stuff up, Jim."

"What else do you have, Joanne?"

"Samantha Long. She and Ted Miller. There's a bit of a twist here, Jim. There's also a recording of Ted Miller with Samantha Long's husband, Aaron Long. He owns Long's Jewelry over on Southern Boulevard."

"A threesome with husband and wife?"

"No, Jim. Separate encounters."

"So, were there any other guests at the party whom Ted Miller had previously despoiled?"

"Antonia Carmelo, the wife of the head pharmacist at St. Peter's. She enjoyed a threesome with Mr. and Mrs. Miller."

"Anything else?"

"No more recorded encounters with guests who attended the party."

"I see you saved the best for last, Joanne, to get me off my focus on Mrs. Beaumont. A professional pharmacist with ready, personal access to phenobarbital, who was at the party, and had good reason for seeking revenge against the people who seduced his wife."

"No, Jim. You asked me to match the guests with the videos. That's what I did. The facts we have on Pete and Antonia Carmelo only raise questions. They don't answer them."

"And they don't put the glasses with the poisoned martinis in the hands of anyone other than Mrs. Beaumont."

"Jim. Try to keep an open mind until all the facts are in. Maybe you're right and I'm wrong about Mrs. Beaumont. But right now, I'd be willing to place a fairly hefty wager on her innocence. Just play out the string before you fashion a noose for her. In any event, Jim, what's next?"

"We interview Mrs. Beaumont. Push her hard. See if see cracks. If she doesn't crack, we study the videos of the folks you just mentioned and see what we come up with."

"Somewhere along the way, Jim, we should interview the caterer." After a pause of several seconds, Joanne added, "Maybe someone on the catering staff saw something . . . or did something."

Chapter 21

MARIA ROMANO HAD told Inspector Milliken that if he wanted to speak to her client, he could do so in her office. She was not dragging her client down to the police station to become the topic of speculation and gossip. Milliken had pushed back, but Romano pushed harder, until Milliken realized that he had no choice, at least not until he arrested her. And he knew that if he arrested her she would be entitled to any and all exculpatory evidence the police had, including the videos of her affection for her friends, her shock and sorrow at their deaths, and the videos of other guests who may have had ample motives for doing away with one or both of the Millers. No, he wanted to squeeze Nicole Beaumont, watch her squirm under his questioning, and maybe say some things that would have been better left unsaid. If he could scare her enough, she might fold and be willing to cop a plea in exchange for a light sentence. Then he could let the judge punish the cheating bitch. He could close the case and move on. Her lawyer would be a problem, but it was worth a shot.

They assembled in Maria's conference room. Maria and Nikki sat with their backs to the afternoon sun, which was shining directly into the eyes of Inspector Milliken and Sergeant Tracey. An old trick, to be sure, and one that was easily addressed by Sergeant Tracey's request that the curtains be drawn. Nonetheless, it told Milliken "You're on my turf today."

Milliken conducted the interview; Tracey took notes.

He started by asking her how long she had known the Millers and when she first became intimate with them. When she answered, he pretended that he had not understood and asked again, in two separate questions, "When did you first become intimate with Mr. Miller?" and "When did you first become intimate with Mrs. Miller?" His follow-up questions suggested all too clearly that he believed she was lying.

"Mrs. Beaumont, you spent time in the hot tub with the Millers that night, didn't you?"

"Yes."

"And you sat on Mr. Miller's lap and kissed him, right?"

"Yes."

"And then you did the same with Mrs. Miller?"

"Yes."

"And you slid your hand inside her swimsuit and fondled her breasts, and she returned that favor for you?"

"Yes."

"And you took selfies of all this?"

"I didn't."

"But someone took selfies?"

"Yes."

"And you expect us to believe that you had never engaged in such conduct with the Millers before that night?"

"I'm just answering your questions as truthfully as I can, Inspector. What you choose to believe is up to you." Then, directing her gaze at Sergeant Tracey, she added, "And what Sergeant Tracey chooses to believe is up to her. All I can do is tell the truth."

"No, Mrs. Beaumont. You can also lie if you choose to."

Maria jumped in. "Enough of your editorializing, Inspector. Did you get your jollies asking my client about her sex life? Unless you can explain the relevance of that to anything you're investigating, I'm going to advise my client to refrain from answering any more questions of that ilk."

"That's your prerogative, counselor. But if your client is not going to cooperate, this investigation is going to take a lot more time."

"My time is your time, Inspector. You mentioned selfies. Are you going to provide us with copies?"

"Your client hasn't been accused of any crime, counselor. If and when she is, I'll comply with my disclosure obligations."

"And, in the meantime, you'll be passing the photos around the station house, like the latest Sports Illustrated Swimsuit Issue, right, Inspector?"

"You don't seem to have much of a high regard for the police, counselor."

"Let's just say that there are some police who have earned the low regard in which I hold them. Now, do you have any more questions for my client?"

"Mrs. Beaumont, how long have you worked at St. Peter's?"

"About 10 years."

"Do you have access to any medication cabinets?"

"Not unless someone gives me the key."

"And who might that be?"

"A physician who asks me to retrieve a med for that patient."

"Do you have your own set of keys for the medication cabinets on your floor?"

"No."

"Do you ever work nights?"

"Yes, I think all nurses do from time to time."

"What do you do if there is emergency during the night shift. How do you obtain medication for that emergency?"

"There's always a physician on duty. Nurses don't prescribe the meds. The physicians do. I would obtain the keys from the physician."

"Once you open the medication cabinet, what's to prevent you from taking whatever you want?"

"My conscience."

"Anything else?"

"Yes. The cabinets are inventoried twice daily. Once when the day shift starts at 8 AM and then again at 8 PM. If the 8 PM and 8 AM inventories can't be reconciled, the pharmacy department checks all the records to see who accessed the cabinets between the inventories."

"Do you know what phenobarbital is?"

"Sure. It's a barbiturate."

"How do you know that?"

"I can't recall when I first heard of it."

"Is there a supply of phenobarbital in the St. Peter's pharmacy?"

"I don't know. I've never had occasion to ask."

"How about the hospital medication cabinets?"

"Same answer."

"Have you ever handled phenobarbital?"

"No."

"When you went home following your night with the Millers, you threw some clothing into a bag, right?

"Yes."

"How would you account for traces of phenobarbital on your clothing?"

Maria Romano jumped in before Nikki could respond. "Mrs. Beaumont, don't answer that question. Inspector, did you in fact find traces of phenobarbital on Mrs. Beaumont's clothing? If you didn't, that question is completely hypothetical and speculative. What have you got to support that question, Inspector?"

"I'm asking the questions here, counselor. If and when the time comes for me to make a disclosure, I'll do what I'm required to do."

"It's not going to work, Inspector. If you had anything, you'd tell us. You're trying to make Mrs. Beaumont think your hole cards are aces. I think they're jokers. Move on. She's not answering that question."

"Mrs. Beaumont, have you ever created a video of yourself having sex with someone else?"

"Where are you going with this, Milliken?" Maria was exhibiting controlled anger. Controlled, but anger nonetheless.

"You'll see the relevance, counselor."

Nikki answered the question, "No."

"Do you know if anyone has ever made a video of you during sexual relations?"

"No."

"You're telling me that sitting here today, you don't know if you were ever videotaped during sex?"

"That's correct."

"How would you feel if that had been done without your knowledge?"

"Maria literally jumped to her feet. "Mrs. Beaumont, do not answer that question. If you have any such videos, Inspector, I want to see them. My client is entitled to know if this interview is based on a bunch of fictional hypotheticals. And if there are such videos, they may contain exculpatory information. Will you produce them?"

"If and when your client is accused of a crime, we'll do what the law requires us to do, counselor. I don't know how many times I have to tell you that."

"You are a Class A jerk, Milliken. I don't know what your problem is." Turning toward Sergeant Tracey, Maria continued, "Maybe your partner knows what's gone haywire inside you, Milliken, but I don't. Maybe she can talk some sense into you. You want to sit on evidence that might exonerate my client until you accuse her of crime you know she didn't commit. That's a true abuse of police power."

"Are you done, counselor?"

"No, Inspector. You are. This interview is over. You know the way out."

Chapter 22

 and embarrassed by the interview. Milliken had resurrected memories of events that had been very personal to her, very affectionate, and he had treated them like fodder for a pornographic movie. He was convinced she had killed her friends, he was a true believer, and Nikki knew enough about human nature to realize that true believers will cling to their beliefs even when all the objective evidence says otherwise.

She looked to Maria for reassurance.

"You did very well, Nikki."

"Huh?"

"He was fishing and he didn't even get a nibble."

"What is he going to do with the selfies and the video he says he has?"

"Well, you knew about the selfies. From what you told me, there's nothing there that would suggest that you were getting ready to murder them. Am I right?"

"Yes, I told you everything about what we did in the hot tub. Why wouldn't he agree to give you copies?"

"Because either there's nothing there to advance his theory of the case, or, there is something that helps to exonerate you. Believe me, if the selfies were helpful to him, he'd agree to hand them over in a heartbeat to squeeze us for a plea bargain."

"What about the traces of phenobarbital on my clothes?"

"He was misleading you without actually lying. But it was a despicable trick. He didn't tell you they had found any traces. He asked how you would account for any traces. Again, he was trying to frighten you. Tell me again, Nikki. Have you ever handled phenobarbital?"

"No."

"Then I would just not worry about that little feat of linguistic trickery by Milliken. But it's that kind of crap that tells me that Milliken is far more interested in convicting you than he is in finding out who really killed the Millers. I hope his partner is more reasonable and can influence him as this thing moves along. What can you tell me about her, Nikki?"

"Nothing, Maria. She has hardly uttered a word. She handed me a pocket package of Kleenex while I sat crying in the Millers' house the morning the police arrived, but we've never exchanged a single word. Do you have anything on her?"

"Not much. Bachelor of Science in Criminology. Joined the department six years ago. Not married. Lives with her mother. A bit of a "gym rat" in her off hours. That's about it. Nikki, do you know whether or not the Millers made a video of your bedroom activities?"

"I don't. I know Ted was professional photographer and videographer, so, if anyone could do it, I suppose it was him."

"Did Maryanne ever tell you that she and Ted made videos of their romantic interludes?"

"No."

"Did Ted ever say, even jokingly, that he wanted to make a video of you and him in bed? Or of you and Maryanne?"

"No, never."

"Nikki, think before you answer this. If he had told you that night that he had recorded your lovemaking, what would you have done?"

"I was pretty tipsy and pretty darn uninhibited that night. I probably would have thought it would be fun to watch later. And maybe asked for a copy."

"Wouldn't you have been angry?"

"Why?"

"Wouldn't you have felt that you had been violated or used?"

"No. I don't think you understand, Maria. I loved her. I adored him. I trusted them. If they made such a recording, I would have had no concerns about it being misused. We probably would have watched it over drinks to get ready for a sequel."

Nikki paused and then asked, "Do you think such a recording exists?"

"Yeah, I do. I don't think Inspector Milliken has enough imagination to fabricate that story. But I also believe that if the video helped him, he'd hand it over. I think there are some things he would prefer we not see until he's done trying to frighten you and me into pleading to a lesser charge than murder."

"Is there any chance of that?"

"Not unless he has a video of you pouring phenobarbital into something they drank."

Chapter 23

THE RIDE BACK to the station was unpleasant for Joanne Tracey. Her approach to witness interrogation was much different from that of her partner. She understood the need to be firm and authoritative, but she also believed in the adage that "you get more flies with honey than with vinegar." More importantly, she believed in honesty. Jim Milliken's question about traces of phenobarbital on Nicole Beaumont's garments crossed that line in Joanne's view.

"Jim, what was the point of that? You know there were no traces of the drug on her clothes."

"Yeah, but she and her bitchy counselor don't know that. Gives them something to worry about, something to make them nervous, maybe make a mistake."

"And all the sarcasm about the sex? Do you enjoy insulting people, Jim?"

"People like her? Sure I enjoy it. Screwing around on the side while her husband is out trying to earn a living? She deserves it. She's earned it."

"Is that how you're going to solve this murder, Jim? You're going to assume Mrs. Beaumont did it and then insult her and plant lies about the evidence until she does something that corroborates your belief that she's just like Lori and, therefore, she's the only one evil enough to have killed them? You call that police work, Jim?"

"Look, Joanne, when you run a case, you can run it your way. This isn't your case. This is my case and I'll run it my way."

"Jim, this isn't your case. This is the department's case. And you need to run it the right way."

They rode the rest of the way to the station in silence.

Chapter 24

MILLIKEN AND TRACEY sat in Tracey's home office. They had spent the day viewing the videos they had found of guests at the Summer Kick-Off party performing *in flagrante* with one of more of the Millers. Unsurprisingly, and notwithstanding Joanne's steady objections, Milliken had come to refer to the videos as the "Sexcapades."

"OK, Joanne. You insisted we look at these. I suppose you think one or more of these people might have been blackmailed by Ted Miller and, realizing that blackmail never stops until the blackmailer stops breathing, took the necessary steps to end it once and for all."

"Yep. And that's the thread Maria Romano is going to pull when you produce these videos."

"You think I'm going to produce them?"

"C'mon, Jim. It'll look really bad if the existence of these videos comes out at trial and we haven't produced them."

"Who's going to say that they exist, Joanne?"

"Me, Jim. Me."

"I can't produce what no longer exists, Joanne."

"Do you want to go to jail over this, Jim? I'm sure there will be quite a few folks waiting to give you a housewarming party there. Now start thinking like a cop."

"Ever the straight arrow. That's you, Joanne. OK. It's your theory. You pursue it. You interview these folks. I won't interfere. Take Officer Hammond with you. Terry can take notes and be your witness. Fair enough?"

"Fair enough, Jim."

Chapter 25

PENNY HAMILTON WAS a bit startled to see two police officers at her door. Joanne turned on her most engaging smile, told Mrs. Hamilton that they wanted to ask her a few questions about Ted Miller, and asked if they could come in. Penny acquiesced, but not with any enthusiasm.

Mrs. Hamilton led them to the kitchen table and offered the usual menu of coffee, tea, soft drinks, or water. Three mugs of steaming coffee were soon on the table.

"How can I help you, Sergeant?"

Joanne explained that they were investigating the death of the Millers and that, as part of their investigation, they were speaking with folks who attended the party the night the Millers died.

"I don't understand, Sergeant. What is it that you're investigating? I know they both are dead, but why are you investigating? Do you think someone murdered them?"

"We do."

"Why me?

Joanne came at the issue directly, "Tell me about your relationship with Ted Miller, Mrs. Hamilton."

"What relationship, Sergeant? Neighbors, friends . . ."

Joanne interjected, ". . . lovers?"

Mrs. Hamilton did not bristle at the question or dissemble in any way, "Ted was a very attractive man, Sergeant. He had many assets that appealed to me."

"How often were you intimate with Mr. Miller?

"I didn't keep count. Maybe five or six times."

"Where?"

"Here or his home. It depended on where our spouses were at the time."

"How often did you meet at his home?"

"Probably three or four times."

"Did you know he made a video of one of your encounters?"

"No. I had no idea."

"Did he ever threaten to expose your affair to your husband?"

"No. Why would he do that?"

"For money. Maybe to extort money from you to keep your affair secret. Or maybe to extort money from your husband to keep your affair from becoming public knowledge?"

"That's a nice theory, Sergeant, but it never happened. Blackmailing me over an affair with Ted Miller? Hell, my husband knew about Ted and me. Do you know what my husband does for a living, Sergeant? He teaches at the local college. He teaches a sociology course on Deviant Behaviors. The students call its 'Sluts and Nuts.' My husband has always said that I am the inspiration for his course, that I am a continuing case study in sluts, up close and personal. Nobody could ever get a dime by threatening my affairs with exposure."

"Your husband doesn't mind?"

"Sluts and Nuts," Mrs. Hamilton said, with a strong emphasis on the "and." My husband is no longer capable of doing what this slut needs. There's a saying, Sergeant—'I'm not the man I once was, but I am once the man I was'? Well, Art can't even make that claim anymore. But he likes to watch, Sergeant. He's one of the 'Nuts,' Sergeant, maybe 'Nut No. 1.' And I'm happy to indulge his voyeuristic needs."

Joanne thanked Mrs. Hamilton for her time and for the coffee. As they shook hands in departure, Penny Hamilton said "I'm really saddened by the deaths of the Millers. They were nice people and I enjoyed my time with Ted. If I can do anything to help you find their killer, please let me know."

"One other question, Mrs. Hamilton. Do you recall what time you left the party?"

"Not really. We did not close down the joint if that's what you're asking. There were quite a few couples still there, some still in the pool or hot tub. The bar was still open and the booze was still flowing."

Joanne turned to Terry Hammond as they got situated in the squad car. "I think we can cross Penny and Art Hamilton off the list of possible suspects, Terry."

Chapter 26

JOANNE AND TERRY waited outside the fitness club where Samantha Long worked. They did not want to interview her at home since her husband was also on their list and they wanted to interview them separately.

Samantha emerged from the club around 5:45 in the evening. As she did so, Joanne got out of her car and approached Samantha. Joanne explained that the police were investigating the untimely deaths of the Millers and asked if there was somewhere private where they could talk. Samantha said that her husband's jewelry shop was open until 8 PM and he usually arrived home around 8:20. They would have enough time to interview her at her home. Joanne and Terry Hammond followed Samantha to her home.

Samantha was effervescent as ever, offering up drinks and asking about the police department's physical fitness requirements and obligations until Joanne could focus her on the business at hand.

After moving quickly through Samantha's lack of familiarity with phenobarbital, which seemed genuine, Joanne opened the door on Samantha's escapades with Ted Miller. "You want to know if I had an affair with Ted Miller? Why is that anybody's business but mine and my husband's?"

Joanne reacted calmly. "You don't have to answer, Mrs. Long. I can't compel you to talk to us. If we empanel a grand jury we can subpoena you and then you'll have to talk."

After waiting a decent interval during which Mrs. Long remained silent, Joanne added, "But in all fairness, you should know that we have a video of you and Mr. Miller in his bedroom. You were not playing checkers."

"You know, Sergeant Tracey, you could have started this conversation with the video. There was no need for you to sandbag me with it."

For a moment, that comment made her feel like Jim Milliken. She did not like that feeling and resolved to avoid any more of Milliken's tactics.

"Did you know you were being recorded?"

"Hardly. Look, he was incredibly good looking and I always had a thing for him. His wife was gorgeous, but I'm not so bad myself and I wondered if he ever thought about a change of pace. You know, short instead of tall. Blonde instead of brunette. More well-endowed up top. More to play with, you know? You never know if you don't ask, so I asked. He was all too happy to oblige. And, my God, was he something. Well-endowed doesn't begin to do him justice."

"How often did you and Mr. Miller see each other like that?"

"Not enough. Maybe six times. It's too bad. I was trying to set something up with him the night he was killed. Wore my best bikini to remind him what I was offering. "

"Did it work?"

"I thought so, but I'll never know for sure. But I swear to you, I didn't kill him. I wanted a lot more of that man."

"When you got together, was it at his house?"

"Mostly, not always."

"You never knew about the video? He never told you?"

"No. If I knew about it, I'd have asked for a viewing."

"He never threatened to disclose the video to your husband?"

Samantha laughed. "Aaron knew about Ted and me."

"How?"

"I told him. We have a pretty open relationship, Sergeant. Always have. I've had my men and Aaron has had his men. Sometimes, they're one and the same."

"And was that the case with Ted Miller?"

"Uh huh."

"What made you think Ted Miller was interested in men?"

"Ted Miller was interested in sex, all kinds of sex. I figured that if he liked to back door women, and I knew that he did, he might like a change of pace there as well. Like I said, you never know if you don't ask, so I asked. He was all too happy to oblige my husband on more than one occasion. Aaron enjoyed it. He gave Ted a really nice tourmaline ring for Maryanne as a thank you. Do you have one, Sergeant? You should. They're really nice."

"No, I don't, Mrs. Long. But I'll look. Maybe I'll drop by your husband's shop and take a look. Thanks. Did your husband know that Ted Miller had recorded their encounter on one of those occasions?

"I don't think so. Aaron never mentioned it to me. But you'd have to ask him to be sure.

Did Ted Miller ever threaten to expose your husband's sexual proclivities?"

"Same answer. Look, Aaron is going to be home in about 30 minutes. You are welcome to stay and save yourselves the trouble of a second trip.

I can sit on the side and keep my mouth shut unless you all ask me something, or I can go to the den and turn on a movie. Your choice."

"Thanks, Mrs. Long. If it's OK with you, we'll wait."

Joanne and Terry were finishing a cup of coffee when Aaron Long arrived. His wife sat stoically, outside his range of vision, while he answered all of the questions Sergeant Tracey put to him. His answers all jibed with his wife's. "No," he was not aware of any videos. "No," Ted Miller had never threatened to expose Mr. or Mrs. Long. "No," Ted Miller had never sought to extort money from Mr. Long to keep his bisexuality under wraps. "No," he had no familiarity with phenobarbital. And "No," he did not kill Ted Miller.

The Longs told Joanne that they were not the last to leave the party, that several couples and Nikki Beaumont were still there. The bartender was keeping them all well lubricated.

Back in their cruiser, Joanne and Terry found the interviews with Penny Hamilton and the Longs to be perplexing. It was difficult to understand why Ted Miller would seek extramarital fun with anyone given the woman to whom he had been married. Maryanne Miller was beautiful and Joanne and Terry agreed that most men would never even think about stepping out on her. But Ted Miller was obviously cut from a different cloth. Terry opined that some men are just tom cats at heart, eager to enjoy pleasure as and where they could find it. Joanne arched her eyebrows as Terry said he could understand how a man could succumb readily to the charms of Samantha Long. She was attractive, with a body that had been beautifully shaped by her regimen of constant aerobics. Nor did her expression relax when Terry added that Penny Hamilton was no match for Maryanne or Samantha in the looks department, but that her world-weary demeanor was incredibly seductive.

Joanne turned in her seat and flashed a quizzical grin in Hammond's direction. "Are you a tom cat, Terry? Are you applying for a job as Ted Miller's replacement?"

Hammond blushed at the suggestion. "No, Joanne. I was just trying to get into Miller's head and figure out how and why all these extramarital liaisons came to be. After all, you're the one who thinks one of Ted Miller's other lovers is a more likely culprit than Mrs. Beaumont."

"Well, Terry, put your tom cat hat back on. You say you can understand Miller's fascination with Penny Hamilton and Samantha Long. But how do you explain Aaron Long? With all of these nice looking women ready and willing to share their beds with him, why did he also have an affair with Aaron Long? Even if Miller were a bisexual, Aaron Long is not an attractive man, certainly not the type of man to which a Ted Miller would turn for bisexual fun."

"Maybe it's as simple as Mrs. Long said, Joanne. She asked him to do her a favor and get it on with her husband and Miller regarded it as a ticket to be punched if he wanted to keep seeing her."

"I think you're right. I think that explains his interludes with Mr. Long. But I think it also suggests that Ted Miller was not, at heart, a heterosexual and that he might have had other male companions. He would not have accommodated Mr. Long if it were completely antithetical to his sexual preferences."

"And you think one of his homosexual trysts might have taken a wrong turn, Joanne?"

"I don't know, Terry. We have no idea how many men were involved with Ted Miller, how, or why. I just think we need to be attuned to that possibility."

That said, as they concluded the discussion in the car, Sergeant Tracey and Officer Hammond agreed that the Longs could be stricken from the list of suspects.

Chapter 27

NIKKI HAD COME to feel as if her life was a continuous loop of lawyers and police officers, and the call from Sharon Riley did nothing to persuade her otherwise.

"Nikki, I have some information on your husband's travel itinerary. Are you sitting?"

"Comfortably, Sharon. Your investigator has given you a report?"

"Yes. Notwithstanding what you've been thinking, Nikki, Jack has not been seeing other women."

Nikki was surprised and more than a little deflated that Sharon's investigation had not dug up any dirt on Jack's nocturnal habits. But before her disappointment could grab hold and sink in, Sharon asked "Did you ever think your husband preferred men, Nikki?"

"What!"

"Nikki, we followed him for ten days. He spent fewer than half of the nights in his room at the Century Plaza. He spent a number of nights at a private residence. He would leave that residence early the next morning, return to the hotel, clean up and change clothes, and then head off to work at the client's facility. In the evening, he would have dinner with one or more company employees, and more often than not head back to the private residence, which belongs to one of his constant dinner companions. He always trails in a separate car, and he arrives a decent interval after the owner."

"Who is it, Sharon?"

"His name is Randy Carmichael. He is the Executive Vice President of Transnational Marine Machinery, Inc."

"He's the client that Jack brought home for the Memorial Day weekend some time ago. Jack said he was going through a rough divorce and it would be a hell of a lot better for him to spend the weekend with friends than in an empty hotel room."

"Do you recall when that was, Nikki?"

"Oh, geez, maybe four years ago."

"That's the time of Carmichael's divorce, according to the public records. What else can you remember about him, Nikki?"

"Tall, slender, good head of hair, nice looking. Good manners. Quite pleasant. An easy house guest. That's about it."

"When did Jack start going on these extended LA trips? The ones that lasted over a weekend? Maybe ten days to three weeks?"

"Oh, Sharon. I can't pinpoint it, but that sounds right. Maybe four years ago. Do the records indicate the grounds for divorce?"

"'Irreconcilable Differences,' which is about as helpful as a blindfold at the movies. We're trying to track down his ex to see if she can or will shed some light on those differences."

"You think Jack has been cheating on me with Randy Carmichael?"

"Nikki, we don't have it on celluloid, but let me give you the pieces of the puzzle. Then you tell me how they fit together. OK, here we go—

First, take my word for this, you are an attractive woman. There are not many men who would say 'No' to you in bed the way you say Jack has.

Second, for the last four years or so, Jack's interest in you sexually has steadily declined to the point where you basically have a platonic marriage.

Third, even on the days when he's returned from an extended trip and you seek to engage him, he has no interest.

Fourth, when he's away, he always calls you at a time that will not interfere with whatever fun he has planned for the evening.

Fifth, he does not often sleep in his hotel room.

Sixth, he often spends the night at the home of an unmarried man. And before you ask, no, they are not joined by female friends.

Seventh, he leaves his friend's home very early, uses his hotel room as a changing station and goes to work, where the cycle starts all over again.

How do you fit those pieces together, Nikki?"

"What do we do with this, Sharon?"

"Let us close the loop, if we can, with Carmichael's ex. If those irreconcilable differences relate to their respective sexual preferences, that will cap off our proof. Then we wait for him to file for divorce and we cross file, based on his adultery. I'd love to be a fly on the wall when he reads your cross claim."

"OK, so we are just waiting for the other shoe to drop, as it were?"

"Yes. I'll keep you posted, Nikki."

Nikki ended the call on her end. She had lost her husband, not to another woman, but to another man. She wanted to cry, but she had long since dismissed Jack as worth any more tears. Then she realized that Randy Carmichael was for Jack what Maryanne Miller had been, albeit all too briefly, for her. She wished that Maryanne could be there, to comfort her as she worked her way through this morass. But Maryanne was gone forever. Her lawyers could not fill that void. She did not see how anyone ever could.

Chapter 28

JOANNE KNOCKED ON Milliken's door and said she had an interim report. He asked her to sit down and brief him. She knew he would be happy. None of the first three guests who had been filmed by Ted Miller *in flagrante* had any reason to kill the Millers. She was down to Antonia Carmelo. Joanne had been surprised by the first two interviews and by the cavalier attitude toward marital vows exhibited by the interviewees. She did not expect a reprise when she spoke to Antonia Carmelo. She would wager a hefty sum that Antonia did not confess her infidelity to her husband and an even heftier sum that Pete Carmelo was not the kind of guy who would derive any jollies from watching Antonia writhe in bed with the Millers.

Joanne had been told that the Carmelos had three children, all of whom attended school or pre-school. She and Hammond arrived at 10 AM in the hope they would hit a window of uninterrupted calm. Their hopes were rewarded. Mrs. Carmelo was alone.

The interview began as the others had—"We are looking into the deaths of the Millers . . . You attended the party . . . Perhaps you saw or heard something that would help us . . . How well did you know the Millers . . .? Do you know if they had any enemies . . .? What did you think of Mr. Miller . . . Mrs. Miller?"

None of those questions generated any visible reaction from Mrs. Carmelo, except for the last two. She began to tear up when Joanne asked what Mrs. Carmelo thought of Ted and Maryanne Miller. Speaking with her residual Italian accent, Mrs. Carmelo said simply, "They were wonderful. I miss them."

"You say they were wonderful, Mrs. Carmelo. How wonderful?"

"What are you asking me, Sergeant?"

"Mrs. Carmelo, we have a video of you and the Millers in their bedroom, on their bed."

"I didn't know they had recorded it."

"Do you mean you didn't know until I just told you?"

"Yes."

"Does it bother you that they recorded you in such a compromising condition?"

"What difference does that make? They are gone. I wish they were here so that I could love them, her, again."

"How would your husband feel about that?"

"Not very well, that's for sure. But Maryanne, she was so sweet, so soft, so gentle, so giving. That day she invited me to lunch alongside her pool, I knew what she was doing. I loved every minute of it. She was wonderful. Bella principessa. "

"And Mr. Miller?"

"He came into the bedroom while Maryanne and I were together. Maryanne asked me if it was OK if he joined us. I said yes. He was so large, and yet so gentle. I know it was wrong. I didn't care. And I still don't care."

"Did your husband know about you and the Millers?"

"I don't think so. He never confronted me about it and, believe me, my Pete believes in the art of confrontation."

"Did Mr. or Mrs. Miller ever mention the recording to you?

"No, I already said I never heard about it until a few minutes ago."

"Did they ever threaten to tell Pete about your threesome?"

"No, not about the threesome or any of the other encounters."

"Others?"

"Yes. Maryanne and I were amante, appassionata."

"Do you know if either of the Millers told Pete?"

"No. Dio mio. Anyone who knows Pete would know better than to do that."

"What do you mean?"

"As I said, Pete can be very confrontational. And he is very Italian. Anyone who challenges the reputation of an Italian man's wife will be in the market for a new set of teeth, if not more. It's in their DNA. Even if the wife is a puttana."

"Mrs. Carmelo, did you kill the Millers?"

"No, Sergeant. On my father's grave."

"What time did you leave the party?"

"I think about 10:30. We left home at 5:45 and I remember paying the babysitter $150. At $30 per hour, that would place us at home at around 10:45."

"It's good to be a babysitter."

"It's the going rate these days, Sergeant."

"Were there any other guests there when you left?"

"Nikki Beaumont was there. I don't recall anyone else."

"Caterers?"

"Oh, yes. A couple of them were packing up the food to put in the refrigerators. And the bartender. He was there. For how long, I don't know. He signaled 'Last Call' as we were headed to the door."

As Joanne and Terry got up to leave, Mrs. Carmelo said "Get him. Whoever this is, get him. She was so wonderful, appassionata."

"We'll do our best, Mrs. Carmelo."

Chapter 29

INSPECTOR MILLIKEN SAT behind his desk while Sergeant Tracey, Officer Hammond at her side, reported on the Carmelo interview. The bottom line was that none of the guests who had any recorded sexual history with Ted or Maryanne Miller were aware of the videos; nor did they seem to care. There was no evidence of threatened exposure or extortion and, so, no ostensible motive for murder. Tracey mused openly about checking their bank accounts to look for large or periodic withdrawals in cash, which might have indicated blackmail, but she and Milliken both agreed that they had insufficient basis for a warrant.

"Do you still think Mrs. Beaumont is innocent, Joanne? You've tried, but you haven't found anyone who had a motive for killing those people."

"And you still haven't come up with a motive for her to have killed them, Jim. And there's plenty of circumstantial evidence that she didn't."

"Yes, Joanne, I know. The tearful reaction to their deaths, the loving "Goodnight" words and kisses, the express hope for future romantic interludes. All of that can be relegated to showmanship if she knew about the video. And the only evidence that she didn't is her say-so."

"Jim, none of the others knew about the videos. Why would the Millers tell Mrs. Beaumont?"

"Maybe the others were lying. Maybe they thought it would make them look even kinkier than they are if they admitted they knew. And who's going to contradict them, Joanne? The Millers are dead."

"Jim, you and I come at this from different perspectives. We're not going to resolve anything sitting here. I've got two more threads to pull. I want to talk to Mr. Carmelo. Then I want to see the caterer."

"Fine, Joanne. Be careful with Carmelo. If he doesn't know about his wife's infidelities, there's no need for you to shatter his illusions about the whore he married."

"Yes, Jim."

Chapter 30

SERGEANT TRACEY AND Officer Hammond settled into chairs across from Peter Carmelo in his office at St. Peter's.

"Mr. Carmelo, I think you know why we're here."

"Yes, Sergeant. You spoke to Antonia and she told me that you were investigating the Millers' deaths and talking to folks who were guests at their party the night they died. Right?"

"Right," said Joanne. She went over some of the details they had obtained from Mrs. Carmelo—time of departure, persons still on site when they left, etc. Mr. Carmelo's answers were close enough to his wife's to ring true. Joanne moved on to virgin territory.

"How well did you know the Millers?"

"Well enough, Sergeant. We would see them at various neighborhood gatherings, you know, barbecues, cocktail parties. Antonia and Maryanne became pretty good friends, I think. Antonia told me that they would occasionally get together for lunch before the kids got home from school.

From what I could tell, Antonia really liked Maryanne. She is probably the better person to ask that question."

"What about Mr. Miller?"

"Nice guy from what I could tell. We had a family portrait done at his studio. He did a nice job. He was very affable. They had dinner at our house once or twice. I could see why all the women loved him."

"What do you mean?"

"Nothing much. Just that he was one hell of a good-looking dude and women's eyes seemed to follow him wherever he went."

"Did you ever see him flirt with your wife?"

"He flirted with all the pretty women, and I think you'll agree, Antonia is a very pretty woman."

"She is, Mr. Carmelo." Carmelo turned to look at Officer Hammond, who smiled and nodded his assent.

"Did his flirting bother you?"

"Should it, Sergeant? Mrs. Miller was very pretty too and I flirted with her as much as Ted flirted with Antonia. It was all harmless."

"Did he ever get out of line with your wife?"

"No. If he had, he would have regretted it. But no, never."

"Do you know if Ted Miller had a reputation for a roving eye?"

"With Maryanne to go home to every night, Sergeant?"

"Well, there are men with beautiful wives who still cat around, Mr. Carmelo."

"I guess, but to answer your question, no. I never heard anything like that."

"Is there anything else about that Saturday night and Ted Miller that you recall?"

"Well, he was pretty well lit, if you know what I mean. But he was a gracious host, even if he felt compelled to give us his standard elevator speech about the evils of the planned mega-mall."

"What elevator speech?"

"Ted headed up some local group called the Citizens' Alliance for Preservation, or something like that. It was his way of trying to unite local businesses and homeowners to oppose the mall. I mean, he was well-intentioned, but he didn't stand a chance in hell of keeping the Zoning Board from voting in favor of the variance requested by the mall."

"When will that vote take place?"

"It already did. It took place the Monday after the Millers' party."

"Did anyone appear for the Citizens' Alliance to oppose the mall?"

"No idea, Sergeant. Local politics bore me. I pretty much assume the fix is in where big bucks are involved. That's why I thought the Citizens' Alliance was a waste of time and effort. I'm sure there is a public record of who appeared."

"Mr. Carmelo, we spoke a few days ago about distribution controls on your pharmaceuticals. Do you recall that?"

"Uh huh. You asked if Mrs. Beaumont had received any phenobarbital recently and I said no."

"Right. Then you checked the computer log for the last twelve months and you said that corroborated your recollection."

"Yes, that's right."

"Is it possible to alter the computer logs?"

"Sure. We modify entries all the time. We make mistakes and we correct them."

"How far back can you go to correct an entry?"

"They freeze the database every six months. After that, the log can't be altered."

"During those six months before it is frozen, is it possible to add a transaction, say, to indicate that Patient A received Medication B on Date C and that the medication was dispensed to Dr. D or Nurse E?"

"Yes."

"And could someone, during that period, delete a transaction that had been previously entered?"

"Yes."

"Who could do that, Mr. Carmelo?"

"I could, or the Assistant Pharmacist, Mark Harnick."

"Is there a record of any such modifications?"

"Yes. We can get a printout of the modifications, if you like Sergeant, at least for the last six months. If you want more, I'll need to work with Records."

"Six months will do fine, Mr. Carmelo."

Carmelo worked at his computer for a few minutes and the printout of modifications emerged from his printer. The officers thanked him, took the printout and left.

As they sat in the parking lot, Terry Hammond looked at Joanne Tracey. "Poor, clueless bastard."

"Let's leave him that way, Terry. Cross him off the list."

Chapter 31

INSPECTOR MILLIKEN LISTENED to the report on the interview of Pete Carmelo and on the officers' review of the pharmaceutical printout, which revealed nothing that was relevant to the case.

"You're running out of playing cards, Joanne. What do you have left, the mega-mall and the caterer?"

"Unless something else pops up to give us a lead, yeah, I'm down to those two."

Terry Hammond asked for leave to speak. Milliken and Tracey nodded their assent.

"One thing that has been puzzling me about this case is the money. I mean, what if this was a professional hit? That costs money. I don't know how much, but I've got to believe it isn't chicken feed. Do any of the people we've been talking to have that kind of financial wherewithal?"

Milliken interrupted him, "We don't know that the killer was a pro, Terry. Let's not base our investigation on that assumption. Besides, these are not poor people."

"I agree, Inspector, but do they have the kind of cash laying around that a hit man is going to demand? Maybe if we get a warrant to examine their financial records we'll find that one of them made a sizeable withdrawal from one of their accounts at or about the time of the hit. But I don't think so. And I agree with Sergeant Tracey, I don't see Nicole Beaumont as someone with the financial capacity to hire a professional assassin. But the folks underwriting that mega-mall would have the money to do that. And Ted Miller may have been a pimple on the ass of progress as far as they were concerned."

Tracey jumped in, "And look at the timing, Jim. Ted Miller was scheduled to appear on behalf of the Citizens' Alliance for Preservation at the Zoning Board hearing on the 24th. He meets his fate in the early morning hours of the 23rd. He cannot appear on the 24th because he is dead. Pimple removed."

"You're going to piss off lot of important people if you go down that rabbit hole, Joanne. Are you sure you want to do that? And are you sure you want to drag young Hammond down into that hole with you?"

"Want has nothing to do with it, Inspector. Didn't you always say that we eliminate all the possibilities and what is left is the truth?"

"Yeah, but I stole that from Sherlock Holmes. That was fiction. This is real."

"But it's still true. We need to eliminate all the possibilities. And the mega-mall is one of them."

"Have at it Joanne. It's your hide."

Chapter 32

TRACEY AND HAMMOND had studied the record and transcript of the Zoning Board hearing. The request for the variance had been filed by "APX LLC" as the owner of the underlying land. There was a report filed with the Board by one of its analysts addressing the application, including the analyst's comments on the opposition filed by the Citizens' Alliance for Preservation. When the analyst had completed her report, the board opened the floor for comments. An individual who represented himself as an attorney for APX LLC went to the lectern and offered to answer any questions the board might have. There being no questions from the board, he returned to his chair. It was announced that Ted Miller had filed a notice of appearance on behalf of the Alliance, but he did not appear. The discussion was closed and a vote taken. The variance was approved by a 7-0 vote.

When they arrived at the offices of APX, they were ushered into the office of Humphrey Holden, the Manager of the LLC. He looked as if he had been plucked out of Central Casting to play the role of a senior magnate at a Fortune 100 company—silver haired, moustache to match, ramrod posture, striped Navy Blue suit with white shirt and red tie, polished winged tips. With him were two gentlemen of a similar ilk, who described themselves as "Members" of the LLC, Lancaster Crawford and Lawrence Frank. After directing the officers to a pair of comfortable chairs and offering liquid refreshments, Holden assumed the role of spokesperson for the triumvirate.

"What can we do for you officers?"

"We are investigating the death of Ted Miller."

"And your investigation brings you to our doorstep, Sergeant?"

"I wouldn't put it quite that way, Mr. Holden. We have spoken to an awful lot of people and now it's your turn. We are trying to figure out if anyone had reason to be pleased by Mr. Miller's demise."

"Well, I'll give you credit, Sergeant. That was about the nicest way you could have asked us if we had anything to do with Ted Miller's death. But, even after you put lipstick on that pig, it's still a pig. What makes you think we had anything to do with Mr. Miller's death?"

"I didn't say we did, Mr. Holden. We're just trying to understand the facts."

"What facts, Sergeant?"

"The zoning variance for your mall project, Mr. Miller's opposition to that variance on behalf of the Citizens' Alliance for Preservation, and his sudden death a day or so before the Zoning Board hearing."

"You realize, Sergeant, that we do not have to answer any of your questions?"

"Yes, sir."

"That we can ask you to leave our offices?"

"Yes, sir."

"OK. Let me start by telling you that neither I, Mr. Crawford nor Mr. Frank had anything at all to do with Mr. Miller's death. Nor did APX, any of its employees or agents, or anyone acting for or on our behalf or at our direction. Am I clear, Sergeant?"

"I understand clearly what you've said."

"Good. Now is there anything else for us to discuss, Sergeant?"

Joanne wondered if Humphrey Holden thought she had fallen off yesterday's turnip truck. She was more than a little annoyed at his presumptuousness and his arrogance.

"Yes, Mr. Holden. Does ATP have any projections of revenues and profits from the mall over the first five and ten years of operations?"

"Of course."

"And if the Zoning Board had rejected your request for variance, how would that have affected those projected revenues and profits?"

"Negatively, of course."

"And Ted Miller was the principal obstacle to getting your way before the Zoning Board, right?"

"Wrong, Sergeant. Ted Miller and his Citizens' Alliance for Preservation were no obstacle to us at all."

"You're telling me that it made no difference to any of you whether or not Ted Miller showed up to make his presentation to the Zoning Board?"

"Correct. No difference at all."

"Why was that, Mr. Holden?"

"Politics is not your game, is it, Sergeant? Or yours, Officer Hammond? You see, politics often devolves into a simple numbers game, How many votes do I need? How many do I have? How many are solid? How many are soft? That's the way it works in Washington. That's the way it works in every state, county, village and town where action requires approvals of some regulatory authority."

Joanne asked him directly. "And you felt comfortable you had the votes?"

"It wouldn't have gotten on the board's agenda if we weren't comfortable. You read the board analyst's report, didn't you, Sergeant?"

"I did, Mr. Holden."

"We were comfortable, Sergeant. We had the votes. Ted Miller was inconsequential. I know that sounds cold and callous, but remember, you came in here asking if we had arranged to have a man killed over a zoning variance. That was pretty cold and callous too."

"We're just doing our job, Mr. Holden."

"Understood. I trust that, as far as APX is concerned, your job is now done. Enjoy the rest of your day."

Chapter 33

AS THEY SETTLED into their cruiser, Terry asked if he should cross APX off the list.

"Terry, the only way we even open the door on them is if we find four or more Zoning Board members who will say, under oath, that Ted Miller's appearance at the hearing on the 24th might possibly have affected their vote. That's never going to happen. But those APX guys give me the creeps. I think Humphrey Holden would run an ice pick through his mother's heart, on Mother's Day to boot, if it would get him another percentage point of profit on one of his deals. So don't cross them off, but don't count on anything coming of it."

"So, we're down to the caterer? Emily Morton?"

"That's it, Terry. Let's go."

Joanne hoped that her conversation with Emily Morton might shed some light on the events of that ill-fated Saturday. Emily was part-owner of Morton & Morrison Catering. She had told Joanne over the phone that she handled the Miller account, had been responsible for all of the food service, and was present throughout the soiree, from the afternoon preparations that began at the Miller home around 4 PM until they wrapped up and left around 11 PM.

"How many folks were on your team that night, Ms. Morton?"

"Call me Emily, please. Eight. Three in the kitchen; three out among the crowd serving; one bartender; and me."

"Were these all regular employees of your company?"

"No. Our business is somewhat episodic. It would be difficult to maintain that kind of staff on a regular basis. The kitchen staff were regulars. You can't afford to risk losing them. Servers can be hired on a job-by-job basis."

"What about the bartender?"

"The bartender is a jobber too."

"So you had four staff who were, as you called them, jobbers that night?

"Yes, that's right."

"Had you used them all before?"

"All but the bartender." Joanne's and Terry's ears perked up at that answer.

"Oh?"

"My usual choice for the job is Danny Dunphy. But he wasn't available."

"Why not, if you know?"

"Danny called just a couple of days before the party, Thursday, I think. He tells me there has been a death in his family and he needs to go out of town. But he says he has me covered. He has a friend who has tended bar professionally for years and can pick up the job. He puts the guy on the phone, we chat, I ask him a few questions to test his mixologist skills, and he passes. He shows up Saturday at the Millers, shows me his ID, fills out some paperwork including his Social Security Number, and goes about the task of setting up the bar."

"His name?"

"Halper, I think. Guy Halper."

"How did he do?"

"He must have done OK. Nobody complained."

"Would you use him again?"

"If Danny weren't available? Sure."

"Who provided the dinnerware, the glassware, the linens, and all of that?"

"We did. That's part of our overall package."

"Wine and liquor?"

"The Millers were pretty particular about what they drank. They did. We provided the mixers and some beer."

"So, when you all packed up and left, the booze stayed behind?

"Supposed to. Did someone complain that some booze was missing?"

"No, Emily. Nothing of that sort. You say you left about 11? Was that everyone?"

"Yes, we loaded up our vans, the team piled in, and we went back to the shop. I paid the jobbers in cash and we all went on our merry way."

"You said that Guy Halper met you at the Millers. So he arrived separately, in his own car?

"Uh huh."

"Did he leave at the same time you did?"

"I don't really remember. Often, the bartender hangs around bit longer, at the hosts' requests. But there was no need for him to come back to the shop. I paid him separately a bit before 'Last Call' and he was free to go directly home."

"Do you know where he was staying?"

"He said he was bunking in at Danny's. You want Danny's contact information?"

"Thanks."

Joanne and Terry went directly to Danny Dunphy's apartment. They knocked. No answer. They knocked louder. No answer. There was a part of Joanne that wanted to locate the superintendent and ask him to open the door. The other part of her—"Sergeant Tracey"—knew that would be a warrantless search and a poor example of police procedure for Officer Terry Hammond.

They returned to the station and reported to Inspector Milliken. For once, he seemed interested and engaged.

"Let me play this out for you, Joanne.

> One—The bartender is the killer.
> Two—He knows from watching all night that the Millers are gin drinkers.
> Three—He also knows that the odds on them taking another drink before bedtime are quite high.
> Four—If they have another martini, it's 'Goodnight Irene' for the Millers.
> Five—If they don't have another drink that night, the phenobarbital is still there waiting in ambush for a Sunday morning gin blossom or a Sunday afternoon Silver Bullet. Either way they're dead ducks.

Six—Our bartender collects his pay in cash, heads out of town, and is never see again.

That's your theory, Joanne, isn't it?"

"Yes, Jim. And that will be Maria Romano's theory. And that will get Nicole Beaumont off the hook."

"Maybe," said Milliken, ". . . unless . . ."

"Unless what, Jim?"

"Unless Guy Halper turns out to be a legitimate, taxpaying bartender who was just helping out a friend. And two more things, Joanne. What the hell is Guy Halper's motive for murdering the Millers and how did he even know about the party or the catering company?"

"What is your suggestion, Jim?"

"Sit tight until Danny Dunphy gets back from the funeral. He should be able to tell us a thing or two about his friend."

Chapter 34

 were busy typing up their reports on the various interviews they had conducted over the last few days. Terry picked the phone that was ringing next to a cold cup of coffee and Joanne did not hear enough in Terry's half of the conversation to pique her interest.

"Let's go, Joanne. That call was reporting a death at the Lakeview Apartments."

Joanne's eyes widened. "Danny Dunphy?"

"Yes. The other tenants were complaining of a foul odor coming from his apartment. When the super used his pass key, he found Danny hanging from the rafters. The super assured me that no one went into the apartment after he opened it. So the crime scene should be pretty much intact."

As Terry drove, Joanne notified Milliken, who said he would dispatch Hank McIntire and a forensics team ASAP. Milliken arrived almost as quickly as McIntire.

Hank was his usual succinct self. "Apparent suicide. Can't be sure. He's been dead for quite some time. Maybe a week or more. I'll need to perform some extensive tests to get to a defensible ballpark for time of death. But one thing is sure—if this was a staged suicide, whoever killed this guy has had plenty of time to get out of Dodge." There were fingerprints all over the place, but Hank did not think there were any that would prove to belong to "Guy Halper," whoever he was.

As they sat around Milliken's desk back at the station, a cute clerk named Diana Lundquist (who clearly had eyes for Terry Hammond) entered the office with some papers and walked over to Milliken and placed a one-page report in front of him on his desk. The social security number that the bartender had given to Emily Morton was indeed assigned to Guy Halper. But Guy Halper had died of pneumonia at the age of 89 in 1994. This killer was a pro, and someone had gone to great lengths to eliminate the Millers. Danny Dunphy was in his way, and he had to be eliminated. Dunphy had undoubtedly called Emily Morton with a gun fast against his head and those were likely the last words he ever spoke.

Jim Milliken was almost ready to eliminate Nicole Beaumont as a suspect. Almost.

Chapter 35

HOWARD COEN HAD disposed of more than two dozen "marks" in the course of his career. Faithless husbands and/or their paramours, cheating wives and/or their lovers, business competitors, a business superior who was blocking access to the Executive Suite, even a candidate for political office, all fell prey to Howard's well-honed assassin skills. Howard's repertoire of lethal techniques was multifaceted—rifles, pistols, knives, explosives, the garotte, and, in the case of two beautiful but faithless wives, his gloved hands. He killed them while looking directly into their eyes, his hands encircling their pretty throats to choke the life out of them while their eyes begged for mercy he was incapable of providing. Just before they lost consciousness, he kissed them, ravenously; it aroused him to know that his kiss would be the last sensory perception of their lives and the pleasure of that arousal outweighed the risk of anyone tracing him through any residual DNA left on their lips. It aroused him further to know that he would be the last image their eyes would take with them into eternity as their lifeless bodies slumped to the floor. Howard was good at what he did, and he loved his work. He would prepare each hit fastidiously, leaving nothing to chance. He had never failed to deliver on a contract. When Howard Coen accepted the contract, the mark was as good as dead. It was just a matter of time before the self-proclaimed "Angel of Death" came calling.

This contract was a bit unique. The customers usually don't want to know anything about the hit, the where, the when or the how. All the contract calls for is the body of the mark on a slab in the morgue. This one was different. The mark was to be hit during a party at his home in ten days. Ordinarily, Howard would not have accepted the contract. There were too many variables, too little time to prepare. But he loved the challenge and, more to the point, he loved the money. $50,000 in cash, tax free, $10,000 paid in advance, was nothing to sneeze at. So he took the contract and began to plan.

He had been given very little information, but it would prove to be enough. He had a photograph of the mark and photographs of the property at which the party would be held. These photos had been taken from various points along the property's 360-degree circumference. He had the name of the caterer and the name of the bartender. It was possible that he could get a line of sight on the mark from one or more of the off-property vantage points, but an open hit of that kind, on that kind of terrain, would increase the likelihood of collateral damage as tipsy guests wandered along the unpredictable paths drawn for them by their cocktails of choice. It would also afford him little time to retreat and escape. The long sniper shot would have to be Plan B for Howard. Plan A was to infiltrate the party and make the hit in a way that would minimize the likelihood of immediate discovery and maximize his time to disappear. It was only because he had the name of the bartender that Howard accepted the contract. It was the one obvious ticket for his admission to the party. Once he disposed of Danny Dunphy, he could finalize his plan for the disposition of Ted Miller.

He did not enjoy killing Danny Dunphy, and there was no incremental fee for Howard in disposing of Danny, but Danny was blocking the only route that Howard had to get in and complete the contract from the inside.

The plan was simple. Howard would serve as an affable bartender, keeping everyone well lubricated. He had tended bar on many occasions, knew all the major cocktails, and could easily pass muster as a mixologist. He would wait until all the guests had left and offer Mr. Miller a nightcap, one that would—shortly but not immediately, and without any outward show of physical distress—induce perpetual sleep. If for some reason the laced nightcap method proved to be problematic, Howard could, and would, resort to his 9mm Smith & Wesson M&P 2 with attached suppressor. Whichever method Howard ultimately used, the remaining $40,000 on the contract would be wired through a number of offshore shell companies owned under fictitious names to Howard's Swiss bank accounts within 24 hours of the hit. Howard would be happy and the unknown principal behind the contract would be happy as well.

Howard did not know who that unknown principal was. He never did. He accepted or declined contracts from a nameless voice of an intermediary who communicated with him via burner phones. In this case, however, given the tight timeline and the unique specifications of the job, Howard wanted to able to contact someone in the event of unforeseen problems that might affect the time and place of delivery. The intermediary did not want Howard communicating with him any further; instead Howard was given a phone number, no name, and instructed to use it only if the delivery on the contract had to be postponed, and only through a burner phone on his end that would be discarded after each use. Both Howard and the principal would know that if a call took place, there would be no exchange of names.

Howard used the time at his disposal to change his features. Since his facial hair grew quickly, he was able to muster a passable, short goatee, which he dyed to a dark brown, along with his hair, to mask its natural salt and pepper coloration. To complete his new look, he added a pair of eyeglasses with faux lenses. He was pleased with the result. While someone who actually studied his face might be able to envision what he might look like sans eyeglasses, sans beard, and sans dye, he doubted that the Millers' partygoers would have any such interest in his face. Their eyes would be focused, if at all, on the drinks he would be handing to them. To his new look, he added a new name, Guy Halper, an ostensible Californian with a California driver's license that Howard retrieved from his cache of false identities and altered to add his new image. When the contract was completed, and before he was next required to present an ID, Howard would shave, wash out his hair, and ditch both the eyeglasses and his identifying papers. Guy Halper would exist no more. In his place, a clean shaven Oregonian named Hamilton Drake would have taken his place.

Chapter 36

 developed, Howard carefully studied Ted Miller's drinking habits. They were nothing if not consistent. Bombay Sapphire gin martinis, very dry, on the rocks, with as many olives as the glass would hold. Little did he know, but Ted Miller had pissed off someone sufficiently to make the last martini of Ted Miller's evening the last martini of his life. It would be dry, very dry, just as he liked it, but with more than a hint of phenobarbital.

As Emily and her staff packed up to leave, Howard counted three remaining guests, the pretty Italian woman and her husband and a woman who had attended solo, without any male companion. Once Emily drove off, Howard receded into the woodwork, occupying a space from which he could observe without being seen by folks who were more than a little bit tipsy. What he observed was that the final guest, the single woman, would not be leaving soon, if at all.

Howard's original plan was to wait until all the guests had left, prepare an individual martini for Ted Miller, and hand it to him as Guy Halper said

"Goodnight" and left the premises. Miller would fall asleep beside his wife and never wake up. It would be a simple, one victim hit. When Mrs. Miller awoke in the morning, her husband would be dead. By the time anyone figured out the cause of death, Howard would be hundreds of miles away, and even if Mrs. Miller remembered what the bartender looked like, "Guy Halper" would have been erased from the face of the earth.

It was apparent to Howard that his plan had been compromised by the presence of the other woman. The "one martini" hit was unrealistic if Miller was not headed off for a good night's sleep. Howard needed Ted Miller to expire in his sleep, not in the middle of an amorous threesome, causing the women to call 911 and shrink the window of time available for Howard's escape. So, as Ted Miller indulged his lustful desires for the women, Howard returned to the bar, opened the gin bottle, which was slightly less than half full, emptied an unhealthy dose of phenobarbital into the gin, then sloshed it around to ensure a decent mixture. He recapped the bottle and receded back into the woodwork. Howard realized that both of the Millers enjoyed their martinis, and that his spiking of the gin bottle could well result in two deaths if Mrs. Miller chose to have a nightcap. That was unfortunate. Howard had no qualms about killing women. He had killed a number of them over the years. But they had all been the designated mark, the subject of his contract. Mrs. Miller was not his target. She would be collateral damage if she chose to have another martini. There was no money in her death for Howard, but sometimes bystanders had to be dealt with as coldly as the mark.

Howard returned to the shadows and remained there, quiet and motionless. He watched as, after an interval of bedroom gymnastics, Ted Miller and the other woman approached the bar, but left with only a Greyhound. The deadly bottle of gin had not been touched.

Howard considered for a moment the possibility that Mr. Miller might not have another martini. If that were to transpire, Howard would resort to his Smith & Wesson. That would increase the body count to three, but again, he could not afford to allow concerns for innocent bystanders to interfere with the contract. But Howard Coen was a patient man and he would use his pistol only as a last resort. Sometime later, he heard Ted Miller call out instructions to his female guest for the making of his martini nightcap. As she followed those instructions and walked back to the bedroom with a tray of drinks, Howard followed silently at an unseen distance with his Smith & Wesson. He listened attentively at the door, prepared to shoot all three of them if necessary. However, when he heard the woman hand out the drinks, express her affection for both of the Millers, and toast the evening, and when Ted Miller complimented her on the bartending skills that had created such a smooth martini, Howard knew his job was done. He retreated from the hall, left the house, climbed into his car and drove away with the headlights off, another contract delivered on schedule.

It was late, and Howard was tired. As he approached Gordonville, he came across a 24-hour service plaza. He stopped for gas and went inside to use the facilities. By the time he reappeared, "Guy Halper" had been transformed into "Hamilton Drake." He drove off until he came to a heavily wooded stretch and looked for a place to pull off and park the car out of the sight of any cars that happened to be passing at this ungodly hour. Finding one, he pulled off, got out, and changed the car's plates so that he would appear to be a visiting Oregonian. He tossed the California plates as far into the woods as he could, returned to the road, and continued driving until he reached the Belvedere Hotel. There, he registered as "Hamilton Drake," paid cash, and repaired to his room. He took a hot shower, wrapped a towel around his waist, and decided to reward himself for a job well done. He took out a sterile syringe, filled it with the fluid that would warm his body and ease his tensions, and pulled with his teeth on the rubber strap to tighten its compression of his left arm. As he often did in the wake of a successful hit, he inserted the syringe and plunged the elixir into his veins. He floated, dreamlessly, into the euphoric netherworld that he so frequently enjoyed.

Chapter 37

 out of the shower early on the Monday morning following his angry call with Nikki and admired himself in the full-length mirror in his hotel room. He had avoided a return home over the weekend, played a round of golf with Randy Carmichael on Sunday, and experienced a night of energetic sex with Randy at Randy's home. Jack had returned to the hotel before sunrise to get ready for another day of legal work at Transnational Marine Machinery, where Randy served as the General Counsel. Randy had the ultimate control over the hiring and firing of outside counsel for Transnational and, in the four years that Jack had been intimate with Randy, Jack's billings to Transnational had increased from roughly $750,000 per year to more than $11 million. Jack got good results for the company, and it was quite happy with his performance. Randy enjoyed Jack's performance on multiple levels. As he admired himself in the mirror, Jack Beaumont understood why.

Jack had always found excitement in other men. One of the benefits of his job, with its heavy travel obligations, was the opportunity to pursue that excitement miles from home, where the likelihood that his secret life would be discovered was much lower, and where he would not need to deal with his wife's efforts to persuade him to fulfill his husbandly duties.

His wife. Jack did not love Nicole Beaumont. He never did. He acknowledged that, viewed through a heterosexual lens, Nikki was a fairly attractive woman. But that was not the lens that Jack used. He was not wired that way. He preferred men. But he believed, rightly or wrongly, that he needed a wife to give him the appearance of normality. Jack thought it always helped in business to have an attractive wife, and he thought that Nikki would do as well as any other. He found his view corroborated frequently by the ogling eyes of many male clients during firm affairs and by their eagerness to dance with her at firm parties and to sit next to her at dinner when the firm purchased a table at some industry or charity affair. Inwardly, he sometimes wished she would succumb to a client's advances, both to reduce her carnal need for Jack and to enhance the prospects for increased business from an appreciative client. He knew it was callous to think of his wife's sex appeal as a potential source of business revenue, but Jack was always on the lookout for any angle that would increase his status in the firm, and his income. Jack Beaumont had three driving forces in his life—money, prestige, and the pleasure he derived from evenings spent with attractive men.

For Jack, Randy Carmichael was the ultimate combination of sexual fulfillment and business success. Before he and Randy had become involved on a personal level, Jack had satisfied his urges, while traveling, with a series of partners that he had met for the first time at local health clubs during his rigorous early morning workouts. Jack would look around the gym to see if any of his fellow workout warriors had fixated on him. If anyone did, and if he caught Jack's fancy, Jack would smile and nod. As he completed his workout, Jack would walk over, introduce himself, and engage in some minimalist small talk. The conversation always ended with a seemingly simple question, "Would you like to get together for a drink tonight?" Often, the evening ended with Jack having been pleased in ways for which his wife lacked the necessary equipment.

Jack's one-night stands came to an end the night he and Randy Carmichael discovered their shared interest in the company of other men. Jack was in town for one of his modest engagements for Transnational and had a conference set with Randy for 5 PM. As the meeting concluded, Jack could see that something was bothering Randy. He asked if Randy wanted to go for a drink, and Randy agreed. Drinks turned into dinner, and for reasons that Jack never fully understood, Randy explained that he had just gone through a difficult divorce. He did not explain the basis for the divorce, except to say that his wife had claimed irreconcilable differences. He was downcast and lonely. He looked at Jack.

"Do you ever get lonely, Jack? I mean, really lonely?"

"I think everyone does at times, Randy, everyone."

"Including you, Jack?"

"Yes, Randy, including me."

"But you're married, Jack."

"Some men can be quite lonely in the company of a woman, Randy."

Randy looked into Jack's eyes and nodded. In that moment, Jack intuited just what those irreconcilable differences were between Randy Carmichael and his ex-wife. He sensed an opportunity not only to find a playmate for the evening but also, perhaps, to enhance his legal practice.

Jack placed his hand on Randy's. "You know, Randy, neither one of us needs to be lonely tonight." Jack knew there was a risk in making such an advance to his client, but he also knew there was tremendous economic upside. When Randy allowed Jack's hand to remain on his, Jack knew the risk had been worthwhile.

Jack gave Randy his room number at the Fairmont Century Plaza, and they left the restaurant in their separate cars. Twenty minutes later, they were facing each other at the foot of Jack's bed, each admiring the sensual opportunity that lay before him.

Jack was a man who took great care of his body. He did not believe in building a heavily muscled body, although from time to time he had enjoyed the company of men who did. Every now and then, he found the power that their well-developed torsos could exert to be tremendously exciting, and he loved the feel of that power inside him. But Jack was more given to a body that was lightly muscled and well-toned, and he adored a male body with abs that would put a washboard to shame. That was the way he had shaped his own body, and it was the kind of body that he most appreciated in another man. A man like Randy Carmichael. Randy was quite a bit taller than Jack. It was easy to see the appeal he would hold for other men. He was lean, well-toned, with great abs, and he was long in the dimension that mattered most to Jack.

Jack walked over to Randy, wrapped his arms around Randy's waist, and kissed him. As he enjoyed the welcoming warmth of Randy's mouth, Jack looked forward eagerly to other oral pleasures that Randy might deliver before the evening was done. They crawled onto the bed and began to explore their respective bodies, using all of the tools that nature provided. By the time they were done, Jack could barely breathe. Whoever had indoctrinated Randy Carmichael into the homoerotic arts had done a superlative job. Jack was resting on the bed, with Randy's arm draped over him.

"When are you going back east, Jack?"

"Friday, Randy."

"So, you'll be here for three more nights?"

"Uh huh."

"Do you have plans for those nights?"

"Do you have something in mind, Randy?"

"Yes, Jack. More of this with . . . you."

Since that night, their relationship had benefitted Jack's business in precisely the manner he had hoped. Jack's firm was receiving significant engagements from Transnational, some of which Jack handled directly, some of which were delegated to other partners who were more experienced with the subject matter of the engagement, allowing Jack better to leverage and monetize his relationship with Randy Carmichael. The new business kept him on the road in Los Angeles for weeks at a time, which provided a convenient respite from the need to gratify his wife in ways that held no appeal or pleasure for him. Instead, he could spend his evenings in ways that were more gratifying, with someone who appealed to him immensely and knew how to please him. On every level imaginable, Jack's relationship with Randy Carmichael was as perfect as he could ever have hoped for.

He and Randy knew that they needed to be discrete. There could be no show of undue cordiality in their business dealings and certainly no reference to their afterhours activities unless the reference was to a get together involving other Transnational or law firm personnel. Randy lived about 40 minutes from Transnational's Headquarters, away from the neighborhoods where most company personnel put down stakes. They agreed it was much safer to meet there than at Jack's hotel, where other company executives might be meeting with customers, or consorts. The pattern was simple—Randy would leave the office for his home; Jack would follow at a decent interval and park his car in the second bay of Randy's two-car garage, the door to which had been left open. He would close the garage door and enter the house through the garage. The next morning, Jack would rise early and depart for his hotel; there, he would work out in the hotel health club, shower, and get ready for the day's work. In the evening, the cycle would start anew. This pattern was not invariable. As indefatigable as they were, they spent some of the evenings apart. Jack tried to keep those evenings to a minimum. Randy Carmichael was the goose that laid the golden eggs that fueled Jack's meteoric rise in his firm's hierarchy. He did not want Randy to feel lonely and, perhaps, seek to ease that loneliness with one of his former lovers or, perhaps, someone new. Besides, Jack regarded the sex with Randy as some of the best he had ever experienced.

The need for secrecy was obvious to both of them. If the company discovered that Randy had bestowed tens of millions of dollars in legal work on Jack Beaumont while enjoying Jack's sexual favors, Randy would be fired, and the legal work placed with Jack's firm would be moved to other firms. Jack would likely be expelled from the partnership, and Nikki—her Roman Catholic upbringing notwithstanding—would divorce him and take him to the cleaners in the property settlement. This was not a fling to be taken lightly. This was a serious relationship based on Randy Carmichael's passion for Jack Beaumont and on Jack Beaumont's passion both for Randy Carmichael and, also, for the financial windfall accruing to Jack from that passion. They adhered assiduously to the rules they had crafted.

Their relationship was in its fourth year. As time passed and the legal business for Transnational flourished, Jack's travel increased exponentially, to the point where he was on the road far more often than he was home. He truly fit the bill of an absentee husband. His marriage had become virtually platonic, which was disconcerting to Nikki, who longed for his nicely sculpted body. She could occasionally cajole him into their marital bed but his lack of enthusiasm was often obvious to her. He was going through the motions of what was, for him, an unpleasant experience, the only purpose of which was to continue his heterosexual charade. More often than not, when he felt compelled to placate his wife, Jack would simply close his eyes and pretend that Randy Carmichael was in bed with him. It facilitated his performance when he did so, which increased Nikki's pleasure, but for reasons to which she was wholly oblivious. Even then, however, Jack would steadfastly dismiss Nikki's interest in anal intercourse, decrying it as distasteful and disgusting in order to mask his hunger for the practice when shared with another man.

Over time, the frequency of their sexual relations declined to virtually zero, which was fine with Jack. His sexual needs were more than satisfied by his nights with Randy Carmichael. Nikki became more and more convinced that Jack had one or more female companions attending to his LA needs, although she had no proof of any such liaisons.

Nikki never gave any indication that she thought Jack's sexual orientation bent toward other men. He was always flirting with Maryanne Miller. Maryanne was exceptionally beautiful, but unbeknownst to Nikki, Maryanne also lacked the physical assets that Jack deemed essential to any meaningful sexual encounter. Jack would constantly double down on his charade by telling Nikki how attractive Maryanne was, how perfect she seemed to be, and how lucky Ted Miller was to be able to take her to bed every night. Plainly, in Nikki's mind, Jack would gladly trade her for Maryanne Miller any day of the week, and twice on Sunday. Nikki did not appreciate Jack's comments about Maryanne, but they were all a part of his act, an act in which he portrayed himself outwardly as a red-blooded heterosexual whose fondest dream was a night with Maryanne Miller. But a relationship with Maryanne Miller, even if he were so inclined, could not put money in Jack Beaumont's bank accounts. His relationship with Randy Carmichael did and, deep within, he would admit that the money was as exciting to him as Randy's bedroom skills.

Chapter 38

NIKKI HAD NOT been crazy about the idea when Jack suggested several years ago—and rather firmly—that Randy Carmichael spend the Memorial Day weekend with them. Carmichael had East Coast business that would run past the Memorial Day weekend and Jack told Nikki that it would be a smart business move to entertain his largest client, who had gone through a difficult divorce.

Notwithstanding Nikki's reservations, Randy Carmichael had proven to be the perfect house guest. When he arrived, he apologized to Nikki for intruding on her weekend, presented her with a bountiful Springtime floral bouquet, and handed to Jack a bottle of Dom Perignon. Nikki found Randy to be handsome, well-groomed, gracious, and well-spoken. He ate what she put before him, complimented her culinary skills, and helped to clean up after dinner. On top of all this, he knew how to make a woman feel beautiful with a few choice words. More than once during that weekend, Nikki fantasized about Randy Carmichael and what it might be like to share her bed with him instead of the cold fish that Jack was fast becoming.

Jack and Randy spent Saturday morning on the golf course and then went, with Nikki, to the Millers for a barbecue. Jack had forewarned Randy to bring his swim trunks so that they could enjoy the Millers' pool and spa, which he happily did. Maryanne and Nikki sported bikinis that displayed their feminine assets to maximum advantage and prompted Randy to comment, in front of the women, on how lucky Jack and Ted were and that he had never seen two such gorgeous women, sitting side by side, in his life. They smiled. Nikki turned to Maryanne and said, "I told you he was a charmer."

With the sun beating down, the men, stripped to the waist, engaged in a spirited cornhole competition. Jack watched intently as he waited to see if his opponent would be Randy or Ted, enjoying the view as their bodies glistened with perspiration and recalling the first time he had met Ted Miller. It was the day that Jack and Nikki moved in. The Millers invited them over for a drink and they hit it off immediately. Nikki and Maryanne could have been mistaken for long lost friends and he and Ted spoke for quite some time about their shared interest in golf and tennis. At some point in that conversation, Jack realized that he wanted to know Ted Miller more intimately. When or how, he didn't know, but his desire for Ted Miller was intense.

As that Saturday evening wound to a conclusion, Ted suggested that the three guys get together on Sunday to play tennis. Maryanne and Nikki excused themselves from that, explaining that they had planned a full day of exploring all of the Memorial Day sales advertised by the local merchants. Ted suggested they hit the courts by 7 AM, to take advantage of the cooler temperatures.

Jack and Randy picked up Ted a bit before 7 and headed to the nearby public courts. It was good that they got an early start, because half the courts were already occupied. They played in round robin fashion for the better part of two hours, then headed to the Millers to cool down. When Randy commented on the soreness in his shoulders, Ted hopped out of his chair and began massaging Randy's neck and shoulders. As he did so, Jack watched, feeling the burgeoning erection in his shorts. Directly across from him, Jack could see that Randy was similarly affected by the touch of Ted's hands. His effect on the men sitting before him was not at all lost on Ted Miller. He knew exactly what he was doing and he was getting precisely the reaction for which he had hoped. After several minutes of shoulder and neck massage, during which he alternated between Randy and Jack, Ted said he wanted to shower before taking a plunge in the pool. As he began toward the house, he turned and smiled at his companions.

"In case you had any doubts, guys, I don't like to shower alone if I can help it."

Jack and Randy followed Ted eagerly. As they entered the shower, their desire for Ted was on full display. Ted stood under one of the shower heads and lathered up, then turned to provide Jack and Randy with a good view. Randy was long, but he was nothing like Ted. Jack was awestruck.

Ted looked from Jack to Randy and then back to Jack. "You know," he said with a grin, "an erection is a terrible thing to waste."

Nothing was wasted that morning. Ted was everything about which Jack had fantasized, and the feel of Ted inside him was nearly incomparable. Jack could hardly contain his excitement as he watched Randy do the same for Ted. They kept at it for as long as they physically could, each one of them enjoying the different ways men could please each other. As they finished, Ted joked to Jack, "We really should play tennis more often, Jack." Then he smiled at Randy lasciviously and said "You need to visit more frequently. Don't be a stranger."

Jack and Randy spoke of that day often, promising themselves a return engagement for the two of them with Ted Miller, but it never happened. And now, with Ted dead, that promise could never be fulfilled.

Chapter 39

MARTINA ODORIZZI WAS close to the end of her shift as a maid at the Belvedere Hotel in Gordonville. One more bed to make, one more room to clean, and then home to her children when they returned from their day at school. She knocked to make sure the room was empty, in accordance with hotel protocol. Hearing no response, she swiped her card to enter the room.

She stopped at the door, frozen. The occupant was seated in the easy chair, vacant eyes staring at her, while a thin rubber strap hung, tightly wrapped, from his left arm. A syringe lay on the floor beneath his right hand. Martina opened her mouth to scream, but nothing came out. She finally composed herself enough to get on her transceiver and tell Security that there was a dead man in Room 777. She knew it happened in hotels, and she heard of it happening in the Belvedere. But it had never happened in one of her rooms.

The police arrived promptly. Officers Tom Corley and Jake Durham took one look and could tell this fatality had been self-inflicted, an overdose of something the corpse had used to lighten his load and brighten his day. The medical examiner would determine what intravenous upper the stiff had elected for his last rodeo, and forensics would gather his effects for inventory if and when anyone claimed his body. The Front Desk said he had registered as "Drake Hamilton" and provided the police a copy of the registration card and "Drake Hamilton's" out-of-state driver's license. Hamilton had prepaid in cash.

Corley and Durham returned to the station, thinking that, apart from the obvious paperwork, "Drake Hamilton" was in their rear-view mirror. The next day, Durham was reviewing the inventory prepared by forensics before closing out his report. Whoever "Drake Hamilton" was, he had four bottles that looked like they came from a doctor's medicine cabinet. They were labeled "phenobarbital." He recalled a bulletin posted a few days earlier asking neighboring departments to report any thefts of phenobarbital. He pulled it up on his computer and called to his partner. "We should report this."

Sergeant Tracey took the call.

"I'm sorry, Sergeant. I don't have much to tell you. A drug overdose, likely heroin. The stiff had some bottles of phenobarbital, or at least it was labeled phenobarbital. We remembered your bulletin, so we called."

Joanne called Emily Morton and explained what had happened. She said this might be Danny Dunphy's killer and could she come with us to Gordonville to make an ID. She readily agreed. "Danny was good guy." Then Joanne advised Inspector Milliken, grabbed Officer Hammond, picked up Emily Morton, and headed for Gordonville.

Two hours later, they were standing around the body of Drake Hamilton. Emily Morton was equivocal. "I can't say 100%, Sergeant. This guy is clean shaven and his hair is salt and pepper. Guy Halper had a beard and dark hair and wore glasses. I think this is him, but I can't be sure."

Sergeant Tracey turned to Corley and Durham to ask if there were any other personal effects. Not much, except for some cash. He had no wallet, no telephone, no credit cards. He had the usual toiletries, and he carried a money clip with about $2,500 in it and a driver's license from Oregon for "Drake Hamilton." By the time Tracey had arrived, the Gordonville police had confirmed what everyone had assumed. "Drake Hamilton" was an alias. Emily could not identify the bills, but the $2,500 in the corpse's possession could easily have included the $350 cash payment she had given Halper at the end of the party.

The only other item on his person were two slips of paper folded inside the bills in his money clip. Each of the slips had a handwritten number, and nothing else. One slip said "4201030." The other, "3424013."

Sergeant Tracey spoke to Officers Corley and Durham and explained the potential significance of the dead man's personal effects. She asked if they could prepare property transfer documentation regarding those effects and the transfer of custody for them to her. They dutifully ran the request up the chain and returned 20 minutes later, saying they had the OK for the transfer. About an hour later, she had the phenobarbital, the money clip, the cash, the slips with the numbers, and documentation establishing the chain of custody for that evidence. The body of Drake Hamilton would also be transferred, for possible identification by other Morton & Morrison employees and for a fingerprint match with the glasses, barware, and bottles collected from the party.

Chapter 40

SERGEANT TRACEY SAT in front of Inspector Milliken, who was reading her report.

"Hank and his team ID'd the bottles as phenobarbital, right?

"Yes, Jim."

"And Mrs. Morton ID'd the stiff as her substitute bartender for the Miller's party, right?

"Possibly, Jim. She thinks so, but she couldn't be sure. We're asking the other Morton personnel to take a look and see if they can ID him as the bartender. If that fails, we can always ask the guests of the party to give it a shot. And we'll look to see if his fingerprints match the barware from the Millers' party."

"If that's the case, then it's likely that the stiff laced the gin, right?"

"Pretty likely, Jim."

"But why, Joanne? He doesn't just come to town, kill Danny Dunphy, take his place at the bar, and leave the makings of a lethal cocktail for the Millers. Do you disagree?"

"I do, Jim. He was paid to do this."

"By whom, Joanne?"

"I don't know, Jim. Not yet."

"Does anyone have any idea what the numbers on those handwritten slips could be?"

"Not a clue. If they have any bearing on the case, they are probably a code of some kind, maybe the location for his payoff. But sitting here today, Jim, we don't have any idea."

"Joanne, bear with me here for a moment. He laces the gin and he leaves with Mrs. Morton's crew. How does he know who is going to have another martini? Or whether anyone is going to have another martini?"

Joanne took issue with Milliken's assertion. "Emily Morton did not say the bartender left with her. He had his own car on site. He's been serving all night, so he knows what the Millers have been drinking. There's no guarantee he didn't hang around, in the dark, to complete his assignment, Jim."

"Here's what I think, Joanne—Someone pays him to spike the gin as he is leaving the party. Mrs. Beaumont knows what he has done because she is the one who paid him. She seals the deal by offering to make a nightcap for her neighbors and delivers the lethal cocktails to them in person. Where's the hole in that story, Joanne? Where?"

"Everywhere, Jim. First, what's her motive. From Day 1 I've been asking you that question and you can't answer it. Second, what proof do we have that she ever met the bartender? Third, what's the going rate for a double murder in this suburban community, where did Mrs. Beaumont get that money, and is there any evidence that she ever paid a dime to Guy Halper or Hamilton Drake, or whoever he is? Fourth, she's a nurse. Surely she could lay hands on phenobarbital directly without all of the rigamarole your theory requires."

"And your plan now is what?"

"There are a number of videos we haven't looked at, Jim."

"Joanne, you interviewed the folks who attended the party and who might have had a motive based on the compromising videos Ted Miller had in his little library of lovers. What do you want to do, interview the whole town?"

"Don't exaggerate, Jim. There were 30 DVDs. We've interviewed Mrs. Hamilton, Mr. and Mrs. Long, and Mrs. Carmelo. There were multiple DVDs of each of them, 12 in all. There are 18 DVDs we haven't reviewed. For all we know, some of those are also recordings of multiple trysts with the same person. It could be as few as five or six more interviews."

"Knock yourself out, Joanne. But be discrete, please."

Chapter 41

JOANNE SAT IN her home office reviewing the remaining DVDs. They recorded Ted Miller's antics with six different bedmates, five women and one man. The recordings, like the others previously reviewed, were indexed by name. The video itself provided the date and time.

Two of the women turned out to be middle aged widows for whom a roll in the hay with Ted Miller was the highlight of their week and perhaps their year. They accounted for eight of the DVDs in all. Based on Joanne and Terry's interviews, Ted Miller's modus operandi for each of them was identical. They had come to his photography studio for a portrait to give to their children for Christmas or some other occasion. He spoke with sorrow of their loss, but he brightened their spirits by complimenting them, expressing amazement at their supposed ages, telling them that he was sure any man would consider himself lucky to enjoy their company, and always making a point of touching them while he talked. He said that if they had any doubts about the validity of his compliments, they should allow him, without charge, to take a few "glamor shots" to demonstrate how well they had retained their youthful good looks, "just for fun." Those photos were like an aphrodisiac for the women. It did not take much more for Ted to bed them. They were happy to have spent the time they did with Ted Miller and, based on the DVDs, he was an enthusiastic but gentle lover with them. No, they did not know he had recorded their romantic encounters and, no, he never threatened to expose the videos or requested money for any reason from them.

Nine of the remaining DVDs involved women on the other end of the age spectrum—three young, single, Latino women, barely out of their teens, who had come to Ted's studio for a portfolio to kickstart a hoped-for modeling career. They explained to Ted that they did not have much money to pay for their portfolios, but Ted told them that there were other ways to pay for his services. Since those photos were in part designed to stimulate the libido, it was easy for one thing to lead to another, and they did. Seven of the DVDs involved Ted one-on-one with one of the nubile nymphs. No. 8 was a class reunion. These women had no careers to speak of and no money that an extortionist could tap. The thought of Ted blackmailing them elicited laughs and a request for a copy of the reunion video. Joanne politely declined the request.

The final video was labeled "Roland Mancuso." On the DVD, Roland Mancuso and Ted Miller proved to be tireless paramours. Mr. Mancuso was an incredibly handsome, openly gay male model who would have been impervious to blackmail based on his overt sexual orientation.

As she conducted these interviews, Joanne Tracey became more hardened in her conviction that Ted Miller had been a satyr, a man with an insatiable appetite for sex without regard to the age, gender, race, or number of his playmates. She acknowledged that she herself was no saint, far from it. Some might regard her as promiscuous, but she had never had a spouse to whom she could be unfaithful. Moreover, notwithstanding the number of lovers who had shared her bed, Joanne had remained faithful to each of them for as long as the relationships lasted. No, Joanne was not Mother Teresa, but Ted Miller's indiscriminate lust was in a class of its own.

None of this was advancing her investigation. These 18 DVDs simply proved to be another dead end. But Joanne was convinced she was missing something, some clue that was perhaps hiding in plain sight. She didn't know where to start so she began anew to review the numbered index of the videos that Ted Miller had so thoughtfully prepared. She started with "No. 1—Penny Hamilton," and worked her way forward. As she did so, she noticed for the first time that the index jumped from "No. 11—Samantha Long" to "No. 13—Aaron Long." There was no record of No. 12. After making a note of that fact, she continued on until she reached No. 24." Here, too, there was no video, no DVD, no CD. But the index listed a name—"Randy Carmichael."

There was no local listing for Randy Carmichael. It was not an uncommon name, but she dutifully looked at hundreds of Google listings, searching for a "Randy Carmichael" who might have some connection to Ted Miller or Nicole Beaumont. Her eyes settled on a Randy Carmichael who was listed as the Executive Vice President & General Counsel of Transnational Marine Machinery, Inc., headquartered in Los Angeles. Joanne began to connect hypothetical dots—the Millers and the Beaumonts were friends; Jack Beaumont and Randy Carmichael are lawyers; Carmichael works in Los Angeles; Jack Beaumont has been working in Los Angeles for weeks at a time. Could there be a professional connection between Randy Carmichael and Jack Beaumont? And could that connection have served to introduce Randy Carmichael to Ted Miller? A lot of "ifs." But if those "ifs" panned out, then another series of questions presented themselves—**if** there actually was a DVD No. 24, and **if** it featured Ted Miller and Randy Carmichael in compromising circumstances, and **if** the DVD No. 24 Randy Carmichael is the Transnational Marine EVP, then the disclosure of the video could possibly have severe personal, professional, and financial consequences for Randy Carmichael. For the first time in this investigation, Joanne felt there might be motive enough for someone to have killed Ted Miller.

She reported the facts and her suspicions to Inspector Milliken. "You've got a fertile imagination, Sergeant, but very few facts. We can't just fly across the country to interview one of hundreds of Randy Carmichaels on a string of suppositions. Let's see if there is any evidence of a link between Randy Carmichael and Nicole Beaumont, either directly or through her husband's business. Right now we have nothing but a name in an index of Ted Miller's Sexcapades."

"OK, Jim. We'll check Mrs. Beaumont's computer and see what pops up when we look for "Randy Carmichael.""

Forensics found three hits, a three-message email string. The first was an email shortly after Memorial Day four years earlier, in which Carmichael, from his Transnational Marine email account, thanked Mrs. Beaumont for a lovely weekend and for being such a gracious hostess. The second was her response, thanking him for the flowers and telling him that he should feel free to visit the next time he came East. The third was his reply, telling her that the flowers paled in comparison to her.

"There's not much there, Jim, but it tells us she knows him. And that's enough in my eyes to warrant another visit to Mrs. Beaumont."

Chapter 42

 place, as before, in the conference room of Maria Romano's offices. This time, Inspector Milliken deferred to Sergeant Tracey and allowed her to conduct the interview.

"Mrs. Beaumont, when we searched your computer, we found a short string of emails between you and someone named Randy Carmichael. Can you tell us who he is and, if you recall, why you were exchanging emails?"

"Randy Carmichael is an executive with one of my husband's clients. He was our houseguest over the Memorial Day weekend some time ago and, as I recall it, we exchanged 'thank you/you're welcome' type emails."

"Do you know if Randy Carmichael ever met Ted Miller?"

"Yes, he did. We brought Mr. Carmichael to the Millers on the Saturday of that weekend for a barbecue, a few drinks, some backyard games between the guys, and some pool time. On Sunday, the guys all went to play tennis. As I recall, they went pretty early, like 7 AM."

"During that weekend, Mrs. Beaumont, did you become romantically involved with Mr. Carmichael?"

"No, Sergeant. Not then. Not ever." Turning to her lawyer, Nikki asked "Should I tell her?"

Maria nodded.

"Sergeant, my husband has threatened me with divorce proceedings, based on my night with the Millers. Well, it is my understanding that, for the better part of the last four years, my husband has been having an affair with Randy Carmichael."

Milliken winced. Joanne struggled to keep her jaw from dropping too far. As Joanne regained her composure, Maria Romano looked at both of the officers and said, "If you think Randy Carmichael is relevant to your investigation, Sergeant, I suggest you speak to him . . . and to Mr. Beaumont. Do you have any other questions for my client?"

Chapter 43

JOANNE TRACEY AND Jim Milliken sat across from each other on opposite sides of Milliken's desk trying to sort out the implications of Mrs. Beaumont's disclosure. Milliken spoke first.

"Mrs. Beaumont tells us Carmichael was engaged in a long-term homosexual affair with his outside lawyer. How do we know it's true, Joanne?"

"I don't think she made that up, Jim. She's in the middle of a divorce. I suspect that her divorce lawyer has had someone investigating her husband's comings and goings. She probably expected the PI to identify a girlfriend or two. I'm sure she was as surprised as we were when the lover turned out to be a man."

"But so what? Where does that take us? Carmichael likes Jack Beaumont and Jack Beaumont likes Randy Carmichael. This is the 21st Century. They aren't breaking any laws."

Joanne interjected. "No, Jim. No laws. But let's pull on this thread. One—Transnational is a client of Jack Beaumont. Two—Jack Beaumont is the long-time lover of Randy Carmichael. Three—Randy Carmichael might be the person in Transnational who doles out the legal work. Four—Maybe, just maybe, Randy Carmichael looks kindly on Jack Beaumont and rewards his affections with significant legal work. Five—The Transnational Board of Directors may not know of Carmichael's relationship with Jack Beaumont. Six—If they find out, Carmichael maybe, no, probably, gets the axe. Seven—a video relating to Randy Carmichael is missing from Ted Miller's library of lovers. Doesn't that add up to a motive for murder, Jim?"

"There are a lot of assumptions there, Joanne. You think Ted Miller was blackmailing Randy Carmichael, and Carmichael arranged the murder of the Millers to keep his relationship with Jack Beaumont secret and protect his job, career, and finances?"

"I'm not so sure he intended to kill Maryanne Miller, Jim. She may have been in the wrong place at the wrong time given the way the killer planned the hit. And Nicole Beaumont would have been collateral damage too if she had a hankering for gin."

"I think you're missing something, Joanne."

"Tell me, Jim."

"Randy Carmichael was not the only one with the motive you've described. Jack Beaumont stood to lose his largest client. He probably would be expelled from his law firm. And he stood to lose his wife, which would have mattered to the extent he cared to continue to cultivate the heterosexual image he had created of himself."

"Carmichael and Beaumont are both in LA, Jim."

"Get yourself a ticket, Sergeant, and coordinate with the Homicide Department of the LAPD. You've got no jurisdiction there."

Chapter 44

IT WAS ONE of those rare Los Angeles mornings when snow graced the top of the San Gabriel Mountains as they sat against a clear blue sky. Randy Carmichael was enjoying the view and musing about his upcoming evening with Jack Beaumont when his desk phone rang. It was his secretary.

"Mr. Carmichael, there are two people here to see you."

"I don't have anything on my schedule, Anna. Who are they?"

"The police, sir."

"Show them in, Anna."

Anna escorted the man and woman into Carmichael's office. They introduced themselves and Carmichael offered them the chairs across from his seat behind his desk. He asked if he could offer them anything to drink and they both declined politely.

"How can I help you, officers?"

Ike Taylor, the LAPD liaison assigned to work the case with Joanne Tracey, took the lead.

"We are investigating a murder, Mr. Carmichael. Actually, a double murder. Tell us what you can about Ted and Maryanne Miller."

Carmichael blanched. "Are they dead? Were they murdered?"

"I'm afraid so, Mr. Carmichael," said Officer Taylor. "I take it from your reaction that you knew them?"

"Yes. I met them over the Memorial Day weekend a few years ago, when I visited with their neighbors, the Beaumonts. How were they killed, Officer?"

"Poison."

"May I ask when this happened?"

"Two weeks ago this past Saturday."

"This is horrible, a tragedy. Such nice people. So young. Why would anyone want to murder them?"

"Well, Mr. Carmichael," said Officer Taylor, "we were hoping that you could provide some information that might help us answer that question."

Carmichael stiffened at Taylor's remark. "Me! I was in Los Angeles that weekend, Officer. Am I correct to assume the Millers were murdered back East?"

Officer Taylor ignored the question. "Were you romantically involved with Maryanne Miller, Mr. Carmichael?"

"No, Officer. Has someone insinuated that I was?"

Again Taylor ignored the question. "Were you romantically involved with Ted Miller, Mr. Carmichael?"

Randy Carmichael just sat, frozen, his eyes darting back and forth from Officer Taylor to Sergeant Tracey. When he didn't answer, Officer Taylor rephrased the question, "Were you sexually involved with Ted Miller, Mr. Carmichael?"

After an interval of silence, Officer Taylor continued. "Before you say anything, Mr. Carmichael, I should tell you that Ted Miller seems to have had a habit of videotaping his sexual encounters. Were you aware of that?"

"No."

"You did have sexual relations with Mr. Miller, didn't you?"

"Yes, but I didn't kill him. I liked him. I liked him a lot."

"How many times did you and Mr. Miller have sexual relations?"

"Just twice. Once just before Thanksgiving last year when I had to travel back East. And on that Memorial Day weekend, when I stayed with the Beaumonts."

"Did he ever threaten to expose your sexual orientation to your superiors?"

"No."

"Did he ever ask for money to maintain your secret?"

"No."

"Did you buy from him any videos in which you appeared performing sexual acts with another man?"

"No."

"Jack Beaumont does legal work for your company, doesn't he?"

"Yes."

"Do you have any idea, even a rough estimate, of how much his firm bills Transnational annually?"

"Well, it varies from year to year. This year, it's already in excess of $10 million."

"Who decides what outside lawyers get your work, Mr. Carmichael?"

"I have the final say on hiring and firing law firms."

"Is Mr. Beaumont in Los Angeles at present?"

"Yes."

"Do you know where he stays in Los Angeles, what hotel?"

"It's the Fairmont Century Plaza."

"Do you know the room?"

Carmichael dialed his secretary on the speaker phone. "Anna, do we know what room Mr. Beaumont has at the Fairmont Century Plaza?"

"It's room 1024, Mr. Carmichael."

"Thanks, Anna."

"Will Mr. Beaumont be meeting here today?"

"Yes, he'll be interviewing possible witnesses here."

"What about tomorrow?"

"I think his schedule is the same tomorrow. I can't be sure."

"Will you be seeing him today?"

"Yes."

"Do your superiors know about your sexual orientation, Mr. Carmichael?"

"I can't really say, Officer. I know there was some speculation at the time of my divorce, and I've never gone out of my way to admit or deny it, so I don't know. But I never worry about it because we have a number of openly gay employees and because California prohibits discrimination on the basis of sexual orientation."

Joanne could see the arrow coming before it left Taylor's bow.

"Mr. Carmichael, have you ever disclosed to your superiors that you have been engaged in a long running sexual affair with Jack Beaumont?"

When Carmichael didn't answer, Officer Taylor asked his last question.

"What would your superiors have done if they knew you were placing millions of dollars in legal work with someone, male or female, with whom you were sexually involved?"

*   *   *

As they exited the elevator into the parking garage, Joanne asked Officer Taylor if he had gone to law school. When he said "Yes," she replied, "It showed." Ike Taylor laughed out loud and said, "And I thought you liked me, Joanne."

Chapter 45

JACK ARRIVED AT Transnational about 45 minutes after the officers had left. He saw immediately that something was wrong. Randy was visibly shaken.

"We have a problem, Jack. Someone knows about us."

"What are you talking about, Randy?"

"Two police officers were here. They said they were investigating the deaths of Ted and Maryanne Miller. They called it a double murder."

"Take it easy, Randy. Slow down. Take me through the conversation as best you can recollect."

"Jack, they seem to think that I had a motive for killing Ted. It seems he had a habit of videotaping his sexual dalliances and the implication was that I was involved in killing him to keep my sexual orientation under wraps."

"Did they tell you they had a video of you with Ted?"

"No, not exactly. But they gave the impression that there was such a video."

"You didn't admit anything, did you, Randy?"

"I'm sorry, Jack. I told the truth. I told them I had been with Ted twice."

"Twice, Randy? Twice! You and Ted got together after our Memorial Day threesome? How could you do that?"

"C'mon, Jack. Are you telling me you kept your hands off Ted when you were home and we couldn't spend our nights together?"

"Did you tell them about you, me, and Ted?

"No, Jack. They didn't press the issue and I didn't volunteer those facts. But Jack, they know about you and me. They asked me directly whether I ever disclosed our relationship to Transnational management. They asked about how much legal work you've gotten from me and what management would do if it knew about you and me."

"Did you tell them we were involved sexually?"

"No. I just didn't answer those questions. I didn't want to admit anything, but I didn't want to lie. Jack, how could they have known? We've always been careful."

"It must have been my wife's lawyer. Nicole has been accusing me of having a chippie or two on the side for quite some time. She thinks that's why I have no interest in her come bedtime. Now that we're divorcing, she must have hired a private investigator to find my girlfriends. They didn't find any, but they found you, Randy. It's my fault. I overreacted to her threesome with the Millers and told her I was going to divorce her. I should have been more supportive. I should have been more understanding. There was no need for me to go nuclear on her. I fucked up. I guess her lawyer told her the best defense is a good offense . . . . Shit!"

"Randy, these guys are trying to make out a case against you for the murder of the Millers. From this point forward, I don't think you should be cooperating with the police. Listen to me. Get yourself a good criminal defense lawyer and follow his advice. Don't talk to the police unless your lawyer is with you and says it's OK. Understood?"

"Yes, Jack, but I haven't done anything."

"That's not what they think, Randy. And their objective is to prove, by hook or by crook, that what they think is in fact what happened. Do not fool yourself into thinking that you're doing yourself any favors by cooperating with the police."

Chapter 46

 day's work in a fog. Everything had gone so well up to now. He had developed a relationship with Randy Carmichael that was sexually gratifying and financially rewarding. It had driven him to the top tier of the law firm's compensation system. His long-held fantasies about Ted Miller had also become a part of his reality. He and Ted indulged their desire for each other following that Memorial Day weekend whenever Jack returned East, ostensibly to rejoin his wife. Why did Ted have to get greedy? Why did he try to monetize their relationship? He cheapened what they had. Moreover, he threatened Jack's and Randy's financial position by threatening to disclose a video of the Memorial Day threesome to Transnational's management.

Jack knew that the video existed. He had seen it. Ted had shown it to him as foreplay for one of their idyllic encounters. It was at the conclusion of that tryst that Ted, glistening with perspiration from his energetic satisfaction of Jack's needs, asked Jack what would happen if Randy's management ever laid eyes on the video. Jack could have responded calmly. He could have dismissed Ted's question based on the legal protections afforded in California to same sex relationships and hoped that Ted did not connect the dots between the sex and Jack's financial situation. But Jack did not respond with calm, and the anger that filled his response told Ted all he needed to know about his ability to extort funds from Jack or Randy, or both, to maintain the confidentiality of their relationship. After that, it became a pure question of how much Ted wanted, and from whom.

"What do you want, Ted?"

"Money, Jack. Money."

"How much?"

"I was thinking in the range of, say, $5,000 per month."

"Forever?"

"Well, until your relationships with Randy and Transnational go away."

"And the video?"

"It's mine, Jack. If I give it to you, I lose all my leverage. And even if I give it to you, you'll never know if I made a copy to show to Randy Carmichael. Maybe he would like to chip in some more cash to ensure confidentiality, Jack. What do you think?"

Jack's jaw clenched at the thought of Ted taking his blackmail scheme on the road to Randy Carmichael. There was firmness in his voice.

"Leave Randy out of this, Ted. Do you want to kill the goose that is laying the golden eggs?"

"An interesting turn of phrase given what's on the video, Jack. But we're friends and I see that you are a bit touchy about me negotiating with Mr. Carmichael. OK. 5G's a month and I leave Mr. Carmichael alone. And don't delude yourself into thinking you can purloin my little cinema verité. The original recording of the threesome is in safe place where you will never find it. If you want, you can take this copy with you to share with Randy. You can use it to get your juices flowing on some otherwise boring evening, if you know what I mean. So, 5G's a month and I leave Mr. Carmichael alone. Deal?"

"Deal, Ted. Why are you doing this?

"Because I can, Jack. And because you can afford it. Why should you be the only one who profits from your relationship with Mr. Carmichael?"

"How do you want me to pay you, Ted"

"You know that I like things that are hard, Jack. So let's make it the $5,000 equivalent of gold or silver coins. They will be less traceable than cash."

"OK, Ted, you win."

Satisfied with his bargain, Ted looked Jack up and down lasciviously as they lay in Ted's bed. Ted grinned.

"What else can I do for you, Jack? Since you're paying for it now, I'd be happy to perk up your spirits again before you leave. You know, the money actually makes you even more exciting."

As Jack looked at Ted, it was obvious that Ted was not kidding about the excitement. And as angry as he was at the extortion to which he was being subjected, Jack could not hide his own erection.

"Come over here, Jack. Let's seal the deal in the most pleasurable way imaginable."

Jack knew he should resist, but he couldn't.

Chapter 47

 forward, there was little outward change in the relationship between Jack Beaumont and Ted Miller. They continued to enjoy their bedroom rendezvous, as before. But every month, Jack Beaumont transferred, in piecemeal fashion, a total of $5,000 from his account at the First Union Bank to the Fairmont Federal Bank, where he kept a separate account with ample funds. Then he withdrew $2,500 in cash from the Fairmont Federal account and transferred another $5,000 from that account to his account at Allegheny Trust Bank. He then withdrew $2,500 from the Allegheny account in cash. The $5,000 in cash was then converted into gold or silver proof coins. Jack delivered the payoff to Ted Miller personally. If Jack was out of town, Ted was accommodating. He would wait until the ritualistic hand delivery could be accomplished. They agreed that Ted would not convert the coins to cash for deposit in in any local bank accounts for at least 60 days and that, even then, Ted would make such deposits in installments to make it more difficult for a forensic accountant to match Jack's withdrawals to Ted's deposits. Ted agreed to these conditions for the simple reason that they would make it more diffi-cult for the authorities to identify and prosecute him as a blackmailer. And the clandestine transfer of gold or silver coins, if not converted to cash, would allow his ill-gotten income to escape examination by the IRS.

The process had been in place for about ten months, enriching Ted to the tune of $50,000. At that point Ted told Jack it was time to renegotiate the deal. Ted threw a figure of $10,000 per month on the table, which was unacceptable to Jack. Jack negotiated Ted down to $7,500. Jack realized, however, that Ted would be back, when he didn't know, asking for more. As he funneled his money to Ted Miller, Jack fixated more and more on the realization that blackmail only ends when the blackmailer stops breathing. As much as he enjoyed his private interludes with Ted Miller, and the blackmail did nothing to diminish the raw pleasure of those encounters, Jack Beaumont enjoyed even more maintaining his bank accounts and the prospect of a future free of Ted's ever-increasing blackmail demands.

At first, Jack thought he could reason with Ted and simply persuade him to quit. Jack was sorely disappointed. Ted told Jack that he meant what he said. When Jack mentioned that the video would be as embarrassing for him as it would for Jack and Randy Carmichael, Ted laughed and said, "Jack, I'm a professional videographer. I can edit the video so that there is not a single frame in which I can be identified as a participant. No one will know I was there. But have no doubt. You and Randy will be front and center. Nothing left to the imagination, Jack. Nothing. You'll pay what I want."

When Jack persisted in resisting Ted's increased payment demands, Ted responded icily, "Don't try my patience, Jack. Either we make a deal or one day soon my little movie ends up in the In Box of the CEO of Transnational Marine Machinery. And I'm not going to wait for you to return from your never-ending business trip to Los Angeles, Jack. Make up your mind and give me your answer—soon."

It was at that moment that Jack decided that Ted Miller had to be eliminated. The question was when and how, and what Jack could do to mask his role in Ted's unfortunate demise.

The "when" was easy. It had to be soon. And there were two upcoming events that would coalesce nicely to create a gaggle of suspects, the Zoning Board hearing on the 24th and the Millers' party on the 22nd that Nikki had begged him to attend. Ted was the spokesperson for the Citizens' Alliance for Preservation, which was attempting to galvanize local opposition against the proposed mega-mall and to secure enough votes on the board to kill the project. Eliminating Ted a day or two before the Zoning Board vote would necessarily raise at least some cause-and-effect questions at the local constabulary. The party fell neatly within the window that would raise questions about the developers and financiers of the mega-mall. But the party had the added benefit of potentially multiplying the suspects, two dozen or so folks who would have had the opportunity to repay their host's hospitality with a kiss of death. Again, the multiplicity of suspects would confound the local police, even more so if it turned out that Ted had compromising videos of others, giving them not only an opportunity to do in Mr. Miller, but a motive as well. All of this would afford the actual killer time to cover his or her tracks and disappear before the police realized what had happened.

And throughout this flurry of activity, Jack Beaumont would be in Los Angeles, without any visible connection to any of those events.

That left only the "how" to be decided.

Chapter 48

JACK BEAUMONT HAD not always been a big law firm litigator. He had started as a public defender, convinced that he would learn more about trying cases there than he would by reviewing terabytes of information and distilling it for senior partners to use at trial. He used his public defender's platform as a springboard to a position with a law firm.

But Jack never forgot his public defender roots or the people he defended. He made a point, at least once every quarter, of visiting the old neighborhoods from which his clientele had sprung, buying a round or two of drinks for the house at their favorite watering holes, and playing a game of pool for stakes he would always be sure to lose. Some might think he was living dangerously, but in Jack's mind, there was no danger to him. He was one of them, he had worked for them, he had defended them, he had won for them. In a way, he was repaying them for the education they had given him.

It was natural, therefore, for him to return to his "roots" to deal with Ted Miller's greed. Unlike Penny Hamilton and her stories of her Brooklyn past, Jack actually did know "guys" who knew "guys" who knew "guys" who could solve any problem. It was only a question of price. It was here that Jack found the solution to his problem. Although their conversation was conducted in codes and hypotheses, the message that Jack got from a would-be go-between was that a professional assassin could take down Ted Miller at his upcoming pool party for $50,000. If it seemed like a lot, Jack needed to understand that the contractor would need to work on a compressed schedule and that the location of the hit meant there would be ample opportunity for guests to identify him. There would be no communication between Jack and the contractor unless the contract proved impossible to perform on time and on-site. In that event, the contractor would leave a message on Jack's hotel room number. The message would consist solely of the burner phone number at which the contractor could be reached. Jack should immediately delete the message and any call by Jack to that number should be made via a burner phone as well. No names would be exchanged during any such communications.

That was it. No muss, no fuss, not a single "Whereas" or "Henceforth." Jack had just negotiated a contract for the murder of his friend and sometime lover without an ounce of remorse. He was still sleeping with Ted Miller; he was enjoying it; he always did; but Ted Miller was threatening the very foundation of Jack Beaumont's professional, financial and personal lives. Ted was poised to ruin Jack's romantic relationship with Randy Carmichael, his professional relationship with Transnational Marine Machinery, his position in the law firm, and his marriage, however counterfeit that union might be. Ted Miller was foolish. He focused on what he could gain from his video. He had given no thought to what he could lose by pushing Jack too far.

Jack had but two duties to fulfill. An aggregate advance payment of $10,000 would be wired in $5,000 installments to two different numbered Swiss bank accounts by the close of business West Coast time the day after acceptance of the contract. If the contractor determined that the contract could not be fulfilled due to the shortness of time to prepare or the demanding nature of the place of performance, the contractor would call the number he had been given and a burner phone discussion would subsequently take place. But the $10,000 was spent money, no refund, no discount, no proration. $5,000 of that advance would be remitted by the contractor to the intermediary who performed liaison between the customer and the contractor. $5,000 was an advance against expenses. If the hit went off on time, Jack would need to wire the remaining $40,000 from separate accounts, in varying amounts, to purchase shares in four offshore shell companies controlled by the contractor under fictitious names, all within 24 hours of the Police Department's announcement of Mr. Miller's death. At that point, Jack's obligations on the contract would be complete. He assumed the contractor would then transfer the payments from the shell companies to the same Swiss accounts, but that was none of Jack's business.

Chapter 49

JOANNE AND IKE Taylor spoke to Milliken following Ike Taylor's interview of Randy Carmichael. She read straight from her notes, lest Milliken accuse her of editorializing, then added her conclusion at the end—Randy Carmichael did not kill Ted Miller; nor did he have him killed. Could she prove that he was innocent? No. But he seemed genuinely surprised by the news of their deaths, and a little sad. Taylor corroborated Joanne's summary of the interview and concurred in her conclusions, adding that he found Carmichael too timid to have orchestrated a murder. They advised Milliken that they would drop by Jack Beaumont's hotel room bright and early tomorrow morning.

Chapter 50

JACK WAS TYING the four-in-hand knot of his Tom Ford silk tie when the knock came on his hotel room door. Upon opening it, he saw two individuals flashing their shields. He asked them in while he examined their credentials, one a Los Angeles detective, the other a police woman from back home. Noting the paucity of seating in the room, Jack suggested that they relocate to the hotel dining room and ask for a remote table.

Although it was 8:00 AM, the dining room was sparsely populated and a table with some modicum of privacy was available. As with Randy Carmichael, Ike Taylor took the lead.

"You were at the headquarters of Transnational Marine Machinery yesterday, were you not?"

"Yes. I've been working on several cases for Transnational for quite some time. This latest trip has had me here for close to a month."

"Did you meet with Randy Carmichael yesterday?"

"Yes. He is my main client contact at Transnational."

"Did he tell you about our meeting with him?"

"Yes."

"What did he tell you?"

"That you are investigating the deaths of my neighbors, Ted and MaryAnne Miller."

"That's correct, Mr. Beaumont. And that's why we want to talk to you."

"Why, Detective Taylor?"

"Well, in cases like this we always look for motives. And in this case, there are all kinds of motives. Did you know, Mr. Beaumont, that Randy Carmichael had homosexual relations with Ted Miller?"

"No."

"Did you know that Ted Miller appears to have recorded a video of at least one of his encounters with Mr. Carmichael?"

"I'm confused by that question, Detective. I said I did not know of Mr. Carmichael's alleged sexual encounters with Ted Miller."

"Fair enough, Mr. Beaumont. Did Mr. Carmichael ever tell you that Ted Miller was blackmailing him?"

"No, he didn't."

"Did Mr. Carmichael ever tell you that Mr. Miller had asked for money to buy his silence regarding Mr. Carmichael's homosexuality?"

"No, and that makes no sense. Mr. Carmichael's sexual orientation is a protected class under California law. He cannot be fired or otherwise disadvantaged at Transnational Marine on the basis of his sexual preferences. It is just not a high-ticket extortion target, Detective."

"Tell us about your physical relationship with Mr. Carmichael, Mr. Beaumont."

"Are you suggesting that if I had such a relationship, I would be a suspect, Detective?"

"Follow the money, Mr. Beaumont. It's not a hard path to track."

"What money?"

"The legal fees you receive from Transnational Marine, courtesy of Mr. Carmichael."

"All of which are supported by detailed daily billing records, Detective. I suggest you get your mind out of the gutter. Let me remind you, Detective, that I was in Los Angeles before, during, and after the murders."

"I'm aware of that, Mr. Beaumont. But, again, please tell us about your physical relationship with Mr. Carmichael."

"Did Mr. Carmichael tell you we had such a relationship, Detective?"

"Why don't you just tell us what you can about your physical relationship with Mr. Carmichael, Mr. Beaumont?"

"I'm going to finish my breakfast, officers. Then I'm going to leave. I won't be answering any more questions. Have a good day."

Taylor and Tracey thanked him for his time. They excused themselves from the table and left the hotel to return to Taylor's station house. On the way, Taylor asked Joanne, "What do you think?"

"He's a cold bastard," said Joanne, "that's for sure. I think he has the cojones to have had Miller killed if the stakes were high enough."

"I agree, but he won't voluntarily give us a thing. Unless we can establish that Miller was blackmailing Carmichael or Beaumont, or both, and that Beaumont had some role in arranging the hit, we've got nothing. We might be able to make out a circumstantial case of blackmail by reviewing Miller's, Carmichael's, and Beaumont's bank records to look for patterns of parallel withdrawals and deposits. But a monetary link to the assassin? Do you know what it is like to try to penetrate what are likely to be Swiss bank accounts? If he's guilty, this guy stands a good chance of getting away with murder."

"Maybe Mrs. Beaumont will come up with something in her divorce case, Ike."

"And maybe Mr. Beaumont discontinues his suit or settles a munificent sum on his wife to make her claims go away. Then what? Do you expect her to keep at it with him just for the fun of it?"

"Not for fun, Ike. For vengeance. She had strong feelings for Mary-Anne Miller. If she thought Jack might get away with murdering Mary-Anne, she might cooperate with us."

Chapter 51

JACK TRIED TO **add up** what the police seemed to have. **One**—Randy and Ted had been sexually involved. It was a given. Randy had admitted to it. Randy should have known better than to answer those questions, but the suggestion of a video had tripped him into answering. **Two**—Randy and Jack were sexually involved. Randy did not admit it, but his refusal to deny it spoke volumes. Moreover, Nikki's fucking divorce lawyer probably had a damned good dossier on his comings and goings to and from Randy's house to make out a pretty strong case for their affair. **Three**—Randy's continuing affection for Jack was a cornerstone of Jack Beaumont's financial success. $10 million a year was a nice, solid cornerstone. **Four**—disclosure of Jack and Randy's relationship to the Transmarine Board of Directors would mean the end of Randy's career at Transmarine and of the cozy business side of Jack's relationship with Randy. It wasn't Randy's homosexuality. The Board probably had tumbled to that during Randy's divorce. But the Board could not tolerate a General Counsel who traded millions in company business for personal sexual gratification.

What didn't the police have? **One**—any evidence of a blackmail threat. But Jack knew this was not ironclad. Although Jack used multiple accounts and converted separate withdrawals into gold and silver coins as payments to Ted, an intensive review of Jack's bank records would eventually reveal a pattern of withdrawals that created a circumstantial record of some type of significant regular payment being made by Jack to someone. And if Ted had converted the coins into cash and deposited it into his accounts, a good forensic accountant could trace the money from Jack to Ted in a pattern that suggested blackmail. On the other hand, if Ted had been smart and simply held on to the coins, then the trail of monetary bread crumbs from Jack to Ted might never emerge. **Two**—no videos of Randy, Jack and Ted. Ted had told Jack the videos were safely hidden where Jack would never find them. That was good. But, again, far from ironclad. He could not control when, how, or why they might surface. But, if they did, they would give rise to a potent motive for murder, particularly when cobbled together with any problematic financial records. **Three**—they couldn't place Jack at the scene of the crime. Again, helpful, but not outcome determinative if they could somehow link him to a paid assassin. Jack had done his best to launder the $50,000 fee through a variety of accounts and "investments," but a dogged forensic accountant could, with enough time and enough energy, trace the breadcrumbs. But to where? To nameless Swiss bank accounts that might well be Jack Beaumont's hideaway for assets he wished to shield from his wife in a divorce, which seemed inevitable.

Jack added it all up. He did not succeed as a lawyer by looking at the world through rose-colored glasses. He knew that defendants can be convicted on the basis of circumstantial evidence. But unless and until the police could identify the hit man and connect him to Jack, he thought the police would have a difficult time persuading the DA to put his reputation on the line in pursuit of a conviction of a prominent and well-respected member of the bar.

Chapter 52

NIKKI SAT IN Sharon Riley's conference room. Sharon had told her, in their brief telephone conversation, that she had three developments to report.

The first was that her investigator had caught up with Rita Carmichael, Randy's ex-wife. She was unwilling to discuss the grounds for the divorce, adding that there was a confidentiality clause that essentially tied her hands.

Also, the police had contacted Sharon.

"They were interested in the source for your statement when you met with them in Maria Romano's office that your husband has been having an illicit affair with Randy Carmichael. They wanted to know if you would be willing to share the information with them to aid in their murder investigation. I passed that on to Maria and maybe we can get her on the phone at the end of this meeting."

Nikki had an interested look on her face. "Does this mean they think that Jack or Randy are involved in the murders?"

"It looks that way, Nikki, but you can never tell. If that's the direction they are taking, it's a good sign for you."

"You said there were three things, Sharon?"

"Yes, Nikki. Jack's divorce attorney called me. They want to put the divorce in the rear view mirror as quickly as possible. They don't want a long drawn out process where the parties are fighting over discovery and assets, making the lawyers rich."

"Oh?"

"They sent over a proposal along with copies of current financial records. It's very favorable for you, Nikki. If you spend wisely, you won't need to work another day in your life."

"I like my job, Sharon."

"Well, this doesn't require you to quit," Sharon smiled, "but it gives you that option."

"What's at the bottom of this, Sharon. One day I'm used goods, a whore, someone he tells to get a good divorce lawyer because I'm going to need one. Today, he's handing me the keys to a damned nice financial future. Help me understand this, please."

"He sees his relationship with Mr. Carmichael as a business problem for him. He wants to keep it under wraps. He wants to avoid discovery. He doesn't want to have to testify at a deposition or, God forbid, have Randy Carmichael do so. I can't read all the tea leaves, Nikki, but it seems to me he wants to buy your silence and limit how much more you can find out about his sexual exploits."

"What about the information we already have?"

"You hit the nail on the head. He wants it all to be covered by a con-fidentiality clause, no disclosure to any third parties. The proposal doesn't say so, but that would include the police."

"So if he was involved in MaryAnne's death and if the file we have on his relationship with Randy Carmichael might help to convict him, this deal would tie the police's hands?"

"Not necessarily, but it becomes more problematic. They'd need a court order and Jack would fight that for sure."

"Let's get Maria on the phone."

Nikki, Sharon, and Maria spoke for about 30 minutes. What it boiled down to in Nikki's mind was whether to take a highly generous financial settlement and walk away or enhance the police's ability to make their case against Jack if he had somehow engineered MaryAnne's death. For Nikki, the answer was clear.

"No deal."

Maria asked, "What about sharing the dossier on Jack and Mr. Carmichael with the police?"

"Maria, unless you tell me there's a very good reason not to share the dossier with the police, I say go ahead and hand it over. If Jack had anything to do with MaryAnne's death, I want him to pay."

Chapter 53

JOANNE HAD RETURNED from Los Angeles. She had provided Milliken detailed notes of the interviews conducted by Ike Taylor and now she was in his office once again, along with Terry Hammond, discussing her conclusions.

When she was finished, Milliken said that the fingerprints taken from the Gordonville stiff could not be matched to those found on the glasses, bottles, and barware collected from the Miller home. No one was surprised. Ever since the Corona pandemic, food service personnel had taken to the use of thin rubber gloves, and Emily Morton had confirmed that she required her staff to do so. But they did have Ms. Morton's somewhat equivocal identification, which was corroborated, with the same degree of doubt, by other members of her staff. They were confident that he was in fact the bartender, but all of the involved police agreed that the staff's subjective confidence was not proof of anything beyond a reasonable doubt. Their only hope for a positive ID was to ask the Millers' guests if they could identify the stiff as the party's bartender. That would take time and it did not hold out much hope.

On the positive side, Milliken said they had a positive identification of the stiff. Based on fingerprints on file with the U.S. Army, his name was Howard Coen. He had served in the Army for four years. There was nothing negative in his Army record, and precious little to suggest a possible future as an assassin. He was assigned to an infantry platoon, was awarded an "Expert" rating for riflery, and received an honorable discharge. After his stint in the Army, he went to community college, got a degree in accounting, and opened his own accounting business in Cincinnati. He was unmarried and they had not yet located any next of kin. They were hopeful of obtaining warrants for his home and office and looking for any information—phone records, internet traffic, bank deposits or transfers—that might potentially link him to someone in Ted Miller's circle of "friends." They were also looking again at Nicole Beaumont's records to see if Howard Coen or information relating to Howard Coen—his home or office numbers or addresses—showed up to create a possible link. They were also doing the same in relation to Coen's alias for that night, "Guy Halper."

Joanne became somewhat animated. "What about Jack Beaumont's records, Jim? Your focus on Mrs. Beaumont is becoming close to maniacal. Shouldn't we be scouring Mr. Beaumont's records?"

"Calm down, Sergeant. I'm only doing what needs to be done. If there are links to Coen or Halper in her records, that suggests culpability. If not, that's another weight on Mrs. Beaumont's side of the scale."

"And her husband, Jim?"

"What do we have to go to the court with to justify a warrant to search his records, Sergeant? A homosexual relationship between the deceased and Mr. Beaumont's largest client, who says that the deceased never threatened to expose their relationship? Mr. Beaumont's likely affair with his client?

This is not the 1940's or the 1950's Joanne. I know your theory about Miller's possible threat to Beaumont's finances and professional stature, but the judge is likely to look at a request for a warrant as nothing more than a prurient curiosity on our part. And what do we have to suggest that there is a probability that Howard Coen can be found in Jack Beaumont's records?"

"Nothing . . . yet."

"Right, Joanne . . . yet. We're not done. Let's play this out. If Mr. Beaumont is involved, I don't want him walking because we obtained a defective search warrant."

Joanne had disagreed with Inspector Milliken on a number of counts in this investigation. But she agreed with him on this. If Jack Beaumont was guilty, he was not going to get away with murder because of faulty police work.

Chapter 54

ARTHUR MILLER WAS Ted Miller's cousin and a lawyer. Arthur had prepared simple reciprocal wills for Ted and MaryAnne and he retained the originals of those wills in his files. Both wills appointed him as the executor and personal representative of the deceased. As such he was able to obtain an order granting him access to Ted's safe deposit box at Fairmont Federal. To his surprise, the box was empty except for two DVDs and gold and silver coins that he had appraised at approximately $65,000. There was a notarized statement from Ted Miller establishing that he was a professional videographer, that he had recorded the events on the DVDs, and that he confirmed the dates and times on the DVDs.

Back in his office, Arthur reviewed the DVDs.

After completing his review, Arthur surmised that the DVDs might possibly have some bearing on Ted's murder, so he drove to the police station and asked who was handling the Miller investigation. Within a minute, Sergeant Joanne Tracey appeared to introduce herself, along with

Officer Terry Hammond. They showed Arthur to the conference room, offered him a seat, and asked if he wanted something to drink. He appeared to be nervous and, when he spoke, it was apparent his throat was dry. Officer Hammond brought him some water.

Sergeant Tracey asked the purpose of Arthur's visit and he told them of his role as Ted's executor, the court order, and his access to the safe deposit box earlier that day. Then he handed Sergeant Tracey the two DVDs.

"Have you watched these, Arthur?"

"Yes, Sergeant."

"Would you mind sitting through these again?"

"I'd prefer not to, but if it will help your investigation, sure. I'll watch."

The first DVD was a "passion play" with two actors. Joanne asked Arthur if he could identify either. He said that one was his cousin, Ted Miller. He could not identify the other man, but Joanne could. She had met him and attended his interview in Los Angeles. It was Randy Carmichael. Joanne quickly concluded that this was the "Randy Carmichael" video "No. 24" that was listed on Ted Miller's master index of videos but missing from the video compilation he kept in his office.

Joanne asked Arthur if he had had any inkling, before he watching the DVD, of his cousin's appreciation for male company. "No, Sergeant," said Arthur, "With a wife like Mary Anne that would have been the furthest thing from my mind."

The second DVD was far longer and far more involved. Three men. Joanne again asked Arthur if he could identify any of them. Again, he identified Ted Miller. He could not identify the other two, but one of them was the same man who had appeared with Ted in the first DVD. There was no mistaking Randy Carmichael. And, from Joanne Tracey's perspective, there was no mistaking Jack Beaumont.

Joanne asked if Arthur had altered the DVDs in any way. He had not. She asked if the police could retain the DVDs as evidence, as well as the notarized statement, and he was none too happy to be rid of them. She asked him to dictate a statement regarding the DVDs, how he came to be in possession of them, and that he had transferred custody of the DVDs to the police. They agreed that Arthur would retain custody of the coins pending completion of the police investigation.

Chapter 55

IKE TAYLOR CALLED Randy Carmichael and asked for a meeting. Carmichael told him that he was represented by counsel, George Bailey, and gave him Bailey's contact information.

Bailey had a reputation for being tough but honest, a fighter but a pragmatist, someone who could recognize a losing hand and work to minimize his losses. "What can I do for you, Detective Taylor?"

"I'm sure you know of our prior meeting with your client. We'd like to follow up. We have some evidence we would like to share with you and your client."

"What kind of evidence?"

"Let's hold that for the meeting, Mr. Bailey."

"When, Detective?"

"At yours and your client's convenience."

"Where?"

"Here. When we meet you'll understand why."

* * *

They settled into the police conference room, Bailey and Carmichael on one side of the table and Taylor and another LAPD officer across from them. A big video screen faced them from the end of the table.

"Mr. Carmichael, do you recall telling us of your sexual relationship with Ted Miller?"

Bailey interjected. "Detective, just so that we are clear in our terminology, what do you mean by a 'relationship'?"

"Fair enough, Mr. Bailey. Mr. Carmichael, you told us, didn't you, that you had engaged in sex with Mr. Ted Miller on two occasions?"

"Yes."

Turning to his fellow officer, Taylor asked him to dim the room lights and start the video. Except for the sounds of the participants on the video, the room was still.

When it was over, Bailey asked for a few minutes alone with his client. Bailey knew about the sex, including the three-way. He did not know about the video and he wanted to make sure his client did not know about it, or any other videos, either. Satisfied with his client's responses, Bailey signaled for the police to return.

Detective Taylor hit Carmichael with a series of questions in quick succession.

"That is you on the video, isn't it?"

"Yes."

"With Ted Miller?"

"Yes."

"When did this take place?"

"I'm not sure. It was around Thanksgiving. Maybe a year and half ago."

"Have you ever seen this video before?"

"No."

"Never?"

"No. Never."

"Before today, did you know it existed?"

"No. When you interviewed me, you said it appeared that Ted had videos of his sexual encounters, but that's all I ever heard or knew about that."

"Did Ted Miller threaten to expose your sexual preferences?"

"No."

"Did he ask you for money to keep quiet about your encounters with him?"

"No."

"Never?"

"Never."

Detective Taylor again turned to his colleague and asked him to dim the lights and start the next video. Again, Randy Carmichael appeared on the screen, again sexually engaged with Ted Miller, but this time joined by a third man.

When the video was over, Detective Taylor asked the same questions, but he asked additional questions about Jack Beaumont and whether Jack Beaumont had given Carmichael any reason to believe that Miller was blackmailing Jack. He had not.

"Detective," said Bailey, "I know you did not ask us down here today to intimidate us with videos of my client in compromising positions that do not violate any laws or give rise to any lawful reason for terminating his employment. So, if I may be blunt, what's the deal?"

"The deal, Mr. Bailey, is that we think one or both of these videos were part of a blackmail scheme to extort money from Mr. Carmichael or Mr. Beaumont, or both of them. We think Ted Miller knew that without secrecy, the sexual relationship between Mr. Carmichael and Mr. Beaumont would get them both fired and possibly disbarred, ruining them financially and professionally. And we think one or both of them arranged a hit on Mr. Miller."

"My client says he didn't do it, Detective. What are you going to do? Drag his name through the mud while forcing me to poke holes in your case?"

"Mr. Bailey, I think we have enough to get a search warrant to access Mr. Carmichael's bank records. We would be looking for periodic payment patterns that tend to suggest blackmail. Ask your client if he would consent to allowing us to access his records without a warrant. If we come up dry, that will tell us to look elsewhere. That's not a guarantee, but it's a logical conclusion."

Bailey and Carmichael conferred in private. Bailey's response was succinct—"If you are willing to perform the review after hours, Detective, we'll consent."

Chapter 56

IF YOU COUNTED everyone connected via Zoom, Inspector Milliken's conference room was getting more crowded by the day. In the room, he had himself, Sergeant Tracey, Officer Hammond, and Norman Brewer on behalf of the forensics team that had been tasked to go back through Mrs. Beaumont's electronic and written records in search of links to Howard Coen and Guy Halper. On Zoom, he had the Cincinnati forensics folks and, from LA, Detective Taylor and a member of his forensic accounting group.

Milliken went down the list of open items.

Mrs. Beaumont's records came up dry. No references anywhere to Coen or Halper. Her bank records were pretty dull stuff, with no significant unusual withdrawals or payments in and around the time of the murders.

Coen's records were equally clean. No reference to Mrs. Beaumont, Mr. Beaumont, or Randy Carmichael. His bank accounts, to the extent they could locate records of any, revealed no significant deposits within the three months preceding the murders or at any time since. If he had one or more overseas accounts, linking him to any would be a long, laborious process with no assurance of success.

Randy Carmichael's bank records showed no patterns that would suggest unexplained periodic payments or cash transactions.

Milliken looked at Norman Brewer and asked again about the slips of paper found in "Drake Hamilton's" money clip. On one slip he had written "4201030." On the other, "3424013."

"Any luck?"

"Jim, this could be anything," said Brewer.

"No, Norman. It has to be significant." Milliken continued, "This guy was a pro. He traveled light. If he had something on his person it was because he needed it, or he might have needed it. Have we checked the airports, bus terminals and railway stations within a 200-mile radius to see if they have lockers with those numbers? Maybe that's where he was to pick up his fee when all was said and done."

Brewer responded quickly, "We did that, Jim. No matches."

Milliken kept pressing, "Telephone numbers?"

Forensics responded, "Standard telephone numbers have 10 digits, Jim, if you include the area code. These are too short. They're seven digits. That's right for a local number, but what good does that do? You'd need to call both numbers in every area code and rehearse some pre-planned patter to see if you got a rise out of anyone. Do we have an army of cold callers to take that job on, Jim?"

Joanne joined the conversation. "Look, he kept the numbers, so they were important. But whatever they were, he would not want them to be obvious. So maybe he takes one large number and breaks it in two, on two separate slips. That's the first step in his masking of what these numbers are. So, let's play along with that hypothesis. Run the numbers together. What do we get?"

Brewer piped up, "You get two possibilities—42010303424013 and 34240134201030."

"OK," said Joanne, "break them down as if they are telephone numbers. What do you get?"

Brewer was in his mathematical element—

"(420) 103-0342 plus 4013

and

(342) 401-3420 plus 1030"

"Now," Joanne suggested, "run them backwards."
Brewer wrote down and read out the results—

"(310) 424-3030 plus 1024

and

(030) 102-4310 plus 4243"

Joanne looked at Hammond. "Terry, call those four numbers. Let's see what we get."

At that point, Ike Taylor said, "Joanne, there's no need. Area Code 310 is out here. I just looked it up on my phone. 424-3030 is the Fairmont Century Plaza. Remember who booked a room there?"

"Jack Beaumont. Room 1024."

Chapter 57

JACK EMAILED NIKKI to tell her that he was returning from his trip. He knew he would not be welcome in the house but he needed to pick up some things to tide him over until they could work through the divorce. He would be taking the overnight red eye from Los Angeles and arriving at 7:40 AM. He should be to the house by 8:45 AM.

The flight arrived on time, but Jack never made it home. By 7:55 AM he was in police custody, hands in zip cuffs, on his way to the station. Upon deplaning, the police had ignominiously presented him with an arrest warrant and read him his *Miranda* warnings right there in the airport. Not surprisingly, the ride to the station was in silence. Inspector Milliken rode "shotgun" while Sergeant Tracey and Officer Hammond flanked Jack in the rear seat.

When they arrived at the station, they booked, photographed, and fingerprinted him. Then they led him to an interrogation room. Milliken had not finished asking the first question when Jack advised them he wanted to speak to his lawyer. They moved him off to a holding cell and waited for Jack's lawyer, Garret Stockton, to arrive. When he arrived, he was taken to his client, with whom he spent about 45 minutes. When he emerged he advised Inspector Milliken that his client would not be answering any questions, that he was asserting his Fifth Amendment rights, that he would plead "Not Guilty" and seek release on bail.

The DA's office opposed bail, but the judge was not moved. Beaumont was a known quantity within the bar, he had no record of prior offenses or arrests, he was married with ties to the community, and he posed no risk of flight to avoid prosecution. Jack was ordered to surrender his passport and post bond in the amount of $100,000. He was on the street by 3:00 PM the next day.

By 3:30 PM he was in Stockton's office, spilling his story in all of its sordid detail. He left nothing out, except for his arrangements for a hit man. Jack assumed that the police would not hold back from Stockton any of the details they had in their possession, and he did not want his lawyer to believe that Jack was trying to mislead him. Stockton told him that the DA had called and asked for a meeting. On the theory that more information is better than less, Stockton had agreed to meet. He strongly urged Jack not to attend, lest he say something he might later come to regret. Stockton would call him at his lodgings when the meeting was over.

As Stockton subsequently explained to Jack, it was not a good meeting unless you were a prosecutor. While it was helpful that Jack was 3,000 miles away when the murders occurred, that fact was not as strong in a murder for hire case. The folks behind those killings almost always found a reason to be far away from the killing zone when the deed was done. The evidence on the prosecution's side was substantial, albeit wholly circumstantial in nature and potentially subject to exclusion at trial.

The motive was one a jury could easily grasp. Jack and Randy had a relationship that would have disqualified Jack from legal representation of Transnational under company policy. It was a conflict of interest for Randy to place millions in legal services in the pocket of his lover. Disclosure of their relationship would have killed the goose that laid Jack's golden eggs.

The police also had evidence that Jack's and Randy's relationship was continuing in nature, in the form of a report from a private investigator hired by the divorce lawyer for Jack's wife. This was evidence that would have destroyed Jack's cozy arrangement with Randy, and it provided a powerful foundation for blackmail. Although he held his tongue, Jack again castigated himself internally for compelling Nikki to engage a divorce lawyer. He should have foreseen the likelihood that Nikki's lawyer would put a tail on him.

The decedent, Ted Miller, had videographic evidence of Randy and Jack's relationship.

The police had obtained a search warrant for Jack's home office and computer, from which they obtained information relating to his various bank accounts, and for the bank records themselves. They also searched Ted Miller's bank records, with the consent of his executor. Jack had done a nice job of bank hopping, but it could be documented that over the past year or so, Jack had withdrawn from several accounts every month an aggregate amount in excess of $5,000. The net effect of all the transfers was that Jack walked away with $5,000 in cash, in two withdrawals of $2,500 each from two different banks. And Ted's safe deposit box contained approximately $65,000 in gold and silver proof coins, which were roughly equivalent in value to Jack's various withdrawals. Ted would not be around to testify, and Jack would sit impassively at the defense table, but a forensic accounting expert would testify that these cash withdrawals by Jack and Ted's ownership of comparable amounts of precious metals were consistent with an ongoing blackmail scheme.

"Garret," said Jack, "if I was paying, why would I kill him and run all these risks? How do they deal with that?"

"Well, Jack, it appears that for the last two months before he was killed, you were withdrawing $7,500 a month. So, their theory is, he got greedy, you saw no end to it, and you decided to put an end to him. It happens frequently in blackmail cases."

"What about my obvious physical affection for Ted Miller? Doesn't that mitigate against me as his killer?"

"It could, Jack, it could. But it's a two-edged sword. Maybe the blackmail incensed you, made you feel as if Ted had used you, that he betrayed your affection for him. And you lashed out. That will be their response."

"Do they know, Garret, who actually killed Ted and Maryanne?"

"Yes, Jack. It was a professional assassin from Cincinnati, named Howard Coen."

"Howard Coen? He sounds like an accountant."

"That's exactly right, Jack. Accounting is his vocation, murder for hire his avocation."

"And just how did Mr. Coen do this?"

"He killed the regular bartender, took his place at the Millers' party, bided his time, then laced the gin so that Ted Miller's nightcap would be the last martini of his life."

"Garret, just how do they say I was able to get Howard Coen the details of the Millers' party, like who the bartender was supposed to be?"

"You provided that information, according to the police."

"And where did I get it, Garret?"

"Your wife told you when she was trying to persuade you to come home for the shindig."

"That's not admissible at the trial is it? She's still my wife. Can't I keep her from testifying against me, Garret?"

"Fortunately for you, in this state you can."

"Then I'll contact my divorce lawyer and tell him to slow roll and stall those proceedings so that the marriage is still intact when the trial comes. Garrett, that's a pretty big hole in their case against me, isn't it? I mean, I won't testify and she can't testify, so how do they connect me with Howard Coen or whoever he is? Have they even found him?"

"Yes, they found him."

"Do we know what he has told the police?"

"He's dead, Jack. Heroin overdose in Gordonville, about 100 miles from your home."

Jack was almost beside himself. They likely could not prove he knew anything about the details of the party, so they couldn't prove he—or anyone—passed them on to Coen. Plus, Coen was dead, and dead men don't talk. He looked at Garret with hope in his eyes. "Doesn't this kill the case against me? I mean, I don't know Howard Coen. I wouldn't recognize him if he was standing next to me. I never spoke to him. I was never in Cincinnati. How do they link him to me?"

"They have two shots, Jack.

First, when they found him, Coen had two small slips of paper stuck between the bills in his money clip. They look like random numbers, but when you manipulate them in a very simple way, one of them is the phone number for your room at the Fairmont Century Plaza."

"So what, Garret? Somebody can manipulate some random numbers to create my phone number. So what? Who's going to testify as to what those numbers were, who created them, when, how they came to be in Coen's possession, and what they meant? Not Howard Coen. And, Garret—I swear to you—I never received a call from anyone in my hotel room other than my damned wife and Randy. The hotel can probably verify that. You're not worth your salt if you can't keep those numbers out of evidence, Garret. What else? What's their second shot?"

"It looks like you withdrew a total of $50,000 in various transactions right before and after the murders. The money went overseas. They haven't tracked all the breadcrumbs but they say it was the payoff to Howard Coen."

"Can they actually put the money in Howard Coen's hands, or accounts he controlled?"

"Not yet, Jack. Right now, all they've got are withdrawals from your accounts that travel overseas at the wrong time. But they haven't yet been able to link the withdrawals to Coen."

"And Howard Coen can't talk. What do we have to lay on the table for the jury, Garret?"

"I haven't seen their potentially exculpatory evidence yet. If Ted Miller liked to video his sexual conquests, he may have more videos, videos of married women or married men, men and women who attended the party and had a motive to kill Miller and retrieve their embarrassing videos, people who were three thousand miles closer to the scene of the crime than you were. Calling those people will certainly cause a stir in the community and provide lots of opportunities for us to distract the jury from you as the only one with enough reason to get rid of Ted Miller. You may not know it, but it's a bit like the murder of the guy who starred in the TV show, *Hogan's Heroes*. He reputedly was quite a ladies' man who liked to record his conquests. He was found bludgeoned to death. The supposition was that a jealous husband gave him his comeuppance. The murder was never solved."

"What are my chances, Garret?"

"If we keep out your wife's testimony and Coen's numbers slips, you've got a decent shot, and if they can't break the trail on your overseas transactions, you have a very good chance of acquittal. But, before you go throwing yourself a party, remember this. You are not going to be a sympathetic defendant, Jack. The jury will not like you and you cannot expect Nikki to sit in the courtroom playing the role of a trusting, supportive wife. Juries tend to acquit people they like. They tend to convict people they don't like."

"Meaning what?"

"Let's look at the exculpatory materials when we get them. Then we can decide whether to fight or bargain."

Chapter 58

JACK HAD MOVED to a residence-style hotel following his indictment. It wasn't home, and it wasn't the Century Plaza, but it was comfortable. The ceiling fan suspended from an overhead beam whirred softly, providing just enough cooling while he worked up notes for his defense counsel on his laptop. He didn't know if they would ever be needed. Trial was several months off and there was ample time for motions *in limine* to keep Nikki's testimony and the number slips out of evidence, and for plea bargaining. At least that was what Stockton had suggested.

He was taking a sip of his Jack Daniels when he heard a knock on the door. He was greeted by a couple of his friends from his public defender days, Hank Martin and Steve Sutton, guys for whom he had secured acquittals, sparing them significant jail time. As they entered the room, they pulled back the hoods on their sweatshirts. Their smiles helped to brighten Jack's spirits.

"Thanks for coming by, guys. I really appreciate it. I think you may be my only friends left. Everyone else is avoiding me like a leper."

Hank was all smiles. "C'mon, Jack. You're our man. How could we leave you out here without a friend? And believe me, you've got lots of guys in the old neighborhood pulling for you. Everyone is interested in what's going on and pulling for you to beat this rap."

Hank was well aware of Jack's drinking preferences and he presented him with a bottle of his favorite Tennessee sipping whiskey, quickly adding "How about a couple of glasses and some ice, pal?" Jack promptly obliged and poured them each a drink. As Jack sipped, Hank expressed interest in Jack's dilemma.

"So tell us, Jack, how are you gonna' beat this rap? You always were able to get us off the hook. Can your mouthpiece do the same for you?"

"Well, they have a lot of circumstantial evidence, probably enough to convict if we draw an unsympathetic jury. We are going to file a couple of motions to keep some of that evidence out and, if we succeed on that, my chances go up considerably. My lawyer says in that event they may be open to a plea bargain, letting me plead to a lesser charge. Then again, if we do keep out that evidence, maybe we don't even bother to bargain. Maybe we just go ahead with the trial or move to dismiss the indictment."

Steve jumped in and said Jack always knew all the angles. After pouring Jack another drink, he said, "You'll figure your way out of this, Jack. You're too smart to let them convict you. Have you had any deal talk with the DA yet?"

"No, Steve. All the chatter has been between my lawyer and the DA."

Hank leaned in and asked in a low voice, as if he were afraid of being overheard, "Does your lawyer know about the arrangements for the hit, Jack?"

"No, Hank. Some things have to remain a secret."

"Right, Jack. Right. Let's keep it that way, pal, OK?"

"Of course, Hank."

"When do you get to put in your two cents worth, Jack?"

"I have no idea, Hank. Trial is several months off."

"What about plea bargaining?"

"Don't know. There's no pre-planned schedule for those sorts of things."

"I guess they could try to negotiate any time, right?"

"I suppose so, Hank." Jack just looked down at the floor. "You never can tell."

They reminisced for quite a while about the old days when Jack made his living and built his career securing acquittals for Hank and Steve and others like them, people the legal system otherwise would have steamrolled. The Jack Daniels seemed to bring the memories vividly to life for Jack, memories of his public defender days, and of his rise to partner in his firm. As he imbibed his Jack Daniels, he happily shared those memories with Hank and Steve, but he kept to himself his memories of how he had used Nikki as a perfect beard to mask his sexual preferences, and his affair with Randy Carmichael.

Jack did not regret his affair with Randy Carmichael. Although he knew he had used Randy, he also had great affection for Randy. Nor did he regret his carnal lust for Ted Miller, which was raw, insatiable, and richly satisfying. What he did regret was his stupidity and the shortsightedness with which he allowed his carnal lust for Ted to mix with his affectionate lust for Randy. If he had kept those relationships separate, he would not be sitting here wondering about his trial, Ted would not be dead, Randy would still be the General Counsel of Transnational Marine Machinery, Jack Beaumont would still be its preferred outside counsel, and Nikki would still be oblivious to his sexual interest in other men. Yes, he had truly fucked up when he launched the first salvo in an unnecessary divorce war with his spouse.

The talk turned back to Jack's legal problems and how he was bearing up under the strain. Slurring his words through the whiskey, he admitted that it was difficult to sit in limbo, wondering what magic his lawyer might be able to work.

"Well, Jack," said Steve, "everybody down in the old neighborhood is behind you, 1000 percent." Looking at his watch, he suggested to Hank that it was time to leave.

As Jack got up to say his goodbyes, he began to wobble from the effects of the Jack Daniels. Hank wrapped his arms around Jack from behind, ostensibly to steady him, but in reality to immobilize him while Steve quickly stuffed a wadded cloth in Jack's mouth to ensure quiet. Jack's eyes opened wide with fright. Hank spoke softly in Jack's ear, unsure of whether the words were making their way through the Jack Daniels.

"I'm sorry, Jack. We can't risk loose chatter. You, my friend, are a risk. It would be quite inconvenient if you were to tell the police how you found Howard Coen."

At that point, Hank moved one of his arms up to Jack's throat and pressed gently until Jack lost consciousness. They removed a rope from Steve's backpack, looped the rope over the ceiling beam, placed the noose around Jack's neck, slowly hoisted his limp form, tied off the rope, and let him dangle and suffocate to death. When he was dead, they removed the cloth from his mouth, turned over the desk chair that the medical examiner hopefully would conclude Jack had kicked out to complete his suicide, knocked over the bottle of Jack Daniels, and then fashioned Jack's farewell note on his open lap top. In it, he expressed "shame and revulsion" for what he had done to Ted and Maryanne. He could no longer look himself in the mirror. He did not "deserve to live." He hoped that God would be more merciful when Jack presented himself, remorseful, before the gates of heaven.

Before departing, Hank and Steve looked at Jack's limp form and addressed him, as if he were still alive. "It wasn't personal, Jack. We owed you a lot, and we liked you. But business is business, and you were a liability." All evidence of their presence in his room left when they did.

Jack's vacant eyes stared at the room. He had never noticed that neither Hank Martin nor Steve Sutton drank a single drop of their Jack Daniels. Nor had he noticed that neither of them had, throughout the visit, removed their gloves.

Chapter 59

JIM MILLIKEN WAS content. His team had solved a double murder. The perpetrator had been arrested and, while the court had released him on bail, justice had been served. Jack Beaumont's suicide note closed the book on the case as far as he was concerned. Others had their doubts. Hank McIntosh questioned how a man with that much alcohol in his system could have secured the rope sufficiently to withstand the weight when the chair was removed. Milliken dismissed those concerns, "Hank, he set up the rope when he was sober, then he got liquored up to give himself the courage to kill himself."

McIntosh persisted, "What about the farewell note, Jim? One minute he's preparing his defense, the next minute he's spilling his guts to anyone who finds him. That's an awfully quick and an awfully final change of heart."

"Hank," said Jim, "Nobody knows what flashes through a suicide's head in his final moments. "Do you have any evidence that other folks were in the room?"

"Not right now, Jim."

"Look, Hank. It's your certificate to sign. You fill it out the way you think best. I think it's suicide. This guy was an SOB. He killed three people. He deserved to die. He saved us all a lot of trouble. He saved some people in this community a lot of embarrassment. Good riddance."

Chapter 60

SERGEANT TRACEY ACCOMPANIED the police team that returned the items that had been removed from the Beaumont home during the investigation. She handed Nikki the manifest and asked her to review it and sign it if was accurate. Nikki said it would take a while and offered the sergeant a seat while she did so.

"Can I offer you something, Sergeant? Coffee, water, coke?"

"Coffee would be nice, Mrs. Beaumont. Black, no sugar."

As she popped a pod into the Keurig, Nikki turned and said, "Now that I am no longer a suspect, I suppose it's OK for you to call me Nikki."

"Then call me Joanne, Nikki."

Nikki handed Joanne her coffee and made herself a cup. They sat at the kitchen table while Nikki pored over the manifest. The rest of the police team had left.

"If there is anything missing or broken, just note it on the manifest. You actually have a bit of time to complete the review if you'd rather not do it now. I can imagine you've got a lot going on inside of you right now and this manifest is pretty low on your list of priorities."

"Thanks, Joanne. How about if we just enjoy our coffee for a few minutes and I'll turn to this when I turn to it?"

"That would be fine." At that point, Joanne opened her back pack and handed a thin package to Nikki.

"This won't be found on the manifest, Nikki, but it's no longer evidence. I know how you feel about what happens to items in the evidence room, so I thought you might like to know that it is not bouncing around in there. Technically, it belongs to the Millers' estate, but I can assure you that their executor was happy to rid himself of it and to have me dispose of it for him."

Nikki stared at the DVD.

"Is this the DVD of that night?"

"Yes."

"Did you watch it?"

"Yes, Nikki. It was part of my job."

"She was beautiful, wasn't she?"

"Very."

"You know, she was the standard against which I evaluated myself. And I always came up short. She was incredibly beautiful. She had a perfect body. She was incredibly smart, with a career that I am sure paid her tons of money. She had a husband who craved her, who lusted for her. I came up short all around. But she loved me anyway, and I loved her. But I only allowed myself to acknowledge our love once before it was snatched away."

Joanne looked at Nikki, at a loss for words. As she had when they first met, Joanne handed her a Kleenex to dry the tears forming in the corners of Nikki's eyes. After a few moments, Joanne found the silence to be unbearable.

"Nikki, I'm sorry for your loss. Apart from my Dad, I've never lost someone that I loved with all my heart. But remember, she loved you. Treasure that. And remind yourself that she didn't love you because she thought you didn't measure up. She loved you because you did. You are a very attractive woman; you turn people's heads; you obviously turned hers. You're smart. You're a nurse. You didn't become a nurse by taking a course from a correspondence school. Yes, Maryanne had a good career; she saved people a lot of money, I'm sure. But you help save people's lives, and that's quite a lot to be proud of. Maybe your husband did not hunger for you the way that Ted Miller lusted for Maryanne, but that was Jack's issue, not yours. If your marriage failed, it was because you were deceived into marrying someone who didn't love you and used you to create a false front to the world around him. Think about that. I hope it helps."

"Thank you, Joanne. It does."

Joanne finished her coffee and got up to leave. She shook Nikki's hand and told her to call when she had completed the review of the manifest.

After Joanne had left, Nikki went to her office. She hooked up her computer and inserted the DVD. Somewhat masochistically, she watched, entranced by the images of a love she would never know again and pained by the irrevocability of her loss. When she was done, she removed the DVD, broke it into pieces, went to her bedroom, and cried until she fell asleep.

Chapter 61

IN THE MONTH that followed, Nikki was happy to re-establish some normality in her life. She resumed her regular shifts at the hospital and enjoyed the camaraderie of her co-workers. Little things, like trips to the grocery store or the dry cleaner, seemed less boring than before. She took more time to enjoy white clouds in a blue sky, the sounds of birds, and the deep glow of sunsets. The crisis had come and gone, she had endured and survived, and her life was her own again. More and more, her face was graced by a smile that had melted many a male heart before she married Jack.

The crisis had left her a fairly wealthy woman. Jack had not been expelled from his law firm at the time of his death, so the $750,000 from the life insurance policy the firm provided for all partners was hers, as were the benefits from the separate $3 million policy on Jack's life they had obtained years before. Somewhat surprisingly to Nikki, Jack had purchased mortgage life insurance, and the house was now hers, free and clear of all debt. There were sizeable amounts in Jack's capital account at the law firm, and in his retirement and investment accounts. She spent quite some time with lawyers and accountants getting a handle on her newfound wealth. No, she did not need ever to work another day for the rest of her life, but she loved what she did and she continued to live as she had before.

She also continued to review the manifest that Joanne Tracey had left with her. When she had completed that somewhat mind-numbing process and consulted with Maria Romano to make sure she had dealt with it accurately, she called the station house and told Sergeant Tracey that she had completed her review. Nikki asked if she should bring it to the station house.

"There's no need to come here, Nikki. I'd think this is the last place you'd want to see. I can come by and pick it up. How about if I come by tomorrow after your shift? 5:30?"

"That will work. Thanks."

Joanne came by on time. Nikki asked her in and offered her something to drink. Joanne declined and they sat at the kitchen table while she quickly scanned Nikki's notations on the manifest. Everything looked to be in order.

"I'm really sorry about all this, Nikki."

"All what, Joanne? There's a lot to choose from."

"Well, we had no control over what happened to the Millers, but I am sorry about that. But we could control how we approached the investigation, and we did not treat you well in that process. Inspector Milliken convinced himself too soon that you were guilty, and he behaved accordingly. I can't undo that. All I can say is I'm sorry."

"You never treated me badly, Joanne, so don't be too hard on yourself."

"Well, I'd like to make it up to you, Nikki."

"No need, Joanne."

"I want to. How about dinner this Friday?"

Until that moment, Nikki had never given a thought to Joanne Tracey's sexual orientation. Now, she quickly came to sense not only that Joanne liked women, but that Joanne liked Nikki in particular.

"Are you asking me for a date, Joanne?"

Joanne's smile turned sheepish in an instant. "I am. I hope I haven't offended you."

"Why should I be offended? After all, I know that you know that I am not completely averse to the company of another woman. Not that I want to mislead you, Joanne. I like men. Always have. What you saw on that DVD between Maryanne and me was the only time I have been with another woman."

Nikki let her disclaimer sink in before continuing, "Look, I haven't been out socially since the night the Millers died. It'll do me good to get out. Sure. I'll have dinner with you. But again, I don't want to mislead you, Joanne. That night with the Millers was the only time I've ever done that. Do you understand?"

Joanne was quick to respond. "Yes, I understand. I don't know what kind of woman you think I am, Nikki, but my intention is to have a nice dinner with someone I think I like. I'm not going to be crawling all over you. Please give me more credit than that."

"Now I'm the one who has to apologize. I'm sorry. Let me put it this way—I would enjoy having dinner with you on Friday, Joanne. Do you think this is going to get you crosswise with the good Inspector?"

"It shouldn't. I can spend my off-duty hours any way I want and with whom I want as long as it doesn't affect an ongoing case. And you've been exonerated. If Milliken has a problem with that, he'll have to learn to live with it."

"OK. It's a date. Where and when?"

Chapter 62

AS SHE PREPARED for dinner on Friday, Nikki felt a pang of remorse for having accepted the date. Joanne had asked her out for the customary reasons that people date—to have some fun, to get better acquainted, to see if there might be a basis for an ongoing relationship. Nikki had none of these in mind. Notwithstanding her love for Maryanne Miller and their one night of passion, Nikki regarded herself as heterosexual. Her interest in an evening with Joanne Tracey had nothing to do with sex. She had no sexual interest in Joanne Tracey. Nikki was looking for information . . . and closure.

As much as Nikki wished to put the entire police investigation in her rear-view mirror, she wanted to know more about the process. She knew it was somewhat masochistic, but she wanted to know what it was about her—Nicole Beaumont—that drove Inspector Milliken to hate her, and she wanted to know what it was, really, that caused the police to continue to place her in their crosshairs when her lawyer had so clearly explained the holes in Inspector Milliken's theories. She wanted to know how the police came to redirect their attention. And she wanted to know what role Joanne Tracey played in each stage of this melodrama. Nikki knew she was using Joanne and, while she felt bad about it, she did not feel bad enough to cancel the dinner date.

Given her utilitarian approach to this dinner, Nikki dressed in a surprisingly chic manner. She wore a black suede skirt that ended two inches above the knee, black sling backs with three-inch heels, and a long-sleeved oyster-white blouse with a scooped neck. A diamond pendant was suspended just above the scoop of her blouse, and three diamond tennis bracelets were layered on her right wrist. A diamond and opal cocktail ring graced the third finger of her left hand, where her engagement and wedding rings used to reside. They had lost all meaning for her. They now sat, on consignment, in a display case in Aaron Long's jewelry emporium.

Joanne arrived at Nikki's front door at 7:45, as planned. Nikki had never seen Joanne out of her police uniform and, at first, she almost did not recognize her. Joanne's hair had always been pulled back and tied off to accommodate her police cap. Now, for the first time, Nikki realized that Joanne had honey blonde hair that rested against the top of her shoulders. In place of her police uniform, she wore pleated, charcoal gray slacks, a wine-colored, long-sleeved blouse, and Gucci loafers. A thin gold chain encircled her neck, suspended from which was a diamond-encrusted onyx pendant. It was obvious to Nikki that Joanne wanted to look good for this date and Nikki was forced to admit that Joanne had achieved her goal. She looked quite stylish. She was no Maryanne Miller to be sure, but she was no longer Sergeant Joanne Tracey. No, she was Joanne Tracey, a woman with a nice smile who wanted to impress her date.

"That's quite a pendant, Joanne."

"It's my Mom's. She thought it would look good with the blouse."

"She was right. Do you live with your mother?"

"We live together. It's my house. I asked her to move in with me after my Dad passed away a few years ago and she agreed. We get along well. She loves me unconditionally and everyone should have someone in their life who does that. For me, it's my Mom."

"That's great. Unfortunately, my folks both passed on some time ago. I was an only child, so since then, it's been me and my husband. And we both know the only person he loved unconditionally—or at all—was himself. Oh well, enough of that. Would you like a cocktail before we head out?"

"No thanks. I can wait until we get to the restaurant."

The drive to the restaurant took about twenty minutes and they filled the vacuum with talk of the weather and how liberating it was for Nikki to be out from under the threat of indictment. When they arrived, Joanne handed the keys to the parking valet and they went in. Joanne did not need to give the maître d' her name. He recognized her immediately.

"Good evening, Sergeant Tracey. We have a lovely table for you tonight."

They were seated at a table along the wall of the restaurant that faced a lake. Lights shimmered on the water, and Nikki thought that the setting would have been perfect for a romantic dinner. She thought, wistfully, of how nice it would have been to share a meal in this setting with Maryanne Miller. Nikki asked how often Joanne came to this restaurant.

"Not as often as that greeting or this table would suggest. But once they know you are a police officer, they treat you well. I guess it's a perk of the job."

The waiter attentively asked if they would like to order a cocktail and they both nodded their assent. Nikki ordered an Angel's Envy Old Fashioned and Joanne a Tom Collins. While they waited for the drinks to arrive Nikki got the conversation going by asking Joanne about herself, her family, her upbringing, her education, and all of the questions that folks feel comfortable answering when they date. It was her hope that, when the conversation turned to the investigation, Joanne would have grown so accustomed to talking with Nikki that there would be no push back. She was right. After a sip from her Old Fashioned, Nikki turned to the investigation.

"Tell me about Inspector Milliken, Joanne. I got the sense he hated me from almost the minute we met."

"He did, Nikki."

"Why?"

"Because you told him that you had cheated on your husband with the Millers. You see, Jim was married to a very attractive woman. He adored her. How can I put this? Lori was the queen of all sluts. She didn't just have an affair. She had lots of affairs. Lots of men. They tried counseling, but Lori found it impossible to keep her hands off any good-looking stud or her body out of their beds. Ever since their divorce, Jim has taken an instant dislike to any female suspect who has violated her marriage vows. He sees Lori in them, and he immediately thinks the worst of them. He transfers his antipathy for Lori to them. That's why he immediately thought the worst of you."

"Isn't there a pretty big gulf between adultery and murder, Joanne? Couldn't Milliken see that, couldn't he appreciate it?"

"Objectively, sure. But not emotionally. Not for the longest time. And you have to admit, Nikki, that there were some pretty bad facts for you here. You were at the murder scene; supposedly, nobody else was in the house; you made the drinks that killed them; and you handed the drinks to them. Leave aside Milliken's judgments about your morality, which are unrelated to the murders, the facts gave you an opportunity to commit the crime that nobody else had and you actually gave them the instruments of their deaths. Put those facts on the table, mix in Milliken's personal bias regarding wayward wives, and it made for a good case in Jim's mind."

"Is that how you describe me, Joanne? A wayward wife?"

"I don't get hung up on labels, Nikki, and I'm no moralist. We all have needs. I'm sure you had your reasons."

"Do you want to hear them?"

"Only if you want to tell me."

"I already told you I had been in love with Maryanne Miller for quite some time. I knew that she loved me, but I had suppressed my feelings for her. And my marriage had been dead for even longer than that, and you know why, but I didn't, not then. That night, we had a bit too much to drink and we started getting playful in the spa. Maryanne asked me to kiss her and, in that moment, everything seemed to come together, years of disinterest from my husband, years of suppressed desire for Maryanne, enough alcohol to eliminate my inhibitions, the warm water, the moon, the feel of Ted's and Maryanne's bodies against mine, the gentle nature of Ted's kiss, the hunger in Maryanne's. None of this makes it right. It just provides context. I could have left at any time, I should have left."

"None of us is perfect, Nikki. You loved her. That was the overriding emotion."

"Tell me, Joanne. Did you ever think that this wayward wife was a murderer?"

"No. I thought you were innocent from the very beginning, and I kept telling Jim that."

"How did Milliken react to your pushback?"

"Not well. It got a bit testy at times. But, to his credit, he did let me run my theories to ground to avoid a rush to judgment on your guilt."

"Why did you feel strongly enough in my innocence to stand up to your boss that way?"

"Lots of reasons. You had made love to these people. They were your friends. People don't usually kill their lovers under those circumstances unless the sex had turned violent. There was no evidence of a struggle. Not a mark on their bodies."

"And their deaths clearly stunned you. I watched the video of that night. When you awoke in the morning, the look of shock and anguish on your face was obvious. I listened to your 911 call. You were hardly coherent. And I watched you as Jim and his team worked the bedroom. You were still crying. By all accounts, you're a talented nurse, Nikki, but you can't be that good an actress. Those were real tears."

"Also, to me, it made no sense for you to stay in the house if you were the killer. The killer would have cleared out, taking all the evidence that might link him or her to the killings. You didn't. You stayed. You lay beside them as they quietly breathed their last. It would have been truly ghoulish for you to have done that if you were the killer. You never struck me that way."

"And there was always the question of motive. No, Nikki, I never thought you did it. Not once."

Joanne paused for a moment and added, "But, Nikki, understand this—if the evidence had ultimately led to you, we would not be sitting here tonight. I'm a cop. If the evidence suggested you were guilty, I'd have arrested you."

Nikki had never spoken with Joanne about the case, and she sat there impressed by Joanne's analysis and appreciative of her faith in Nikki's innocence, and by her honesty. They continued to talk about how the focus shifted from Nikki to Randy Carmichael and then to Jack, the videos of Jack, Randy Carmichael, and Ted, and whether Nikki had ever thought that her husband was interested in other men. Nikki admitted to her own naivete and to her belief that Jack's real libidinous interest was in Maryanne Miller and whatever girlfriends he entertained in Los Angeles. Joanne told of the bulletin she had sent to neighboring police departments and how they got lucky when the killer OD'd with phenobarbital among his effects and even luckier when he got sloppy and failed to destroy the slips of paper, which he apparently never used, which they deciphered to link Jack's hotel room to the assassin.

"We don't think the contract included Maryanne Miller. Ted was the target. Maryanne was collateral damage. And you would have been collateral damage too if you were a gin drinker. Thankfully, you prefer Greyhounds, and that's why you are alive and sitting across the table from me tonight." Joanne took a moment, looked directly into Nikki's violet eyes, and smiled. "I'm very happy that you preferred Greyhounds that night, Nikki. Very happy."

Nikki thought about the slim divide between life and death and how survival can result from choices that we make that are, when made, innocuous. A Martini? Death. A Greyhound? Life. If Maryanne had taken Nikki up on her offer of a Greyhound, she would be alive and she might be sitting where Joanne was sitting tonight. But Maryanne wasn't there, and she never would be there.

Nikki asked about Jack's death. She knew it had been ruled a suicide, but she was interested in Joanne's opinion. Frankly, Nikki believed that Jack was too egomaniacal to have taken his own life.

"The official pronouncement is suicide, Nikki. My opinion doesn't matter."

"It does to me, Joanne. You were right about so many things in the case. Your opinion would be meaningful to me."

Joanne blushed at the compliment. She had received plenty of compliments from the women she dated, particularly after they had shared each other's bodies. While they could be profuse in their appreciation for Joanne's bedroom skills, none had ever expressed the kinds of opinions about Joanne's intelligence and professional competence that Nikki offered. As she looked across the table at her dinner partner and listened, Nikki's compliments affected Joanne like an aphrodisiac.

"No, Nikki. I don't think that Jack killed himself. His suicide note was typed on his laptop immediately under notes he had prepared to share with his trial lawyer. Those notes suggested a certain confidence in escaping conviction. Given that optimism, why the quick turnaround into the ultimate act of depression? There's just no evidence that helps us make the leap from 'I can beat this rap' to the erosion of all hope. None."

"If you're right, who murdered Jack?"

"I have no way of identifying the murderer, or murderers. My suspicion is that it was someone who was connected with the hiring of the substitute bartender to get rid of Ted Miller. Maybe they were concerned that Jack would say something in attempting to plea bargain his way out of this that might have implicated one or more of his accomplices. They obviously regarded their own skins as a heck of a lot more valuable than Jack's, so better safe than sorry. He had to go."

"And Milliken didn't care who killed Jack?"

"No, Nikki. And frankly, neither did I. Jack was an evil man. He was callous, cold blooded, and calculating. He wanted to get rid of Ted Miller for mercenary reasons and he did not care who else got hurt in the process. Like Maryanne. And like you."

"But . . ."

"No buts, Nikki. Leaving aside the niceties of the law, Jack got what he deserved. Tell me honestly. Did you mourn his passing? Did you cry yourself to sleep that night?"

"No, he had killed the only woman I ever loved, and he hurt me more than anyone ever had, or could. I didn't mourn."

"And based on what we heard from Jack's lawyer, Jack's defense at trial would have laid bare the skeletons in a host of Highland Estates closets, all designed to besmirch other folks' reputations, fabricate motives for their elimination of Ted Miller, and divert attention from Jack's motive for Ted's murder. No, I'd say that whoever fashioned the noose around Jack's neck did the community a favor."

While Nikki ruminated on Joanne's seeming appreciation for the societal benefits of Jack's unexpected demise, the waiter cleared the remnants of their main courses and delivered the steaming chocolate soufflés with vanilla ice cream they had ordered when selecting their entrees. Joanne punctured her soufflé to allow the steam to vent, spooned out some of its delectable contents, cooled it with a dollop of the ice cream, and closed her eyes in obvious enjoyment as she began to consume her dessert. As much as Nikki wanted to explore the warm flavorful confection sitting in front of her, she wanted even more to explore what it was that made Joanne Tracey tick.

"You enjoy police work, don't you, Joanne?"

"Yes. I can't think of anything else I'd rather do."

"Why? It's a dangerous profession."

"It's hard to say. It can be exciting, and I like excitement. And I've always thought that people had a right to be safe, and police work was a way to make that happen. I really can't explain it any more directly."

"Has anyone ever shot at you, Joanne?"

"Once. We were responding to a domestic disturbance call. To me, those are always the worst. Emotions run high and they are completely unpredictable. We get there and we seem to have the guy calmed down and ready to let his woman go and throw down his gun when he freaks out and just starts firing. He hits me and I go down from the force of the shot into my Kevlar vest. My partner doesn't hesitate. He squeezes off three shots and they all hit home. I might not be here if he hadn't. Great guy—Carmine Faraldo. Twenty years on the force and that was the first time he ever fired his gun in anger. He retired within the year."

"And you still want to do this kind of work?"

"It's my life, Nikki. It's what I do."

"Have you ever needed to fire your gun in anger, Joanne?

"No."

"Do you think you could?"

"That's what we train for. But I hope I never need to find out if I could, or how it would affect me if I did."

Nikki admired Joanne's lack of false bravado. She was honest enough to admit that she might not be up to the task when the moment of truth arrived. For reasons she could not explain, Nikki concluded that Joanne would do what needed to be done if and when the time came.

As they lingered over coffee, Joanne turned the conversation to Nikki, her upbringing, her education, her nursing career. Joanne listened intently and asked follow-up questions that reflected a genuine interest in the woman seated across from her. Nikki found it refreshing to be able to answer questions that were not designed to trap her into admissions that might be twisted or contorted by a prosecutor at trial. And she found Joanne's interest in her to be endearing. She liked Joanne.

They finished their dinner and Joanne beat Nikki to the check. "I asked you out, Nikki. My treat."

Chapter 63

 the ride to Nikki's home was as predictable as the sunrise. The food, the wine, the service, follow-up questions regarding snippets of the personal life histories they had exchanged. As would be expected, Joanne kept her eyes on the road ahead. Nikki did not. She shifted in her seat so that she could look at Joanne. As the night time shadows and the lights from oncoming cars passed in alternating fashion over Joanne's face, Nikki struggled to find the words that best described that face. Joanne was not a pretty woman. She certainly was not the kind of woman who would have been selected to man the "Kissing Booth" at an old time county fair. Like a lot of women with average or ordinary looks, however, her face could be transformed by a smile. Nikki was no linguist, but when Joanne smiled, she could be somewhat "fetching." Yes, "fetching" was the right word. It fit. Joanne was a nice woman, amiable and engaging, with a fetching smile. The small, faint scar alongside the left corner of her lower lip only made that smile more interesting and invested it with character.

Joanne was not only fetching, she was smart. She had impressed Nikki with her doggedness in pursuing other suspects based on their "star turns" in Ted Miller's video extravaganzas and with her decision to send the notice to neighboring departments regarding phenobarbital. That notice had combined with sheer luck to cough up Jack's hotel number among the personal effects of the heroin-addicted faux bartender.

As the ride continued, Nikki suddenly realized that she found the woman with whom she had just shared dinner to be quite appealing. The closer the ride took her to her home, the more Nikki realized that she did not want the evening to end quite yet. Although she was late in coming to this realization, her night with Maryanne had forever shattered Nikki's ability to deny her suppressed bisexual urges. As a result, she found herself thinking of Joanne Tracey as someone with whom physical intimacy might be fun tonight. And whether it was the period of extended celibacy that she had endured since that night with the Millers, gratitude for Joanne's faith in her throughout the investigation, her desire for the touch of another woman, or that fetching smile, Nikki began to wonder whether Joanne's body would prove to be as fetching as her smile. Nikki could feel her pulse quicken as she thought about what she might do to obtain an answer to that question. She had never tried to seduce another woman. The thought had never crossed her mind, but she now wondered whether her choice of attire for the evening reflected, all along, a subliminal desire to do just that. Nikki resolved that, one way or another, she and Joanne would become much better acquainted before the night was done. Nikki found herself surprisingly thrilled by the thought of enticing Joanne Tracey into her bed.

Joanne turned into Nikki's circular driveway and stopped outside Nikki's front door. Before Joanne could utter a word, Nikki asked Joanne in for a nightcap.

Chapter 64

JOANNE LOOKED AROUND and realized that Nikki's place was large enough to hold two or three of Joanne's home.

"You certainly have a lot of room, Nikki."

"Yes. Don't ask me why. I assumed Jack wanted the space for business entertaining, but he never really did much of that. In any event, it was a short commute for me to the hospital, and I had Maryanne next door."

As she said it, Nikki realized her mistake. Talk of her deceased lover was not the right springboard for a seduction of Joanne Tracey. Seeking to move on from her faux pas, Nikki said that, with her husband dead, the house was now hers. She was thinking about selling it and buying a smaller place, either a condominium or a townhouse, preferably closer to St. Peters Hospital.

"I have a townhouse," said Joanne. "I like having a small, low maintenance yard where I can plant a flower garden."

"You like to garden?"

"I like flowers and it is cheaper to grow them than to buy them."

Nikki walked into the dining room and Joanne followed. As Nikki approached the liquor cabinet, she asked Joanne what she would like.

"I know you are a fan of Greyhounds. I've never had one. Can you make me one?"

Nikki made two tall Greyhounds. She moved to the end of the dining table and pushed the chair next to her away from the table, and then pulled it close to hers on a diagonal, as an invitation for Joanne to sit beside her. Joanne thanked Nikki for the drink and sat down. Joanne took a sip of the Greyhound. She raised the glass ever so slightly in Nikki's direction and smiled. "I like it."

Nikki kicked off her heels and crossed her legs, hiking her skirt high on her thigh to give Joanne a good look. Joanne looked, then she looked away, focusing instead on Nikki's eyes. Nikki allowed the silence to linger for a few moments, smiling demurely at Joanne. Joanne realized that Nikki was flirting with her, but other women had flirted with her in this manner and gone no further. Nonetheless, Joanne regarded the possibility of a night with Nikki Beaumont as worth the disappointment if Nikki were simply toying with her. She was determined to play out this scene. She returned Nikki's smile and took another look at Nikki's thigh, a long, lingering look. Joanne could not hide her interest. She didn't even try, and her interest excited Nikki.

"Tell me, Joanne, why did you ask me out?"

Joanne blushed. "I like women, Nikki. And I was attracted to you from the moment I first saw you."

"At the Millers'? Disheveled and crying? You were attracted to that?"

"Yes. I don't know how to explain it. It was easy to look past the tears and see that you were a pretty woman, and I like pretty women."

Nikki liked the direction in which this conversation was heading. "Thank you for the compliment. It's nice to hear someone tell me that. My husband sure didn't."

"He had other interests, Nikki. Believe me, no one interested in women would ever find you to be anything other than attractive. Very attractive."

Joanne went on, telling Nikki in some detail why she found Nikki to be so appealing. "I think maybe I saw you as sort of a damsel in distress, a pretty damsel in distress who needed someone to make sure she was treated fairly, to be protected from Milliken's bias against women who find comfort outside of their marriages. As the investigation went on, I learned more and more about you. Every time you were interviewed, you projected intelligence, strength, and grace. I admired that and I came to realize not only that I was attracted to you physically, but that I liked you. And every person who I interviewed spoke highly of you, that you were a kind and caring person, a top notch nurse, and a good friend. It confirmed everything that I thought. So, I swore to myself that, when the investigation was over, if you were exonerated, I would try to see if you might have any interest in getting to know me better, as I had come to know you."

Joanne paused, not sure of how to continue. As she had spoken, she noticed that Nikki had never lost eye contact with her. Joanne hoped that this was not a mere courtesy, and that is reflected a genuine interest in what the night might hold in store for them. Nikki did not say anything. She continued to look at Joanne intently and, after what seemed like an eternity to Joanne, Nikki flashed a flirtatious smile that encouraged Joanne to continue.

"I know that I'm not a pretty woman. I know that. I don't have a face that grabs and holds someone's attention. I wish I did, but I don't. Maybe

I am deluding myself, but I live with the perpetual hope that a woman like you might find me to be interesting and that, perhaps, you might find something about me that was attractive. I hope you do."

"Why do you think I asked you in for a nightcap, Joanne?"

Before Joanne could respond, Nikki laid her hand on top of Joanne's as they sat at the table. Joanne felt a rush of emotion and hoped that Nikki felt the same. Nikki left her hand in place. Joanne did as well. It seemed like forever before either of them spoke.

"Is there anyone special in your life right now, Joanne?"

"No, no one special. I don't have a ton of admirers lined up outside my door, Nikki."

Nikki could sense the longing in Joanne's response. She wanted to let Joanne know that, tonight, she was with someone who did admire her. Even more, Nikki wanted to telegraph in no uncertain terms that she did not want Joanne to be going home, at least not anytime soon.

"I find that hard to believe. From the moment I opened the door when you rang the bell until now, I've been admiring you. There's a lot to admire. Your smile. And your eyes. A person could get lost in those beautiful blue eyes."

As she spoke, Nikki found herself increasingly drawn to Joanne Tracey, with feelings of affection she had not anticipated when she embarked on what she expected to be a purely physical seduction. Joanne's eyes were mesmerizing. Without breaking eye contact, Nikki took Joanne's free hand and slowly guided it under Nikki's skirt along the top of her exposed thigh. It electrified Joanne in a way she had not felt in quite some time and she emitted an audible sigh as her hand moved up the firmly toned flesh of that gorgeous thigh. It was clear that Nicole Beaumont, the Nicole Beaumont whom she had desired from afar, actually wanted Joanne Tracey, at least for tonight. Joanne's heart began to race. It raced even faster when Nikki leaned forward, eliminating the gap between them. Nikki placed her hand under Joanne's golden tresses and gently pulled her neck ever so slightly forward until their lips met. Nikki slid her tongue slowly, first back and forth across Joanne's moist lips, and then between those lips into the moist warmth beyond.

In that moment, as their tongues touched, Nikki discovered that Joanne knew how to reciprocate a kiss. Nikki had always enjoyed kissing. For her, it was an essential first act in lovemaking. In fact, before she married Jack, many a would-be relationship cratered on the shoals of an uninspired kiss. That would not be the case tonight. Joanne Tracey knew how to kiss, and she knew how to be kissed. That discovery made the prospect of this encounter all the more thrilling for Nikki. When their lips parted and Nikki pulled back, she was transported by the scent of Joanne's perfume.

"Your perfume? It's Angel, isn't it, Joanne?"

"Do you like it, Nikki?"

"It's intoxicating. And so appropriate. Angel perfume for the guardian angel who kept Inspector Milliken from railroading me to an indictment."

Nikki's voice had dropped and she was now speaking in a breathless near whisper. "How can I thank you, Joanne? What can I do to show you how much I appreciate what you did? How does a damsel in distress reward her rescuer? Just ask me. Anything you want."

"I'll take your gratitude if that's what you're offering, Nikki. But what I really want is for you to like me, and to show me you like me in a special way."

"There's nothing I would enjoy more, Joanne."

As Nikki spoke, Joanne slid her hand further up Nikki's thigh until there was nowhere else to go, stroking it gently. When she probed beyond the wet elastic of Nikki's satin briefs, Joanne elicited an gasp of pleasure from Nikki that encouraged Joanne to continue, heightening Nikki's ever-increasing desire for the pleasures yet to come.

The feel of Joanne's fingers inside her was glorious and Nikki had no desire for Joanne to stop. When Joanne withdrew her hand, Nikki pleaded with Joanne to resume her exhilarating caress of Nikki's inner sanctum. But Nikki's protestations were quickly quieted when Joanne pressed her moist fingers against Nikki's lips and into her mouth, where Nikki enjoyed, for the first time, a taste of her own femininity. Joanne then cupped Nikki's face in her hands and kissed her. It was a passionate kiss, one that communicated in no uncertain terms the hunger that Joanne had for the woman she was kissing. It was a kiss to which Nikki knew she could easily, and eagerly, become accustomed, a kiss that was both giving and demanding, a kiss that foreshadowed the far more intimate kisses that Nikki planned to share with Joanne Tracey that night. Nikki had no desire to delay further the ultimate satisfaction of the lust that had been building with every smile, every look, every compliment, and every touch that they had exchanged. Nikki stood, took Joanne by the hand, and led her to the bedroom. They removed their clothes, neither of them losing sight of the other as they disrobed, each of them smiling at what the other was offering.

It was in this bedroom that Nikki had experienced so much disappointment with Jack. There would be no such disappointment tonight. She was transfixed by the sight of the woman standing before her. Joanne was nothing like she had expected. Nikki had only been with one woman, Maryanne Miller. Joanne's body was nothing like Maryanne's. Joanne was much taller and it was only now, having removed her heels, that Nikki realized just how much Joanne towered over her. Nikki was not short, clocking in at 5 feet 6 inches, but Joanne had her by at least five inches, maybe more. Maryanne had been soft and slender, with the body of a swimsuit model. Joanne was not slender and she would never pass for a model. Her frame was thicker, which was hardly surprising given her height, but she could never be described as "soft." There did not appear to be an ounce of excess anywhere. Her entire upper body was firm and hard, the contours of her muscles obvious and impressive. Joanne had clearly worked hard to create the body on which Nikki now fixated. It was beautifully muscled, but without bulk. She had broad shoulders, a hard core, and well-developed arms. The words "chiseled" and "ripped" entered Nikki's mind. She had seen men whose bodies fit that description, including Jack. She found them to be incredibly attractive and, before her marriage, she had succumbed with great enthusiasm to a number of such men. Those hard bodies were hard to resist and Nikki never put up much of an effort to do so. She wanted those men, she loved the feel of their bodies against hers, and she gave them full rein over her body while doing her best in return to please them in every way imaginable. But this was the first woman she had ever seen up close and personal who fit that bill and Nikki could not believe the surge of excitement and the feral hunger for Joanne that began to consume her as she drank in the taut, sinewy female body that Joanne was offering to share with her.

Joanne's legs were long, befitting her height. Those legs would not cause heads to turn the way Maryanne's did, but they were firm and nice enough to cause Nikki's eyes to linger as she envisioned what it would be like to nestle between those rock hard thighs and please Joanne as she had Maryanne on that fateful night. As her eyes moved up those legs, Nikki saw that Joanne's pubic hair had been reduced to a thin blonde vertical strip decorating a beautifully curved and muscled abdomen.

Nikki had never been a fan of ink or piercings. All of that changed in an instant. A colorful tattoo of an orange and black Monarch butterfly graced the space below Joanne's right clavicle and a red rose decorated the top of her left thigh. A glittering diamond adorned her navel. Nikki marveled at the unanticipated effect the body art had on Nikki's desire for Joanne.

Nikki congratulated herself on her decision to seduce Joanne Tracey. Everything about Joanne's body appealed to Nikki—not just the well-defined musculature of her torso, but also the rest of the physical package—the honey blonde hair, the blue eyes, the long legs, the broad shoulders, the ink, the pierced navel, the smile . . . and her kisses. Unlike her night with Maryanne Miller, her desire for Joanne Tracey was not driven by love, or anything akin to love. They were essentially strangers. But with every minute that passed between the time Nikki watched the shadows crossing Joanne's face on the ride home until now, Nikki's lust for Joanne had been building, rising within Nikki like magma prior to a volcanic eruption. Nikki thought it curious that she could want another woman as much as she desired Joanne right now without love factoring into the equation. But she did. Nikki found Joanne's body to be riveting. She could not take her eyes off it. She could not wait to feel the press of Joanne's firm flesh against hers and to explore, in every way possible, the most intimate recesses of Joanne's impressive body. Nikki's seduction of Joanne Tracey was going to be incredibly enjoyable.

Joanne, in turn, enjoyed the sight of Nikki's naked body, a body that she had seen during the investigation, in her review of Ted Miller's digital library. Joanne had long desired to share that body. But Joanne's desire for Nikki was not purely physical. Nikki was attractive, yes, but Joanne had shared the night with many women, dating back to her college years. As Joanne struggled to find someone with whom she could share her life, she had been with younger women, older women, married women; beautiful women, pretty women, plain women; submissive women and dominating women. These playmates had their own unique charms, all in varying degrees, and they were happy to share them with Joanne. And Joanne was happy to revel in those charms and to reciprocate. It broke the cycle of loneliness that too often dominated her existence. But these were casual liaisons. None of them evolved into anything approximating a meaningful relationship. Moreover, as attractive as many of those women were, and as satisfying as some were in the bedroom, no other woman had ever occupied Joanne's thoughts on a continuing basis the way that Nicole Beaumont did. In her dreams, Joanne frequently burned with envy as digital images filled her nights, images of Maryanne Miller fondling Nikki and of Maryanne writhing as Nikki raised Maryanne's bottom and buried her face between Maryanne's legs. Joanne had long ached for that same experience and now her lustful dreams of Nicole Beaumont were about to become Joanne Tracey's reality.

Joanne walked toward Nikki. She placed her hands on Nikki's shoulders and ran her nails lightly down Nikki's back, causing Nikki to shudder. Then Joanne turned Nikki around so that her back was facing Joanne. Joanne wrapped her left arm around Nikki's waist from behind and let it travel down to the moist, ultimate object of Joanne's desire. As the fingers of Joanne's left hand stroked her, Nikki placed her own left hand on Joanne's and directed Joanne's long, slender fingers inside her once again, allowing them free rein to probe at will and eliciting soft moans from Nikki that impelled Joanne to probe ever more deeply.

While her left hand heightened Nikki's desire, Joanne used her right hand to cup Nikki's right breast.

"They're small, Joanne."

"They're lovely." Joanne toyed with Nikki's nipple and repeated her assessment—"Lovely." Joanne then leaned her head forward, drinking in the scent of Nikki's Black Opium. Joanne found herself intoxicated by the hints of orange blossoms and jasmine, all of which enhanced Nikki's allure immeasurably. With her tongue, Joanne slowly traced an arc around the back of Nikki's right ear. Nikki shivered with excitement as Joanne did so, and she shivered even more as Joanne proceeded to nibble on Nikki's earlobe and then to do the same, with considerably more force, on the back of her neck and on her soft white shoulders. Nikki felt a rush of pleasurable pain as her knees weakened.

Joanne spoke in whispered tones, "I want you, Nikki. I want to do things to you that no one has ever done . . . I want to please you like no one ever has. I don't want you ever to forget this night. Ever."

In an instant, Nikki realized, in a manner that was beyond her control, that the script for this seduction had been flipped. Nikki was no longer the one doing the seducing. Nikki was more aroused than she ever could have imagined by Joanne's body and by the thought of being taken by this tall, powerful woman. She was fascinated by Joanne's tightly muscled body and she wanted to be taken, taken in any way that Joanne chose, taken in every imaginable way that one woman could impose her libidinous will on another.

Joanne turned Nikki around so that they were facing each other. She again wrapped her arms around Nikki and pressed her body sinuously against Nikki's slender frame. It was an embrace from which Nikki could not escape, and one from which she did not want to escape. The thought of being physically and emotionally dominated in the bedroom by another woman had never crossed her mind, but now, with Joanne's arms wrapped around her and her head resting against Joanne's shoulder, Nikki luxuriated in that prospect. She looked up and found herself drifting into the cerulean sea of Joanne's eyes. They kissed again. Joanne's prior kiss, as enjoyable as it was, paled in comparison. Nikki knew it was only her imagination, but she felt as if Joanne had reached into her very soul, lighting a fire that burned with an orgiastic desire unlike any Nikki had ever known. As their tongues intertwined, Nikki quivered, helpless in the arms of a woman to whom she wanted to submit, a woman to whom she wished to surrender herself completely.

Joanne scooped Nikki up with ease and placed her gently on the cool, crisp sheets. Joanne walked to the other side of the bed, climbed on and knelt, bidding Nikki to kneel as well, their bodies facing each other. Joanne took Nikki's face in her hands, and ran her tongue slowly across Nikki's lips. Joanne then placed one of her hands on Nikki's breast and began to fondle it gently, while her other hand reached around to softly caress Nikki's bottom. After a while, Joanne moved her hand from Nikki's breast to the bottom of her abdomen and lingered there, allowing her fingers to enjoy the wet warmth that told Joanne how much Nikki was enjoying their foreplay.

They moved from their knees and stretched out on the bed, locked in the kind of embrace for which Joanne Tracey had ached since she first laid eyes on a tearful Nicole Beaumont in the foyer of the Millers' home. And now, here she was, in bed with Nikki and holding her close. But, as responsive as Nikki was to Joanne's touch and to her kisses, Joanne could sense a tension in Nikki, a tension that she feared would impede Nikki's ability to enjoy the pleasure that lay before them. And Joanne wanted Nikki to enjoy this, to enjoy it like nothing she had ever experienced, to enjoy it in a way that would keep Nikki coming back for more. Joanne wanted to be the ultimate narcotic for Nicole Beaumont's lustful needs.

The tension she sensed in Nikki was not unfamiliar territory for Joanne. A number of her lovers had exhibited this type of initial anxiety when Joanne had induced them into their first lesbian experience. Although this was not Nikki's first time with a woman, she was far from experienced. Joanne rolled Nikki onto her stomach, kneeled over her, and began to massage her neck and shoulders. She massaged slowly and deeply using her strength to exorcise Nikki's anxiety. As she did so, Nikki—like those who had preceded her in Joanne's bed—sighed softly and relaxed visibly. The apprehension dissipated, as if the touch of Joanne's powerful hands had forced all of the tension out of Nikki's body. Joanne whispered softly in Nikki's ear, "What would you like me to do for you?" Nikki rolled onto her back, gazing up at Joanne.

"Whatever you want, Joanne . . . anything . . . everything . . . whatever you want."

"Anything, Nikki?"

"Anything, Joanne."

The surrender in Nikki's eyes elicited a feral lust within Joanne, a lust to savor Nikki's sweet surrender, to take her and ravish her, to have her way with Nikki's supple body, and—by pleasing her in every way possible—to own her.

Joanne had no expectation, when she asked Nikki to dinner, that they would end up in each other's arms. She had always fantasized about it, but she did not expect it, and certainly not this soon. But Joanne accepted Nikki's surrender with unbridled passion. Joanne was determined to justify Nikki's complete submission to Joanne's aggressive lust for her. Joanne drew on her experience with all of those other women to make this a night that Nikki would never—could never—forget.

Nikki was spellbound by the strength she felt in Joanne's hands as they explored the rest of Nikki's body. When Joanne's hands had left no part of Nikki's body unexplored, Joanne rolled Nikki onto her back and knelt bestride her, her knees alongside Nikki's hips. Joanne bent forward and focused all of her attention on Nikki's breasts. She traced a series of circles around the nipples with her tongue, then began to flick the tip of the nipples, alternating between them. Nikki had always regarded her breasts as the least of her assets, but Joanne had described them as "lovely" and she left no doubt that she had meant it. As Nikki's nipples became even harder and more erect, Joanne took them gently between her teeth and bit lightly. Nikki was startled at first and winced as she felt Joanne's teeth grab hold. But the initial stab of pain soon gave way to an incredible sensation of pleasure as Joanne slowly, and with the slightest pressure, dragged her teeth the length of the nipple, from base to tip, and proceeded to repeat that delectable journey several times. The pleasure only increased as Joanne transitioned her enthusiasm for Nikki's nipples from biting to sucking. She sucked hard, like an infant demanding the life giving sustenance of a mother's breast. Nikki moaned in delight and pleaded for more. "Don't stop, Joanne. Please don't stop." She didn't.

When Joanne had finished enjoying Nikki's breasts she moved forward on the bed, still kneeling, but with her knees now alongside Nikki's ribs. She reached out for Nikki's hands and, as their hands met, Joanne interlaced her fingers with Nikki's. Joanne then slowly but firmly pushed Nikki's arms down on the bed, their hands above Nikki's head. Nikki could not move, but she had no desire to move. Joanne leaned forward, kissing and biting Nikki's neck, throat, and shoulders, and then returning again to her lips and mouth, more aggressively than ever. The desire in that kiss was unconstrained and frenzied, and Nikki was consumed by Joanne's carnal desire for her, writhing as if she wanted to escape but knowing full well that escape was the last thing she wanted.

After what seemed like an enjoyable eternity, Joanne pulled back and, as she did, she released Nikki's hands. But she did not release Nikki. Instead, Joanne raised up and placed her hands on Nikki's shoulders, pinning her to the bed as if she were Joanne's prisoner. Nikki did not know where this interlude was headed, but she was eager to find out. As Joanne pushed Nikki fast against the bed, her lust for Nikki's total submission found full expression. As Nikki gazed up, Joanne ordered Nikki to declare her hunger for Joanne. In an insistent and strident tone that suggested a threat of corporal punishment for any wrong answers, Joanne demanded that Nikki confirm her desire for this tall, domineering blonde and her unconventional lovemaking:

> "Tell me you like me, Nikki."
> "Tell me you want me, Nikki."
> "Tell me you want more of me."
> "Tell me what more you want, Nikki."

Nikki did not understand why Joanne needed such reassurances. The response of Nikki's body to what Joanne was doing provided all the assurance that Joanne should have needed. Nonetheless, Nikki knew that something inside of Joanne needed to hear Nikki tell Joanne that she was desirable and that Nikki had not yet had her fill of Joanne Tracey. Nikki wondered whether this insecurity manifested itself when Joanne was with other women or whether it was unique to her communion with Nikki on this night, as if Joanne doubted her appeal to Nikki and her ability to please Nikki. There was no need for any such doubt. Nikki did find Joanne to be irresistible; her kisses were intoxicating; her lovemaking was breathtaking; her dominion over Nikki was electrifying; and Nikki wanted more, much more. She wanted more of Joanne's kisses, more of her incredible body, and more of the physical control and domination that she found so enthralling. To assuage Joanne's doubts, Nikki breathlessly affirmed each of Joanne's demands, not only because Joanne needed it, but also because Nikki could not, in good conscience, have answered in any other way.

When Nikki told Joanne what "more" she wanted, Joanne dropped from her knees, moved down and slid her hands underneath Nikki's bottom. She lifted Nikki ever so slightly and nestled her head where she could give Nikki the "more" she had asked for. As Joanne's tongue found its mark, Nikki lost all sense of time and place. She entered a kaleidoscopic realm in which images of Joanne Tracey and Maryanne Miller merged and dissolved into one another. One moment, Nikki was enjoying the taste of Joanne's kiss. The next, Maryanne Miller was caressing her in the shower, covering her with a rich lather, and exploring her body inside and out. Then she saw Joanne Tracey massaging her neck and shoulders to dispel Nikki's anxieties and prepare her for her fevered surrender to Joanne's will. She saw Maryanne Miller, her tanned legs dangling in the water of Nikki's pool as Maryanne confessed her love and her desire for Nikki. She saw Joanne Tracey's hand moving up under the soft, black suede of Nikki's skirt. She relived Joanne's enticing first kiss, a kiss that confirmed for Nikki the inevitability of where and how this night would end. That image faded and it was Maryanne Miller's turn once again to tantalize her as Nikki sat on her lap in the spa and kissed her for the first time, enjoying the touch of Maryanne's breasts as she did so. Image after image of Joanne and Maryanne making love to her passed in and out of view, each one intensifying the pleasure of the moment. When Nikki came, she pressed her hands against Joanne's broad shoulders and dug her nails into her muscled back. When Nikki's body convulsed with orgasmic pleasure, Joanne continued until Nikki cried out and shuddered a second time.

Joanne rolled onto her back, breathing heavily and smiling. Though she was looking at the ceiling, she was speaking to Nikki. "Show me how much you like me, Nikki."

Although she lacked Joanne's experience, there was nothing lacking in Nikki's enthusiasm for Joanne's body. And Joanne responded in kind, undulating with increasing rapidity and moaning with delight as Nikki proved to be an incredibly quick study in Sapphic love, using her hands, fingers, mouth, and tongue to explore every muscled contour of Joanne's body. Unlike Nikki, Joanne did not wrestle with images of any of her past lovers. She lost herself in the realization of her desire for Nicole Beaumont.

Nikki glistened with perspiration as she disengaged. She lay on her left side, facing Joanne. Nikki's left arm was bent at a 90 degree angle from the elbow, her head resting in her hand as she admired the taut body of the woman to whom she had just made love. She looked at Joanne with a smile that Joanne would later describe as radiant. Before tonight, Nikki had never thought she could enjoy making love to any woman other than Maryanne Miller. Joanne had thoroughly disabused her of that belief. The pleasure and release she experienced from her submission to Joanne Tracey was more than she thought to be possible. Nikki could no longer think of herself as heterosexual or simply "bi-curious." The pleasure she found in Joanne Tracey, and her desire for more of Joanne, would have made any such self-appraisal delusional.

"As first dates go, Joanne, I'd have to say this was pretty spectacular."

Joanne laughed. "Does that mean you'll give me a second date?"

"Frankly, Joanne, I'm not ready for our first date to end."

"Meaning . . . ?"

"I see three choices. One—you can get dressed, get in your car, and go home. If you do, I will be very disappointed. Two, we can kiss goodnight, pull up the covers and enjoy sleeping together. That's inviting, but I prefer No. 3 because I am too revved up to sleep and I want more time to be with you, to talk to you, to get to know you better, and to understand why I find you so irresistible. So, I suggest we pull on some warm robes and go sit on the sofa in the living room. I'll light a fire and then open a bottle of wine that's been waiting for a special occasion. I'd say this qualifies as special. And when we're done, we can return to the bedroom and enjoy our first night of sleeping together. What do you say?"

When Joanne nodded her agreement, Nikki went to the closet and came out with two knee- length terry cloth robes. She wrapped herself in one and handed the other to Joanne.

Chapter 65

JOANNE SETTLED ON the couch, her legs tucked under her the way that women do when they are truly comfortable. Having started the fire, Nikki went to the kitchen and returned with an open demi-bottle of chilled white wine. She poured the wine into two smallish glasses and handed one to Joanne.

"What is this, Nikki?"

"It's a dessert wine. A sauterne, I think. Chateau something or other. Jack bought it. He was an awful man but he had good taste in wines and he said that this was one of the best." As she too settled comfortably on the couch, close to Joanne, Nikki asked, "Do you like it?"

Joanne sipped and her smile answered that question. "Very sweet."

"Not as sweet as your kisses, Joanne."

Joanne cocked her head, raised her eyebrow and asked, "How many times have you used that line, Nikki?"

"Are you interrogating me, Sergeant?" Nikki smiled, an honest smile, and added "Never, Joanne. Never. Have you?"

Joanne blushed. "Yes, I have. Women love to receive such compliments. And I like to please my lovers."

"Based on my experience, you are quite successful at that."

"I've had my share of lovers. None of them ever lasted."

"Why not? I don't see what more anyone could want."

"The sex was usually good, sometimes incredibly good, but I wanted more than that. And it's really hard to find what I am looking for."

"What's that, Joanne?"

"I think you know. It's what most people want in life."

"What about men, Joanne?"

"I don't dislike men. I've been with men. And I've enjoyed them. I guess that makes me bi-sexual, but that's not how I think of myself. On a couple of occasions I've had girlfriends ask if their husbands could join us. I said yes because I wanted to please my girlfriends. It was obvious that the husbands enjoyed watching their wives get it on with another woman and, when my girlfriends and I finished, the wives would watch with equal enthusiasm as their husbands took their turn with me. It was amazing how wide-eyed with excitement the women could become when they watched their husbands fucking me. The women liked to watch. And I have to confess, I liked having them watch. It turned me on to fuck their husbands while they watched. The look in their eyes contributed immensely to my ability to get off with their men."

Joanne tried to read Nikki's reaction, but she couldn't. After a few moments' pause, she asked Nikki, "Does that make me a whore, Nikki?"

"Why would I think that, Joanne? Isn't that what I did with Ted and Maryanne Miller? I know just how exciting that can be."

As Nikki spoke, visions of Nikki taking Ted Miller inside her in every way imaginable while Maryanne watched filled Joanne's thoughts. She immediately regretted her candor regarding her history of threesomes. The last thing that Joanne wanted to do tonight was to resurrect in Nikki's mind memories of Maryanne Miller, or memories of the pleasures Nikki enjoyed with men. Joanne had pleased Nikki, there was no doubt of that, and she wanted memories of tonight to drive Nikki's sexual yearnings in the days and weeks to come. Joanne quickly sought to move on from her mention of the mixed threesomes she had enjoyed. But Nikki

"Would you like to do that with me, Joanne? A threesome?"

"I would hope that if I were in a relationship with a woman for whom I really cared, if what we had was more than physical, then neither one of us would need anyone else. That wasn't the case with the threesomes I told you about. Those women and I were bedmates who enjoyed each other's bodies and including their husbands was just another way to please my girlfriends. They wanted it and I wanted to please them. So I did. But I don't enjoy men the way I enjoy women. I prefer women. By a wide margin. I particularly like pretty women. Pretty women captivate me."

"Do I captivate you, Joanne?"

"You're very pretty."

"I could get accustomed to this."

"Do you mean me or women in general?"

"I mean you."

Nikki hesitated for a few seconds. "When you stood there at the foot of the bed, I was stunned by the effect your body had on me. It is so different from mine. Tell me, honestly, don't you prefer being with women with bodies like yours?"

"I like women with strong bodies, but I find someone like you far more exciting. You see, you have exactly the kind of body that I've always wanted to have." Nikki smiled and inched closer to Joanne. Joanne added, "Does that surprise you?"

"It does, but it pleases me."

Nikki moved still closer, so that their knees were touching as they spoke, She reached her free hand inside the folds of Joanne's robe and said, "Frankly, I'm finding it hard to keep my hands off you."

"Then don't. I like the feel of your hands on me."

Joanne stared at the fireplace and smiled, watching the flames flicker and dance. The heat thrown off by the fire felt good, a perfect complement to the feel of Nikki's hand inside her robe. She paused for a moment, leaned over to give Nikki a tender kiss, and then went on, "I was never a pretty girl. Let's face it, apart from the way I've developed my body, my looks are pretty ordinary."

Nikki tried to interrupt, but Joanne continued.

"I was not blessed like you with a slender, willowy frame or nicely curved legs that catch the eyes and cause them to linger in admiration. I wish I had been. I always envied girls and women with that kind of body. I was drawn to women with that kind of body and I wanted to have that kind of body so that other women would be drawn to me. But, try as I might—and I tried very hard—I could never shape my body to get anywhere close to what you have. So I decided to give up that chase and do something different, to set a goal that I actually could accomplish and make me feel good about myself. I started weight training when I was in college. I liked the results I was seeing. So did some of my female classmates. It opened the door to a number of relationships for me. I was amazed at how curious some very pretty co-eds were about a roll in the hay with a woman with a well-developed body."

Joanne hesitated for a few seconds, trying to read Nikki's reaction. Nikki sat silently, in rapt attention, her desire to learn as much as she could about Joanne evident on her face. Joanne continued.

"I liked being wanted, I liked being touched by other women, and I liked pleasing them. So I've kept up the training. Maybe it's egocentric, but I like the way I look. It's me. And I like it when other women find me to be attractive, when they eye me at the gym and try to gauge my interest in them. I liked the way you looked at me when I undressed. You liked what you saw and that was exciting to me. Frankly, I was concerned that you might find my body unattractive. More than a few women do. They say that a body like this is too mannish."

"Their loss. What I saw was strength and power. It was irresistibly seductive and incredibly thrilling. I felt that strength when you held me. I was helpless and . . . you know what? . . . I liked that feeling. I'm 34 years old and I've never had that feeling of pleasurable helplessness, and I certainly never expected it with another woman. I enjoyed the aggressive nature of your lovemaking, the intensity, the control. It was unlike any experience I've ever had."

After a few seconds of silence, Nikki made sure that Joanne understood what Nikki meant.

"I want to experience those feelings again, with you."

"I know that there are people who think my approach to sex is warped, but they don't understand. When another woman is willing to submit to me, to allow me to have my way with her completely, to dominate her, it intensifies my desire for her, and it increases in me my need—my obligation—to please her."

Joanne looked at Nikki, with an admixture of hope and trepidation.

"I did please you, didn't I, Nikki?"

"Do you have any doubts?"

"Did I hurt you?"

"I'd be lying if I said you didn't. I winced more than once, but I was surprised by how stimulating it was. I enjoyed every moment . . . every moment from beginning to end." Nikki hesitated for a moment before adding, "I don't think there is anything that you might do to me in the bedroom that I would not willingly embrace."

Joanne looked at Nikki quizzically.

"Nikki, tonight barely scratched the surface of how I like to make love, what I've done with other women, and what I would like to do with you. It's not for everyone."

"I'm not everyone, Joanne. You gave me a taste tonight of something I've never experienced. And I loved it . . . I loved it . . . and I want more. I said I was game for anything with you, Joanne. Anything. Do you understand what I am telling you?"

"I understand what you're saying, Nikki. I'm not sure you understand what that means."

"I think I do. I haven't been living in a cloister. I know what BDSM is."

"Do you? Are you willing to find out if you really do? Knowing about it and experiencing it are worlds apart, Nikki."

"I don't have any preconceived boundaries."

"None?"

"None."

"How can you say that, Nikki?"

"Because I trust you, Joanne."

Joanne clutched Nikki's hand, leaned in and kissed her lightly.

A silence fell over them. They finished their wine and, as the fire began to burn down, they returned to the boudoir. They lay together in a reverie that neither of them had anticipated when they had agreed to have dinner. They kissed goodnight and Nikki rolled onto her side, her back to Joanne. Joanne nestled her body against Nikki's and wrapped her left arm lightly around her. The warmth of Joanne's body against hers was, for Nikki, a pleasant and fitting way to end a date that she had accepted with some reluctance and had taken an unanticipated and delectable turn. Joanne could scarcely believe that she was actually would sharing the night next to Nikki and greeting the morning with Nikki by her side. As was her wont, Joanne said a silent prayer before surrendering to whatever dreams awaited her. Tonight, she prayed that Nicole Beaumont might see her as more than a satisfying sexual playmate. Joanne had always wanted more. She prayed that—someday—Nikki might be the one who provided the "more" that Joanne had long sought. Joanne drifted off to sleep knowing that, for the first time in her life, the reality truly exceeded the fantasy.

Chapter 66

 Nikki was not in the bed. Joanne pulled on the robe that Nikki had given her and followed the aroma of the coffee. Nikki approached Joanne with a mug of steaming coffee.

"Black, no sugar, right?"

"You have a good memory, Nikki. Maybe too good."

"What do you mean?"

"You can't shake your memory of making love with Maryanne, can you?"

"What makes you say that, Joanne? You seemed to be so happy last night."

"I was. But in the middle of the night I heard you calling her name in your sleep. And not just once." Joanne paused for a moment, then added, "And not just her name, Nikki. You asked her to do things to you, things that we did last night. You told her you loved her and pleaded with her never to leave you." As Nikki absorbed what she had just heard, Joanne continued, "It hurt, Nikki. A lot. I considered just getting up and leaving, but I couldn't bear to do that. I owed you an explanation. So I cried myself to sleep and now here we are."

Joanne trembled as she spoke.

"This was a mistake, Nikki. I never should have asked you out and we never should have done what we did last night. It was too much, too soon. I can't compete with your memory of Maryanne Miller, not now, maybe never. She was beautiful. I'm not. She was a model of graceful femininity. I certainly am not. She was perfect. I'm not. And she'll always be beautiful and perfect to you because that's the way she was when you fell in love with her, that's the way she was when you made love to her, and that's the way she was when she died. And I'm afraid that she would always be there, lying between us in the bedroom, your body with me, but your mind and heart with her."

"Look, Joanne, this was not a mistake. I accepted an invitation to dinner with you." She stressed the word "**You**" in her answer, as she did with increasing fervor in each of her responses. "I asked **you** in for a nightcap. I led **you** to the bedroom. Do you know why I did those things? Because I like Joanne Tracey and because I wanted Joanne Tracey. I wanted **you** in my bed and I wanted **you** in my arms. I wanted **you** last night and I want **you** now. **You**, not Maryanne Miller."

Nikki words did little to ease the hurt in Joanne's heart. Nonetheless, Nikki continued on, doing her best to explain why Joanne was wrong.

"Joanne, Maryanne's gone. You're here. **You**. Not the ghost of Maryanne Miller. **You**. Can't you accept that?"

"I've always wanted someone special in my life, Nikki. And I want to be the special person in someone else's life. But I fear that Maryanne was and always will be your someone special. I need to go."

"Please don't. Stay and talk through this with me. You need to know how much last night meant to me, how much I want to spend time with you, to get to know you better, to see if last night can be the beginning of something for us."

"I can't. I don't think you know how much it hurt me to hear you call her name time and again after what we shared."

Joanne returned to the bedroom and got dressed. Tears were now streaming down her face. Nikki followed, asking her again to stay. When it became apparent that her efforts had failed, she tried another approach.

"Joanne, I know you are hurting too much to talk now. Can we try to work this out later? Come for dinner tonight. Nothing fancy, nothing formal. Take the day to let the emotions die down and then we can talk. What do you say? I don't want us to end like this. I don't want us to end at all."

"I don't think so. As much as I care for you, as much as I have longed for you since the day I met you, and as much as I enjoyed you last night, I don't want to compete with a ghost. I can't. I won't."

"Can I call you?"

"Not now."

"Can I kiss you goodbye?"

Joanne simply said "Goodbye," and walked out the door. Nikki watched Joanne sit behind the wheel for several minutes, as if she was contemplating returning to the house. Nikki continued to watch disconsolately as Joanne drove off.

Chapter 67

JOANNE WALKED IN the door as her mother was fixing breakfast. She saw the tears running down Joanne's face and asked her to sit down and share a cup of coffee.

"Mom, I'm too upset."

"I can see you're upset, dear." She walked over and wrapped her arms around her daughter, trying to console her as best she could. "Tell me about it, sweetheart. Maybe it will help if you get it all off your chest." She handed a cup of coffee to Joanne and guided her to a chair at the kitchen table.

"I know you were excited about this date, Joanne. Was she not what you expected?"

"Mom, she was more than I had any right to expect."

"Then why the tears?"

Joanne took a sip of coffee and, through intermittent sobs, proceeded to tell her mother about her date with Nikki. She held nothing back. Her mother had long been her confidante and her best friend. She was the one person to whom she could express her innermost feelings. When Joanne was done, her mother asked her, very simply, whether she still had feelings for Nicole Beaumont.

"Yes, Mom. God help me, but I do. But I know she will never be able to reciprocate."

"I don't think you know that, Joanne. You fear it, that's for sure, and that's a reasonable fear given what you said. But do you really know it? Joanne, you have two choices. You can write this off as a bad experience and forget about Mrs. Beaumont or you can take a chance on her and risk having your heart broken. Frankly, sitting here listening to you, I don't think you can easily forget Mrs. Beaumont. I think you may end up spending your life wondering if she was the one God intended for you. And while she may break your heart, she might not; she might be a source of great joy in your life. It's your choice, Joanne. Look, take a nap. You need it. When you waken, let's talk some more." She kissed her daughter and led her to the bedroom. She closed the drapes and made sure that Joanne slid under the covers to give sleep a chance.

Mrs. Tracey stood silently for a moment at the door before closing it and returning to the kitchen. She had watched her daughter struggle with her emerging sexuality in her teenage years. She had seen Joanne deal with the snickers and looks of disgust from girls she had thought were her friends. It was a painful period for Joanne. "She survived that. She will survive this," thought Mrs. Tracey. Her daughter only wanted what most of us want, someone special who thought that she was special and wanted to be with her, to make her happy. So far, she had searched in vain for that person, settling instead for casual dalliances with women who provided a respite from loneliness, but no interest in or ability to form a meaningful relationship. Mrs. Tracey did not know Nicole Beaumont; they had never met; all she knew was what Joanne had told her. Maybe Mrs. Beaumont was like the others—happy to enjoy the pleasures of the night with Joanne, but nothing more. That wasn't how it sounded when Joanne recounted their date, but Joanne was there; her mother was not. Joanne would need to decide for herself whether to turn the page and move on.

Chapter 68

NIKKI'S MORNING WAS no better than Joanne's. Her thoughts returned time and again to the previous evening. The dinner, the conversation, the lights of passing cars illuminating Joanne's face, Joanne's hand on her thigh, Joanne's kisses, her taut and nicely muscled body, the serene surrender of her entire being to Joanne, and the incredible combination of strength, dominance, and tenderness with which Joanne had made love to her. She sat at the kitchen table and looked out the window. Soon, the trees would be barren, the days would be short, and the temperatures would drop. She had always loved the Fall and, sitting alone in that big empty house, she wondered which of the seasons was Joanne's favorite. She wondered what it would be like to sit in front of a roaring fire, snowbound on a cold winter night, with Joanne by her side, the scent of her perfume stimulating Nikki's senses. She wondered if she would ever have the opportunity to find out.

Nikki tried to distract herself from the morning's events by occupying herself with more of the humdrum Saturday chores that she had tended to neglect during her legal travails. It was hard to ignore Joanne's tearful departure, to go on as if nothing had changed. She wanted the kind of life people can enjoy when stress does not dominate their existence. Yes, the investigation was over, her malevolent husband was dead, and it was time for her to move on. Yes, she could sell the house and find something more suited for a single person. Yes, she had inherited all of Jack's accumulated wealth and knew that she would be financially secure for a lifetime and a half. Those were nice developments, but they were not altogether satisfying. She had no one with whom to share her newfound wealth, or her new life.

She got in her BMW and started to drive. To where, she was unsure. She was hoping, somewhat irrationally, that a drive in the crisp Autumn weather would stimulate her thoughts and generate a cure for her depression.

Chapter 69

JOANNE AWOKE AROUND 2 in the afternoon. She showered, pulled on a pair of jeans and a Cornell University sweatshirt, and went down to the kitchen to look for her mother.

"Feeling any better, Joanne?"

"Somewhat, Mom."

"Resolve anything?"

"No."

Just then, the doorbell rang. It was a delivery from the local florist for "Ms. Joanne Tracey."

"Are these your way of trying to brighten my spirits, Mom? You needn't have done this, really. I'm 30 years old. I'm a big girl. I'll get over this."

"They're not from me, Joanne."

Joanne opened the box to find a dozen orange sweetheart roses. There was a note, handwritten in an elegant feminine script. As she read it, Joanne's eyes misted over. She handed the note to her mother—

Last evening I had my first date ever with another woman. It was wonderful. She was wonderful. She is intelligent, honest, and sweet. As the evening wore on I was increasingly drawn to her in ways that I had not anticipated. I had an irresistible urge to kiss her, and I did. When she reciprocated, when she wrapped her arms around me, I wanted to—and needed to—surrender my entire being to her. It was something I have never done before with anyone and I want to experience that sweet surrender again and again, with her. I know it was one night. But it was a special night. I hope Joanne will allow me to see her again, to see if that special night might have opened a door to something more between us.

Chapter 70

 out the window, looking at everything and seeing nothing. Her phone buzzed and she picked it up without looking to see who was calling.

"Nikki?" The sound of Joanne's voice, halting as it was, caused Nikki to smile.

"Hello, Joanne. I'm so happy to hear your voice." Trying her best to sound matter of fact, she added, "How are you feeling?"

"The flowers are beautiful. Thank you. And your note was more beautiful than the flowers."

"I'm glad you liked them."

"I've been thinking about last night, Nikki. And about this morning. I guess I overreacted. None of us can control what we see in our dreams or say in our sleep. I can't. I shouldn't expect you to be able to do that. I asked myself whether, if I were in your shoes, I could have erased all memory of the only woman I had ever loved and the only woman with whom I ever had made love. The answer was 'No.' I suspect you will have feelings for and memories of Maryanne for the rest of your life. You can't change that. I can't change that."

Nikki wanted to speak, but she sensed that Joanne had more to say and that listening was far more important than talking at this point.

"What you can do is allow yourself to find someone new with whom you can make memories that will be new, fresh. Maybe that's me. Maybe that's someone else. Maybe it's a man. Maybe another woman. I don't know. What I do know is that there was nothing in how you touched me, how you kissed me, how you let me love you, and how you loved me in return, that suggested that walking away from you was the right thing to do. Sitting here, I realize that was a decision I would come to regret. Life is a series of gambles, Nikki. You are a chance I'd like to take."

Nikki listened intently as Joanne finished. Tears formed in the corners of her eyes. Nikki said simply, "Dinner is at 7, Joanne. Come as you are. Can you make it?"

Joanne smiled on the other end of the line. "Can I bring anything?"

"Yes, Joanne, your toothbrush."

And that's exactly what she did.

Chapter 71

 dated for the next several months, getting to know each other as well outside the bedroom as in. A number of men sought Nikki's company, but Joanne had extinguished Nikki's interest in men and she and Joanne fell easily into an exclusive relationship. They shared the holidays, welcoming in the New Year with a toast to the future, a warm embrace, a kiss that spoke volumes about their mutual affection . . . and more. What Nikki came to discover was that, apart from Joanne's unique ability to please Nikki in the bedroom, Joanne was a sweet, considerate, gregarious woman who was easy to like. As the months passed, Nikki became convinced that, had they met under different circumstances, they inevitably would have become great friends in any event.

When they were together, time flew. They spoke of their childhoods, their parents, their youthful indiscretions, the loss of their virginity, their likes, dislikes, aspirations, phobias, disappointments, and fears. They talked about TV shows, movies, books, music, history, politics, and religion. Nikki asked Joanne to teach her how to shoot a pistol, not because she thought she would ever need to do so, but because it was something she could share with Joanne. Joanne in turn happily took up tennis, not only because Nikki enjoyed it so much, but also because it gave Joanne the opportunity to drink in the sight of Nikki's legs as she gracefully bounced around the court in her tennis dress. Nikki learned very quickly that Joanne was a natural athlete. Her tennis game was quite good for a beginner, displaying the same agility and quickness on the tennis court as she did as the first baseman for the Police Department's softball team.

Nikki had given up any interest in team sports after suffering a broken nose in a high school soccer game, but Joanne was an avid fan of football and baseball, and Nikki found it easy to watch the games with Joanne, admiring (and trying to absorb) her knowledge of the rules and strategy. She watched Joanne as much as she did the games and was bemused by the fervor with which she rooted for her favorite teams and the intensity with which she castigated the inevitable "poor officiating."

They learned that they were both capable of disagreeing without anger and without harboring a grudge and of using humor to smooth over the few rough patches they encountered. A good sense of humor was a personality trait that they shared, and neither of them was afraid to let go with a good laugh when the situation warranted it.

Joanne introduced Nikki to Joanne's mother, and she and Nikki hit it off from the start. Mrs. Tracey liked Nikki for a variety of reasons, primary among them being Nikki's unique capacity to make Joanne happy. The three of them spent considerable time at Joanne's house during the week, often sharing meals and dinnertime chores. They regularly set aside time for some highly competitive games of Rummy, Uno™, and board games like Scrabble,™ Trivial Pursuit,™ and "Cards Against Humanity,"™ a game that exposed Mrs. Tracey's penchant for off color humor. They often devoted a night to movies, either at the local multiplex or streamed with microwaved popcorn at home. On Sundays, they would attend church together. Joanne and her mother were Episcopalians and Nikki, while raised as a Roman Catholic, found it easy to attend services at a church that shared many of the rites of Catholicism but was more receptive to same sex relationships. Following church, they often enjoyed brunch at a nearby restaurant, where smiles and laughs were always on the menu.

Friday and Saturday were usually "Date Night" for Nikki and Joanne and, however they started, they customarily ended in the primary bedroom of Nikki's house. Joanne schooled Nikki in the art of lesbian love, exposing her to everything Joanne had learned from her previous lovers. Joanne was a fan of bedroom fantasies, something that was new to Nikki, but which she took to readily. Nikki soon found both amusement and pleasure in playing her assigned role in games like "The Professor and the Coed," "Sorority Sister Initiation," "The Secretary and the Boss' Wife," and—to no one's surprise—"The Prostitute and the Police Officer."

They often supplemented their lovemaking with toys of every size and shape; toys to stimulate every part of the body, inside and out, front and back; toys that could simulate any manner of sexual play that anyone, men included, could provide; toys large enough in every way to displace any residual nostalgia that Nikki might ever have had for the feel of a man inside her; toys that Nikki had never even conceived of. Nikki's relationship with Joanne was, in effect, a prepaid admission to a "Toy Land" of sensual delights. That said, Joanne's inventory of toys, impressive as it was, did not deter them, every now and then, from browsing together some of the better known internet sites in search of new devices that would help to keep their assignations fresh, provocative, and hedonistic. Before she had embarked on her relationship with Joanne, hedonism was just a word to Nikki. Now, it had become a lifestyle—one into which she was being indoctrinated on a nightly basis and one that she enjoyed to the hilt.

Joanne was an unabashed dominatrix, and more than a few of her toys reflected that, from blindfolds to handcuffs to chains and clamps of various kinds, with more than a little emphasis on leather, real and faux. There were leather restraints, leather collars, leather to impose discipline, and leather vests, corsets and body suits that tantalized Nikki when stretched tightly across Joanne's muscled torso. Nikki thrilled at the sight of a leather-clad Joanne Tracey kneeling above her and pinning her to the bed in anticipation of a painful pleasure unlike any other. Nikki knew that other women had experienced that thrill but she could not understand how, once they had, they would ever want to live without it.

Before that first night, Nikki never would have predicted her reaction to Joanne's aggressive control over her in the bedroom and the pain that typically preceded the overwhelming pleasure of their lovemaking. But having experienced it, Nikki now craved it. She ached for the uncommon passion that accompanied the complete surrender of her body—and her soul—to the physical force, fervor, and controlled frenzy that Joanne brought to their bed. True to her word on that first night, Nikki never hesitated, objected, or asked Joanne to stop as she imposed her will on Nikki. To the contrary, she enthusiastically indulged Joanne's penchant for bondage, discipline, and submission, confident that Joanne would never do anything that would push Nikki beyond the realm of extreme pleasure and into the darkness of unwelcome pain. And she never did. Yes, there was pain, but it was not unwelcome. To the contrary, Nikki embraced the pain. She embraced it because she knew it fulfilled a deep-seated need somewhere in the recesses of Joanne's soul and Nikki wanted, more than anything, to please Joanne and to prove to Joanne the depth and intensity of Nikki's desire to please her. Submission to Joanne's will, however it might manifest itself on any given night, was a way for Nikki to prove her devotion.

Nikki's willing acceptance of the pain was not only to sate a need in Joanne's soul. Nikki came to realize she shared a similar need. She could not fully explain it to herself, but the need was palpable. In part, she felt that she deserved to be punished for her sins in allowing Jack to deceive her and for sacrificing ten years of her life to marital gullibility. And her rejection of Maryanne's offer of a loving relationship until it was too late, she reasoned, was another sin that demanded penance. Her penance, which she willingly accepted, was to offer her body on the altar of masochistic discipline at the hands of Joanne Tracey. This discipline came in many forms, but at it most aggressive it entailed the use by Joanne of a short handled riding crop with a leather tongue to lash the firm flesh of Nikki's cheeks and thighs.

Aside from the psychological underpinnings of Nikki's hunger for the pain that Joanne administered, the pain aroused Nikki in a manner that no previous foreplay ever had. With each wince, each quiver, each moan, each tremble, and each sob, her desire for the woman inflicting her pain intensified until the rush of ecstasy that accompanied the pain overwhelmed it. In the past, Nikki would have shuddered at the thought of submitting to such treatment. Now, her entire being shuddered from the painful pleasure she experienced with Joanne. Whatever Nikki's ever evolving boundaries were—and even she was unsure of where they ultimately might lie—she and Joanne had yet to find them. But they enjoyed the quest for those boundaries immeasurably, and they embarked on that journey often.

Joanne did not only assert control when she was ravishing Nikki. Even when she was on the receiving end of their love-making, Joanne orchestrated the sexual gymnastics as if she were the dictatorial director of a steamy scene in a XXX-rated film. But Joanne had a softer side to her sexual psyche as well. Sometimes, having had her way with Nikki, Joanne would roll onto her back and abandon her dominating posture. She would stroke Nikki's face softly, pleading with Nikki to love her tenderly, as if she were a virgin surrendering herself to the ministrations of another woman for the first time. As much as Nikki relished her role as the victim in Joanne's BDSM games, Nikki enjoyed the opportunity to be soft, gentle, and patient when she sensed Joanne's need for delicate and soothing treatment at the hands of her lover. Nikki could leaven passion with tenderness in a way that no previous lover ever could for Joanne.

After years of loneliness and frustration in her bedroom, Nikki enjoyed a sex life unlike anything she had ever dreamed possible. Joanne had unleashed, from a place deep within her that Nikki did not even know existed, a voracious and increasingly curious sexual appetite, an unorthodox and kinky appetite at which her night with the Millers had scarcely hinted. She loved what Joanne did for her and, perhaps even more, she loved how Joanne did it. In the space of little more than a year, Nicole Beaumont had been transformed from a dutiful wife in what she thought was an unhappy, loveless, but conventional marriage, to the one-time bisexual participant in a threesome with her best friends, and, finally, into an unashamed and confirmed masochistic lesbian who wanted nothing more than to probe the depths of her sexual curiosity and the limits of her tolerance for pain with Joanne Tracey, a towering blonde dominatrix who did things for her—and to her—that no one else ever had. Nikki had no need or desire for anyone else, man or woman, in her bedroom. After years of seeming celibacy, Nikki's physical hunger for Joanne Tracey and for her distinctive form of lovemaking was close to insatiable.

For all of that, Nikki often wrestled with the internal articulation of her feelings for Joanne. She liked Joanne; she liked her a lot. In fact, there was nothing about Joanne that Nikki did not like. Outside the bedroom, Joann exhibited none of the domineering characteristics that Nikki found to be so enthralling under and on top of the sheets. To the contrary, Joanne was sweet, kind, affectionate, and loving toward Nikki. Nikki's affection for Joanne was, in turn, true and genuine. She admired Joanne, her commitment to her career, her courage and honesty, and the love and respect that she exhibited toward her mother. Joanne had the unique ability to brighten Nikki's days, and she energized Nikki's nights with unbridled mutual lust. Nikki struggled with whether this amalgam of affection, admiration, friendship, respect, and lust was love. She thought so. Her feelings were far stronger than any she had ever had for Jack, even back in the beginning, and stronger still than those she had for Maryanne. But Nikki was afraid. One of those prior loves was obtained through lies and her life had nearly been destroyed by that deceit; the other was the victim of a cruel fate. As much as her behavior toward Joanne said "I love you," Nikki was, as yet, too paralyzed by fear of another ill-fated relationship to speak those words.

Joanne suffered from no confusion regarding her feelings for Nikki. Nikki did more than inflame Joanne's passions. Joanne enjoyed being near Nikki, holding her hand while they watched TV, and inhaling the scent of Black Opium whenever Nikki was near. When they were apart, Joanne would spray a light mist of the perfume on her pillows to provide the illusion of Nikki's presence at bedtime. Joanne cherished the easy friendship that had developed between Nikki and Joanne's mother. Joanne loved to see Nikki smile and it made her happy to realize that she—Joanne Tracey—played a part in putting that smile on Nikki's face. She admired Nikki's commitment to her nursing career and the way that she spoke with compassion about the patients to whom she tended. She was beguiled by Nikki's intelligence and her ability to articulate her thoughts without a hint of egotism or condescension. And she could not believe her good fortune in having a woman as pretty, as sexually curious, and as willingly submissive as Nikki for her lover.

Nicole Beaumont was everything that Joanne Tracey ever wanted. After years of casual sex with a carousel of lovers, Joanne found with Nikki the "more" she had always sought in those unfulfilling relationships. But for all that they shared in and out of the bedroom, Nikki had never told Joanne that she loved her. Joanne longed to hear those words, and because of Nikki's inability or unwillingness to utter them, Joanne lived in constant fear that her relationship with Nikki would end like all the others. Each night, Joanne thanked God for bringing Nikki into her life, for imbuing her with hope for a loving future. She prayed that Nikki would not grow tired of her, that Nikki's fascination with Joanne's sculpted physique and uncommon sexual needs would not wear thin in favor of a woman more reminiscent of Maryanne Miller. She prayed that no other woman would ever again experience the joy that she had known in sharing her bed with Nicole Beaumont. She was afraid to utter the words for fear of pushing too hard and driving Nikki away, but Joanne was deeply in love with Nicole Beaumont.

Chapter 72

AS SPRING TURNED to Summer, they spent an increasing amount of time in and around the pool behind Nikki's place. On occasion, after dark, they would heat the spa to 101 degrees and slip into the water unclad. Nikki would sit on Joanne's lap and tell her how much she enjoyed their relationship, how important Joanne was to her, and how happy she was to have Joanne in her life. Joanne treasured these quiet moments, alone in the dark with her lover, drinking in the compliments that Nikki directed her way. As the water pouring from the spa's jets washed over their bodies and delivered its pleasant warmth, Nikki would gently fondle Joanne's breasts before seeking the warmth of Joanne's mouth and the magical tongue that never failed to excite Nikki. These were moments that Joanne wished she could freeze in time, moments in which she was as happy as she had ever been. She did not want them ever to end.

Late on a Saturday afternoon in early July, Nikki and Joanne sat in the spa, enjoying the warm water, watching the sun begin its descent in the West. Nikki had thrown away the bikini she had worn the night of the murders, sporting instead a bright yellow model that nicely complemented both the rich tan she was developing and the colorful hummingbird tattoo she had recently acquired atop her right thigh, below her bikini line. With Joanne's encouragement, a diamond now pierced Nikki's navel and shimmered beneath the sparkling water. Nikki liked her new body art and she liked displaying her body to Joanne like this, in the privacy of their yard, in a pool on which no neighboring properties had a line of sight. Unlike Jack, Joanne made Nikki feel beautiful, alive and vibrant. These feelings had been missing from her life for quite some time and she reveled in their return. She reveled even more in what she saw when she surveyed Joanne, with her beautifully sculpted body and that fetching smile, a smile that always brightened Nikki's day.

Nikki enjoyed the views—of the sunset and of Joanne—as they sipped their Greyhounds. Nikki decided it was time to raise an issue she had been mulling for several weeks. Her memories of Maryanne Miller remained, but they no longer crept into her dreams. They were fond memories, but they grew faint in comparison to the vibrant and far deeper reality she had in the here and now with Joanne Tracey. She positioned herself so that she was kneeling on the spa bench, facing Joanne, her knees hugging Joanne's thighs. Nikki took off the white Panama hat she was using to shield her face from the sun and placed it, at a flirty angle, on Joanne's honey blonde tresses. "It's a good look for you, Joanne. You need this hat. It's yours." Then she kissed Joanne, sweetly on the cheek, and allowed her hands to fall softly atop Joanne's shoulders as if she were preparing to deliver a lecture.

"We need to talk."

Before the look of concern could form fully on Joanne's face, Nikki put her at ease.

"Joanne, we should not be living apart. I want you to move in here, you and your mom. There's plenty of room and, frankly, I don't ever like to leave you at the end of the evening when I visit your place. I feel alive when I am with you, and lonely when I leave. I miss being able to kiss you good morning and I want to kiss you goodnight before my head hits the pillow. I miss the comfort of your arm across my body as I fall asleep."

"Nikki, this is your home, not mine."

"Only because you're not here. If we live together, this will become our home. We'll have our bedroom; your mom will have hers. We can redecorate the house to give it a new look, our look, something we create together. We can reconfigure the home office to accommodate us both. We can add a nice gaming table and some swivel chairs in the Rec Room for Game Night. There's already a Hi Def big screen TV for movies and sports, and the house has two fireplaces. Want more? I've talked to a contractor about creating a home gym in the basement, with all the equipment you need, to make exercising all that much more convenient for both of us."

"Both of us?"

"Yes, both of us. Don't expect me to be as religious or aggressive about it as you are. I just want to make sure that you continue to like what you see when you look at me. I want you to continue to want me the way you do now. And I'm going to love watching you work out. We'll have mirrored walls like they do at the health club. That way, I can ogle you to my heart's content . . . while keeping you away from my competitors."

"You don't have any competitors for me, Nikki."

Nikki smiled at Joanne's response, but what followed betrayed Joanne's ongoing insecurity about their relationship.

"Like I said, Nikki, you don't have any competitors for me. But I'd bet there are plenty of men and women who would welcome what I have in you. I know you've had offers. Let's face it. You could probably have just about anyone you wanted. I know I'm lucky to have you. Sometimes I feel like pinching myself to assure myself this isn't a dream. But I don't know if I am enough for you. I don't know if I'm good enough for you. I fear that one day you'll wake up and realize you can do better and that someone better will come along and take you away from me."

Nikki placed her hand alongside Joanne's face and turned Joanne's head ever so slightly so that they were eye-to-eye.

"Joanne, look at me. I'm the lucky one. I don't want anyone else. Do you remember what you told me that day you dropped off the search warrant manifest? When I told you I always compared myself to Maryanne and came up short? And you said I shouldn't think that way because Maryanne obviously did not think I came up short? Well, think about what you told me then and listen to what I have to say to you now—no one could possibly be better for me than you, Joanne Tracey. I have never found you to come up short. Since our first night together, I've not given a first thought to anyone else."

Nikki leaned forward and kissed Joanne, lightly. "You're the one I want, and I don't want to live apart from you anymore."

As enticing as Nikki's offer was, she still had not uttered the words that Joanne longed to hear. Had Nikki told Joanne that she loved her, Joanne would have said 'Yes' in a heartbeat. But she was afraid to make such a huge change in her life if love was not the motivating force. So, out of self-protection, she summoned up reasons why co-habitation might be problematic.

"I don't know, Nikki. What do I do with my house?"

"Rent it out. Become a landlord. Make some money on the side. Let your property work for you."

"Well . . ."

"I've spoken to a landscape architect. He's going to create planting beds back here that stretch out in a V-shape from both sides of the patio toward the ends of the pool, with low stone walls behind them." As she said that, she pointed to the patio and explained where the walls would be and how the planting beds would follow them. "And he's going to suggest a garden of shrubs and flowers along the front of those walls and some flowering trees behind them to give us continuous colorful blooms from April to late October. I know you like flowers. We can have tulips, lilies, daffodils, geraniums, begonias, salvia, roses, mums. We can have dogwoods, red buds, cherry trees, crepe myrtles. Maybe a couple of magnolias. Whatever you like. You can work with the architect to figure out what you want."

"This is too expensive. I can't afford to help pay for all this."

"I'm not asking you to, Joanne. Given what I inherited from my late, unlamented husband, this is chump change. And I want to do it. For you. For us. It will make me even happier than I am—and I'm very happy."

"Nikki, I can't do this if my mom doesn't want to move."

"I know. Talk to her, Joanne. I'll talk to her if you like."

"No, I'll do it."

When Joanne spoke to her mother, Mrs. Tracey did not share her daughter's reluctance. She urged Joanne to go ahead.

"Joanne, you love her, don't you?"

"You know I do, but . . ."

"But what, sweetheart? You love her and I think she loves you, even if she hasn't told you so."

"Mom, I want to be loved. I want someone who is not afraid to look at me and say, 'I love you.' Is that too much to want?"

"Of course not. But, Joanne, you're afraid to say that to her too, aren't you? Aren't you asking more of her than you're willing to do yourself?"

"But, Mom, what if I tell her how I feel and she doesn't reciprocate? I'm not sure how I could handle that."

"For what it's worth, Joanne, I think she is head-over-heels in love with you. I really do. But as much as she cares for you, remember, she gave her heart to her husband and he shattered it. She was ready to give her heart to her best friend and fate denied her that opportunity. She'll tell you when she's ready. I suspect she only intends to say 'I love you' one more time in her life. And I think it will be to you that she says it, Joanne. Be patient."

"What about moving in with her under the circumstances? Not knowing if she will ever tell me what I need to hear?"

"You have nothing to lose. If it doesn't work out, you'll still have your own house. But it's going to work out. And, if I can be selfish, I'd like to be around to watch as my daughter finally enjoys what she's wanted for so long. Not that I'm planning on checking out of this life early, but if you've found your one and only, I can die happy."

The move was easy, the contractors performed on time, and a new "family" took occupancy of 2172 Highland Estates North. It was a happier family, by far, than the one that preceded it.

Epilogue

ONE FRIDAY IN November, before Thanksgiving, Joanne was working her usual shift. Nikki had the day off. But Nikki was not at home when Joanne finished her work for the day. Nikki arrived about 30 minutes later. As they enjoyed their dinner, Joanne asked where Nikki had been.

"An errand. Just something I had to do."

"Was it important?"

"To me, yes, Joanne. Very important."

"Are you going to tell me?"

"Later."

Later that evening, when they repaired to their bedroom, Joanne again asked, somewhat nervously, about Nikki's undisclosed errand.

"Why are you so curious, Joanne? Is something bothering you tonight?"

"Nikki, you know how jealous I am, how fearful I am of losing you."

"I told you, Joanne. There's no reason for you to be afraid."

"Tell me then, where have you been?"

"Can't I have any secrets, Joanne?"

"It depends. Have you been seeing someone?"

"Yes."

"Man or woman?"

"Man."

Joanne felt her whole world crumbling around her. The one fear that haunted her, the fear that Nikki would grow tired of her and look elsewhere for her life's partner, had come to materialize. Sadness consumed her. Even so, she felt compelled to ask the question.

"Who?"

"Do you really want to know, Joanne?"

Joanne did something she rarely did with Nikki. Ignoring the twinkle in Nikki's eyes, Joanne raised her voice to a near scream. "Yes, damn it, I want to know who you've been seeing."

At this point Joanne was nearly beside herself and on the verge of tears.

"I've been seeing Aaron Long, Joanne."

Joanne was dumbfounded. She did not understand what Nikki and Aaron Long could possibly have in common or what Nikki would find to be attractive in him. She just looked down at the floor and said, "Oh, Nikki, how could you?"

"Oh, I think you'll find it in your heart to forgive me, Joanne."

"I don't think so."

"I do."

By now, the twinkle in Nikki's eyes had broadened into a smile, a smile that had always brightened Joanne's disposition but was doing nothing to ease Joanne's distress. She approached Joanne, reached up to wrap her arms around Joanne's neck, and pulled herself up so that she was standing on her toes. "Kiss me, Joanne. Kiss me like you mean it." Somewhat reluctantly,

Joanne kissed Nikki as if it were the last one they would ever share. When their lips parted, Nikki said, "I have something to show you."

Nikki handed Joanne a little velvet box with gold lettering that said simply, "Long's Jewelers." Joanne opened it to find a gold eternity ring encircled with diamonds large enough to illuminate a dark room. The engraving inside the band said simply, "Joanne and Nikki, forever."

Joanne stood mute, staring at the ring in apparent disbelief. Then she looked up at Nikki and the tears began to flow. "Don't ever do that to me again. Don't you realize how much I love you and how much it would hurt me to lose you?"

"I love you too, Joanne."

Although she had longed to hear those words, Joanne was speechless, particularly since they came on the heels of what Joanne had assumed was the end of their love affair.

"I love you, Joanne. Unconditionally. More than words can express. I want to spend the rest of my life with you. Joanne Tracey, will you marry me?"

After what seemed like an eternity to Nikki, Joanne looked up, her face lit by that fetching smile.

That December, on the Friday before Christmas, Joanne and Nikki pledged their love in a small ceremony in their church. Neither of them had the slightest doubt regarding the vows they exchanged that day, not then, not ever.

About the Author

JOHN CHIERICHELLA IS a native New Yorker who relocated to Virginia in connection with his military service and has resided there ever since.

He received his bachelor's degree from Cornell University and his law degree from the Columbia University School of Law. Following his law school graduation he served as an Attorney/Advisor to the Secretary of the Air Force in The Pentagon, where his work focused on the acquisition of major weapons systems. Upon leaving the Air Force, he continued his focus on the legal aspects of Government procurement as a partner in several international law firms. Over the course of his career he was admitted to the practice of law in New York, the District of Columbia, California, Wisconsin, and Virginia. He has served as the lead attorney in connection with legal projects relating to fighter aircraft, the Stealth bomber, helicopters, naval destroyers and other surface ships, surveillance satellites, submarine subsystems, and plant machinery. He has consistently been included on a variety of "Best Lawyer" lists, both in the metropolitan DC area and nationally.

He currently serves as the Founder and Manager of Chierichella Procurement Strategies LLC, a consulting firm through which he continues to serve the needs of contractors in dealing with the Government. Information regarding the firm can be found at *www.chierichella.com.*

He has co-authored one book and written dozens of articles on a variety of Government contracting issues. His first novel, "Triangles of Fate," was published in 2023. "The Last Martini" is his second novel.

He currently resides with his wife Shannon and their three children on a small farm in Warrenton, Virginia, in the foothills of the Blue Ridge Mountains.

Book Synopsis

NICOLE BEAUMONT IS staring at an invitation from her neighbors, Ted and Maryanne Miller, to a pool party to kick off the summer season. As she looks at the date on the invitation, she realizes that her husband, Jack, will still be on another of his extended business trips to Los Angeles. Jack is a lawyer, a very successful lawyer, and he spends more time on the road than he does at home. Although Nikki is an attractive woman, Jack's career and his monetary success are the driving forces in his life. His physical interest in his wife has waned to the point where their love life is virtually nonexistent.

Whenever Nikki asks Jack to interrupt his travels to spend time with her, he lectures her about the importance of travel to his business and to his ability to provide Nikki with a beautiful home, a pool, a BMW, jewelry, and other trappings of success. Nonetheless, she calls him that evening and virtually begs him to come home for the Millers' party. He brusquely rejects her request.

Nikki calls Maryanne to RSVP her "regrets," but Maryanne won't take "No" for an answer. Maryanne is Nikki's best friend, a gorgeous and successful professional whose husband is a professional photographer and videographer, and every woman's secret fantasy. Maryanne is Nikki's closest confidante and she is aware of the problems in the Beaumonts' marriage. She persuades Nikki to come to the party and allow herself to have a good time.

The party is a gala affair with plenty of good food and good conversation. After cocktails and dinner, Ted announces that the pool and spa are open for business. By the time all of the other guests have left, Nikki is alone in the spa with Ted and Maryanne. Before long, Nikki is sitting on Ted's lap and Maryanne is encouraging her to kiss him. Maryanne then invites Nikki to sit on her lap and kiss her. Although she regards herself as heterosexual, Nikki has long harbored a secret desire for Maryanne. Now, under the moon, in the warm water, fueled by several cocktails, Nikki abandons all inhibition. She kisses Maryanne with a fervor that transcends friendship, slides her hand under the bra of Maryanne's bikini, fondling her lovingly, and asks if she can spend the night. They exit the spa and head for the Millers' bedroom, where Nikki Beaumont engages in the first threesome of her life, a sexual "round robin" of lust and love that stands in marked contrast with the hollow shell of her marriage to Jack.

Before turning in for the night, Nikki asks if her friends would like another drink. They ask her to mix them each a martini. As she does so, she makes herself a greyhound and returns to the bedroom where they drink a toast to their evening. Nikki heads to the shower and, when she is finished, she climbs into bed between Ted and Maryanne, who are asleep. Nikki falls asleep thinking about the morning and how her future will play out with the Millers.

But there is no future. When Nikki awakens, Ted and Maryanne Miller are dead.

As the police investigate the scene of the crime they discover that Ted Miller—a professional photographer and videographer—had recorded the evening's events. The video shows Nikki handing the Miller's their drinks, offering them a toast, and then heading off to the shower before joining them in bed. The martinis were laced with phenobarbital and Nikki's fingerprints are on the tumblers.

Inspector Milliken focuses immediately on Nikki as the prime suspect. There she was, in living color on Ted Miller's recording, handing her neighbors the drinks that would kill them. Moreover, in the Inspector's view she was a slut, someone who cheated on her husband while he was working hard to earn a living, just as his ex-wife had done to him repeatedly. She was a woman who deserved to be punished and it would please him to help serve up that punishment.

Milliken's partner, Sergeant Joanne Tracey, is dubious of Nikki's motive for and thus her involvement in the murders. Moreover, a search of the Millers' home uncovers a library of video recordings in which Ted and Maryanne Miller can be seen repeatedly indulging their physical desires with a host of their friends and neighbors, male and female, several of whom were present at the party preceding the murders. Inspector Milliken scoffs at Sergeant Tracey's suggestion that these videos provide others with a motive for the murders, but the sergeant is bent on running the back story for those videos to ground.

Nikki finds herself fighting two heated legal battles—one to avoid indictment for the murders of her best friends and a second to address Jack's suit for divorce based on her documented adultery. How these battles play out, whether Nikki can survive them, and—if so—whether and how she can return to anything approximating a normal life are the questions that provide the balance of the plotline for the book.

www.ingramcontent.com/pod-product-compliance
Lightning Source LLC
Chambersburg PA
CBHW031527150726
47990CB00001B/82